Desert Mara

Gordon Landsborough

© Gordon Landsborough 1976

Gordon Landsborough has asserted his rights under the Copyright, Design and Patents Act, 1988, to be identified as the author of this work.

First published in 1976 by Allan Wingate (Publishers) Ltd and Tandem Publishing Ltd.

This edition published in 2018 by Endeavour Media Ltd.

GENERALS ARE as good as their captains, a saying sometimes quoted in officers' messes and always, curiously, by captains. Among Field-Marshal Erwin Rommel's captains was a bold young Hauptmann, Kurt Braunschweig.

Hauptmann Braunschweig had proved in many a skirmish in the desert against the British and their Allies that he had no nerves. His idea of war was to get stuck into any enemy he could see and demolish them before they knew what was hitting them. It was a policy which could lead to fatal results, and not just to an enemy, but Field-Marshal Rommel encouraged it because overall it paid dividends—the dividends of war.

One hot early afternoon Hauptmann Braunschweig stood in his open car, dust goggles above the long peak of his cap in the style popularised by his general, quarter of a mile into the desert from Siwa Oasis . . . Siwa, four hundred miles south into the Sahara from Derna, Tobruk and the Mediterranean coastline.

Ahead of him a fierce fire blazed. It was an isolated palm grove— probably date palms, he thought, though he knew little about palm trees because he and his men had only recently arrived in Siwa. To do so they had had to drive out the British from this paradise of greenery in the vast hot desertland.

Hauptmann Braunschweig was responsible for that fire. His mortars had lobbed their shells in amid the tall palms, causing great devastation and setting light to the mass of dried leaves that had fallen to the sandy earth. Some Arab owner was going to be very unhappy about losing his investment, but if people cultivated trees in the midst of open desert they could expect warring soldiers to occupy them and turn them into a battlefield.

At this moment the Hauptmann was not sure the place was a battlefield any longer. The injured British Tommy—a very crude and unpleasant fellow—who'd been brought into the German H.Q. by reward-hungry Arabs, had talked and what he had told them resulted in the swift mobilisation of forces under Hauptmann Braunschweig and a race out to this innocent-looking palm grove.

Desert Marauders

The innocent-looking palm grove had promptly sprayed them with machine-gun bullets, proving that the incredible story of the unpleasant Tommy was correct. A strong force of British soldiers was impudently camping out right on the doorstep of this German-occupied oasis. The Hauptmann then gave orders designed to make the enemy wish he was very far away from Siwa at that moment.

His infantry debussed in a swift flowing wave of desert-green uniforms, to merge into the sandhills and begin an advance on the enemy. Braunschweig's Spandaus were mounted and began a deadly spraying of the palm grove and an enemy as yet unseen. Then his mortars came into action and trees toppled and then the fire began, and that was exceedingly to the Hauptmann's satisfaction. He did not think of the analogy of rats being driven from hiding by the flames—to Braunschweig, a professional soldier, an enemy, especially if he was Nordic, was a man to be honoured, though killed because that was part of the game. The fire, he thought, would soon drive the Britishers into the open where his superior forces would quickly put an end to their impudence. As a soldier he could admire them for their daring, but also as a soldier he had to remove them as a threat to his army's security.

The fire raged, and a great pall of smoke came to sully the perfect blue of the Sahara sky, but the still unseen defenders maintained a fierce and heavy fire with machine-guns and rifles from behind shelters within the perimeter of the palm grove. Braunschweig ordered his men to work their way around the grove, eventually to encircle it and thus cut off the enemy. The manoeuvre proved too slow or too late.

Abruptly, no more than five minutes after the attack had been mounted, all firing ceased from within the palm grove. It took some minutes before the Hauptmann began to suspect that the enemy had withdrawn from his positions and this was no lull in their firing. Even then, though the pace of the advance was quickened, it was quite a while before the first of his infantry ran inside the burning grove and reported that this part, at least, was clear of desert raiders.

Thereafter the advance was swift, the German infantry dodging amid the blazing trees until finally they came out beyond the grove and declared it free of enemy presence. They also reported evidence of a large camp within, which apparently had been used by a considerable force of men, thus confirming the injured British Tommy's story.

Even before the infantry Leutnant brought his report, Hauptmann Braunschweig had further confirmation of the enemy's withdrawal. Two lightly armoured patrol cars had caught up with him and had deployed on either side of the burning palm grove. In a few minutes one reported by radio that a dust cloud was heading south, telling of the passage of vehicles over the desert.

'South?' thought the Hauptmann immediately, and got out his map. But there was no way of escape for them to the south! Here, for hundreds of miles, stretched the Great Sand Sea, a barrier of loose shifting sands which no vehicle, according to German Intelligence, could cross. What was this manoeuvre, then, of the enemy? Had they some stronghold on the edge of the Sand Sea, or did they, after all, know of some secret path across it unknown to German cartographers?

Hauptmann Braunschweig, being Hauptmann Braunschweig, speculated no more than two seconds on his theories. To him action was everything. There was the enemy, fleeing. Therefore he would go after them and bring them to battle. He had little doubt of the result. By the injured Tommy's testimony there were about thirty men in the desert raiders' party, and only four open trucks for transport. He had two well-armed patrol cars, magnificent for this terrain, a dozen troop carriers and well over a hundred men under his command. Once the Hauptmann came to grips with the enemy they would soon by crying *Kamerad;* and even if his own force had been smaller than the Britishers', the Hauptmann's decision would have been the same.

Get after them—fast!

He had water and provisions for two days. In that time he would destroy the enemy who had so daringly raided the Siwa garrison H.Q. and made off with eight British P.O.W.s. He gave an order and the empty infantry carriers came rolling up and the men were recalled and mounted their vehicles, and then the pursuit began.

One way or another Hauptmann Braunschweig's force had given the desert raiders—what had the Tommy called them? G.G.C.U.? A new guerrilla unit to be operating in the Sahara—an hour and a half's lead. It was always surprising how much time was taken in making sure an enemy had truly gone and was not in ambush, and then more time rounding up one's own troops and getting them moving again.

But now they were rolling, taking a route south, leaving the crackling and fire-swept palm grove and entering upon a time of torment. The going was soft and firm at first, clean, almost golden sand, carved into beautiful shapes by an almost constant wind, giving good grip to their ersatz rubber tyres. But it was hot. The wind that brought little eddies of sand hissing like writhing snakes close to the desert's surface also brought heat. It hit them in their faces, crouching though they were in their infantry carriers, so hot it was frightening. Their skin dried and began to flake, and their throats grew parched to a degree that was intolerable, and no man spoke because tongues were scaly and rasped against palates that were equally desiccated. They huddled in their misery, wistfully thinking of the cold clear springs of the lush Siwa Oasis and wondering Germanic thoughts about the folly of war, and what were they doing here in Africa, anyway?

The patrol cars had kept the receding dust cloud in their glasses, but in any event the desert raiders could hardly give them the slip because one thing about sand, it did leave clear impressions of tyre treads. All they had to do was follow; in the end the tracks would bring them to the enemy. Hauptmann Braunschweig was confident that he would have the speed on the British and he had no doubts that the raiders' present lead of ten miles would soon be whittled down to nought.

He reckoned without that desert.

By mid-afternoon, with that still distant but much nearer dust cloud to entice them along, the going had changed. The colour had gone out of the desert, they all noticed—now it was grey where before it had been an inviting yellow. There was more rock outcropping through the sand; and the sand itself seemed curiously loose.

With increasing frequency their vehicles got into a wheel-spin, tyres racing round unable to get a grip, and fountains of dry sand spraying out under the treads. The going became slower with the passing of time, and now the Hauptmann's eyes kept looking at the sun's position, while he wondered anxiously if he would be able to catch up with the raiders before dark.

Braunschweig still thought they were gaining on the enemy, but he knew it was not as much as earlier, where the going over firm sand had been better. He suspected that with the raiders were men who knew the desert and knew how to cope with wheel-spins. But then these British always did seem at home in these wild lands, unlike his own men with their limited desert experience. One thing, though, the Hauptmann kept telling himself obstinately, soft sand or no soft sand, where the *verdammen* Britishers could go they could go, and in time, he swore, they would get within range and destroy them.

It was not, however, to be that night. Of necessity they had to make a halt, though it was a mere ten minutes, just sufficient time for refuelling and for food and water to be rationed out. Then they were away and catching up again. But now the sun was falling towards the western horizon with disconcerting speed, and that dust cloud hardly seemed to get any nearer.

The going grew even more difficult. A vehicle would get into a mad wheel-spin and halt. Those vehicles behind would sometimes be brought to a halt, too, and then men had to get down and dig away at sand and shove until their lungs nearly burst before clambering aboard their moving vehicle again.

In time Hauptmann Braunschweig evolved a drill to maintain a faster pace. His four-wheel-drive patrol cars now hovered on the edge of the column, tow ropes ready. The instant an infantry truck seemed to be getting into difficulties, men were down and out with the ropes, dropping them over tow-hooks and the four-wheel-drive vehicles getting the truck moving. By later afternoon—a bit too late—they were becoming quite expert and the column was travelling at more satisfying speed. At any rate, the dust cloud ahead was coming noticeably nearer—various calculations now placed it as close as six miles away, but Braunschweig thought this might be touched with optimism.

Darkness came too suddenly for him, though welcome with the relief it brought from that terrible sun. For a time the Hauptmann even tried to press on and catch up in the dark with the unsuspecting enemy, but all at once they seemed to run into very soft going and the men were forever clambering down with the tow ropes until they seemed hardly to be progressing at all.

Sensibly, Hauptmann Braunschweig decided to call it a day. His men were worn out; they could not keep up this pace much longer. If they did catch up with the enemy, what good was that if his men were too exhausted to fight? So reluctantly Braunschweig brought the column to a halt and they leaguered up for the night. Food, coffee and rest for their weary muscles, and in the morning the pursuit would be on. Lying under the stars, shivering now because they had no blankets with them, Hauptmann Braunschweig did his calculations. If they didn't catch up with the enemy by the following midday, pursuit would have to be abandoned.

Water, if not fuel, would run out too soon, and he wasn't going to die of thirst in this awful desert.

He had his men up before dawn, so that with the first crack of light his column was moving, and another day of anguish began for them. The relentless pursuit was on.

Disappointingly the British force was up just as early, as they saw when the light became good enough. The dust cloud still hovered miles ahead of them.

All that morning the Hauptmann drove his men ruthlessly, inspiring them to maintain the pace, killing, heartbreaking though the effort was. The sun burned on to their backs, that intolerable thirst gripped them, but Braunschweig never allowed the pace to drop. *He had to catch up with that column by noon or abandon the trail*. The Hauptmann was not a man to ease off so that an enemy could escape.

By eleven that morning, in a heat greater than they had ever experienced before, it began to look as if they had lost the race. That elusive dust cloud was coming closer, true, but not fast enough. It was still probably four or five miles ahead. Grudgingly the Germans had to admire the desert craft of these bold raiders and the way they kept their ungainly trucks on the move over this treacherous surface. By eleven-thirty they knew there was no hope of catching them at this pace. Still the dogged Hauptmann carried on. He had decided to pursue till midday and he would keep to his plan and hope that within that time some miracle would occur to halt the fleeing enemy.

At twelve noon, reluctantly, he gave the order to halt. They had lost the race. The guerrilla force was too smart for them and had got away with their cheek. Wearily Hauptmann Braunschweig said they would rest during the heat of the day, finding shade under their vehicles, and also the men could eat and partake of their small ration of water.

So the German force got down and dragged their tired limbs to food and drink and then into the little shade available to them. But even this was better than struggling to keep heavy trucks on the move.

The Hauptmann ate his tasteless field rations, squatting against a tyre that gave off a sour odour in that heat. He had no shade, but there was too little shade and what there was must go to his men. He would suffer the sunshine during the halt.

His eyes, brooding over the distance, never left that dust cloud. He hated it. It mocked him. A fierce vengeful spirit stirred inside him all the time he looked. He swore awful German oaths to himself to express his frustration at being outwitted. All this effort—this terrible struggle through the desert—and at the end nothing to show for it. Again he prayed for a miracle, but quite unknowingly the miracle had already occurred.

When half an hour had gone by, the dryness in his mouth making a mockery of that recent ration of water, the thought came to Braunschweig that the dust cloud seemed scarcely any further distant than when his column had drawn to a halt. It took a while for the thought to register, and then he sat up and watched more intently. Quarter of an hour later he was quite sure. The dust cloud was as high as ever but it seemed to be hanging over one place, hardly moving at all.

Hauptmann Braunschweig came lurching to his feet, depression gone, fierce exultation now possessing him. Startled eyes saw their captain with all his old vigour, that vigour now turned upon them.

'*Aufstehen!*' he roared and they rose at his command, tired men though they were, and hating the prospect of more hours of desert torment. He told his Leutnants that the pursuit would be resumed. The enemy was perhaps one hour ahead and not moving. In one hour, he promised them, they would wipe out the intruders.

The miracle for Hauptmann Braunschweig had happened. The desert raiding force had indeed run into trouble. At this moment, here in the arid Sand Sea, it had got itself bogged down in a lake.

*

They came to Captain John Offer about nine o'clock that morning, the day after their escape from the palm grove outside Siwa Oasis. Until that time they had been unaware of pursuit, though that fact was not remarkable.

As the four Chevrolet trucks entered the Great Sand Sea, sharp eyes watched behind. Divided among the trucks were thirty-one men and one officer, though that officer—Offer—was no more entitled to his three pips than any of his ruffianly followers. Four of these men were from the celebrated Long Range Desert Group, those masters of the Sahara, and mightily valuable on this Sand Sea crossing. Their hosts, the Glasshouse Gang Commando Unit, had rescued them from German hands while held P.O.W. in Siwa.

With all this talented soldiery aboard the Chevs, Hauptmann Braunschweig's pursuing force ought to have been spotted the moment they made chase after the commandos. The pursuit, however, was not immediately detected because of the wind, which was blowing north, though gently so. Travelling as they were across the Sand Sea in an almost direct line south, the wind thus ensured that the dust cloud dispersed behind the Chevs, and the gentleness of this northerly wind was such that the dust cloud dispersed with infinite slowness, hanging haze-like over the desert for what seemed hours.

All this meant that the watchers on their trucks looked back along their deep-rutted trail through a dust cloud that rose thickly immediately behind them and even at a distance was a thin fog that was still considerably obscuring. Added to this, of course, was the vision-distorting effect of refracting air currents dancing up from the hot desert soil.

So all the first day, aided by distance, Hauptmann Braunschweig was able to follow the commandos without being detected. By the following morning the commando had become lulled into a sense of security, sure that no one was on their tracks.

Even so their R.S.M., Angus O'Keefe, had them out of their blankets before dawn. It was no good moving before daylight, of course, not on that treacherous, winding track, but still it was sound sense to get cracking as soon as possible before the day got hot.

Two and a half hours after moving out, the R.S.M. called a halt. Now, two and a half hours is a long time at one stretch in uncomfortable wagons with a torrid sun getting hotter every hour, but O'Keefe liked to cram a lot into the first move after daybreak. After that they could rest up for a good hour, then another drive forward until midday, when everyone would get under shade and they'd do no more trekking until it began to cool some time after four o'clock.

Nice plans, but they never came off, not that particular day.

This time, because they rested, there was no dust cloud being thrown up, and towards the end of their breakfast even the distant dispersing dust grew thinner and less obstructive to the eye. Perhaps, too, the wind shifted for a moment and cleared a path to the north of where they halted. Whatever the reason, one of the L.R.D.G. with them, so recently a P.O.W., spotted the advancing German vehicles.

His eye first caught the billowing cloud of dust, then through the dancing air currents he was able to make out the dark shapes of vehicles. They were five or six miles away, but five or six miles looks no distance in the desert.

The L.R.D.G. man gave a shout and pointed, and instantly everybody was rolling to their feet, grabbing guns and looking towards the possible danger. R.S.M. O'Keefe came running up at the first whiff of trouble.

He was a remarkable man, this Augus O'Keefe, a former L.R.D.G. sergeant who had been busted to private for beating up his old enemies, the Military Police, while on leave in Cairo, and slapped into the Glasshouse.

Now O'Keefe unslung the glasses he habitually wore, a habit of his L.R.D.G. days, and trained them on the advancing column. They merely confirmed what they already guessed—these were pursuing Germans, and uncomfortably close upon their heels. What he did not like were those turreted vehicles, for some patrol cars in the German army had four-wheel-drive and that could keep them going over loose sand where conventional vehicles, depending on rear-wheel-drive, got bogged down. Neither did he like the twin machine-guns that poked from those turrets. He had had personal experience of the havoc those guns could cause to soft transport such as their own.

O'Keefe said to himself, 'Captain Offer must be wakened.' Their commanding officer must know about this. But in anticipation of orders the R.S.M. bellowed out a command, 'Prepare to move!' There could be no leisurely halts after this, not while those tenacious Germans dogged their trail.

He ran round to where Captain John Offer lay on his blankets stretched out on a truck. Thoughtful men had draped another blanket over their mounted machine-gun and this threw shade over most of their officer. Clambering over the side, R.S.M. O'Keefe gently shook the captain's shoulder. Gently, because no one knew, not even their medical orderly, Arab Ward, what bones were broken within that tough body.

John Offer, who had lost the King's Commission and served a memory-searing sentence in Sharafim because he had flogged Q stores to civilians and had had a happy time on the proceeds—this morning John Offer looked terrible.

His face was a mass of bruises, his eyes lost in mounds of puffed-up flesh, the flattened nose—a screw in the Glasshouse had broken it with his boot—looked like pulp and showed black along the nostrils where blood had congealed. But probably Offer's worst injuries were to his body, where a boot had gone in again and again as he had lain unconscious in that palm grove outside Siwa Oasis.

Captain John Offer had taken the second worst beating of his life a few hours before being driven out of that palm grove by Hauptmann Kurt Braunschweig's Panzergrenadiers. A rabbit had done it, alone in the dark. A rabbit six-foot-two with tattooed forearms which answered to the name of Private McTone.

McTone had resented Offer's leadership of this gang of army deserters. He had become truculent, unpleasant, threatening, so Offer, a forthright man, had knocked the big boxer out with one unexpected blow, smashing McTone's jaw in the process.

In turn, a pain-wracked McTone, broken jaw supported by a head bandage whose knot gave the appearance of rabbit ears, had waited for Offer in the dark. Then he had put his captain out of action very painfully before going off into Siwa to give himself up to the Germans there so that he could get medical attention. They were a hard bunch, these Glasshouse men, inclined to play rough with each other.

His men had put Offer on some blankets in one of the Chevs when they took flight from the palm grove, and there he had lain ever since, whether sleeping or unconscious no one really knew. At times Arab Ward came to give him some attention, but the most solicitous among the men was Offer's newly made-up sergeant, Eddie Walker. Walker and Offer had shared the same cell in the Glasshouse, and Walker, ruffianly *ex-palais* bouncer though he was, thought the world of the smaller man. It was Walker who came every hour or so and roused Offer and poured water down his throat.

It was curious that in this emergency, tough, lean Angus O'Keefe should turn to John Offer for instruction, for his captain, by all evidence, was in no condition to take command. But O'Keefe knew his superior officer, and knew the toughness of the man under that battered exterior. He also had the most sublime faith in Offer's ability to extricate them from any situation—a wild man, O'Keefe, especially where Military Police were concerned, and yet he too, like Eddie Walker, gave unswerving devotion and loyalty to John Offer.

So now he shook him gently, and gradually Offer wakened, and when O'Keefe saw those sharp eyes peering at him through folds of bruised flesh, he said, 'Sir, the Germans are close behind us. I thought you'd like to know.'

The swollen lips moved painfully and O'Keefe only just got the words. 'Are they, b'God!! Then we'd better do something about it.' He held out his arm, a silent invitation to be hoisted erect. And that was typical of John Offer. He was a wreck of a man who should have been in bed in a hospital, but the one word of danger was sufficient to bring him to his feet and take charge.

They stood him up and it was obvious the pain he went through, yet he made no sound in protest at the agony. The R.S.M. held his glasses to those painful looking eyes, and slowly Offer adjusted them.

'Germans all right.' Offer pulled his head away from the glasses. 'All we can do is keep ahead of them if we don't want to get hurt.'

It was scarcely a brilliant solution to their problem, but O'Keefe was satisfied. His commanding officer was back in circulation, and he knew that later, if there was a chance to turn the tables on the pursuing Germans, this smaller, incredibly ingenious ex-actor would grab the opportunity in a flash.

So they moved, and once again the column sent up a great dust cloud, advertising their presence and giving the German Panzers a target for their endeavours. An hour later the R.S.M., sitting beside a silently suffering Offer, said, 'No doubt about it, sir, they're gaining on us.'

They were losing time. The going was so bad the men spent more of their time shoving the trucks through soft sand than sitting in them. It was an exercise which took the guts out of them, labouring in that dehydrating heat, and Offer knew that, pursuit or no pursuit, they'd have to make halts and take rest or his men would simply collapse through exhaustion.

Towards noon it became apparent that if the Germans just kept on long enough they were bound to overhaul the Glasshouse Gang, and then, with all that infantry and the two armoured cars, they could do pretty well what they liked with the commando.

Offer said, in that careful way he had of speaking, 'It's hardly a cheerful position.'

O'Keefe was more abrupt. He said it was bloody horrible, and watched with gloom the slow efforts of nearly exhausted men to shove sand channels under wheels which only sank deeper into loose sand when they tried to dig them clear. The men had had enough. They simply must be given rest. But rest with that grim force upon their tail?

Sergeant Maye was listening to their conversation. He was one of the four L.R.D.G. men who had been released from captivity in that daring raid in the Siwa H.Q. by the Glasshouse Gang. He was also the only man who knew this terrible trail across the Great Sand Sea. He looked a dead tired man, too, for sergeants' stripes were of little account in that desert. If you had a shoulder you put it to the wheel like any other man, that is, if you wished to get through alive.

Maye now said, 'So far this has been a picnic.'

Offer turned with a carefully controlled movement calculated to reduce the pain of his aching body. 'You're joking, old chap.'

'Old chap isn't joking,' Maye assured them grimly. 'Any time now we have to cross the Lake of Sand.'

'You'd better tell us about it,' advised Captain Offer, which Sergeant Maye did.

Nowhere on the Sand Sea crossing was there an easy part, but some places were more hellish than others. Perhaps the most notorious lay just ahead, christened by the L.R.D.G. the Lake of Sand.

'You know how soft the sand is here, how easy it is to sink into it?' The straining efforts of the men right at that moment were sufficient illustration of his statement. 'Well, you get on to the Lake of Sand and you'll really be moving over a quicksand. Nothing stays on the top, nothing of weight. And things don't go down for a foot or two—they keep going down . . . and down.'

O'Keefe said it was charming and then asked the obvious question: 'Then how the hell do we get across?'

Sergeant Maye, who had twice made this awful crossing with an L.R.D.G. patrol, did his best to explain but neither of his audience thought it held too much conviction.

The theory in the L.R.D.G. was that there seemed to be some vast basin within the Sand Sea which had filled with this particular brand of quicksands. Yet across this 'lake' was a ridge of firmer ground, very narrow but if they kept to it they could struggle over. Discarded empty petrol tins marked the way, and it was highly advisable not to stray from the marked route, Maye told them. Offer wondered how on earth the L.R.D.G. had found that ridge across the Lake of Sand. Had they gone probing with long sticks until they'd charted a pathway? Remarkable bods, these L.R.D.G., he thought, not for the first time.

'But don't have any illusions,' Maye warned them. 'When I talk of a ridge of firmer ground, it's only comparative. If we make a hundred yards in an hour, we shall be mighty lucky.'

Offer lifted his weary head and stared through the heat haze back the way they had come. Again the wind had shifted, clearing away the dust cloud thrown up by spinning wheels, so that Captain Offer was able, quite clearly, to see the tiny vehicles. They appeared to have halted. Certainly there was no cloud of dust rising from them now. Well, thought Offer, if the Hun could find time for rest, so could they, and he told O'Keefe to stand the men down for twenty minutes and serve out an extra ration of water.

To Sergeant Maye he said, 'If that's all the pace we can make, old Jerry will be up with us in no time and we'll really be sitting ducks.' But what else was there they could do but go on?

So they had their break and then resumed their weary way, and within half an hour the going was so bad that Sergeant Maye said they must already be on the Lake of Sand. At the news Captain Offer looked round. He had never seen anything so desolate in his life. Grim grey sandy hills stretching to the horizon in every direction, shimmering in the oven-like heat of Central Sahara. Nothing seemed to exist in this terrible land, and what form of life would choose to live in such inhospitable terrain, anyway?

The men put their backs to it, but it was slow work, and most of the time their vehicles were running on sand channels. Even the sand channels sank at times and the vehicle tilted and came off them and heroic efforts then had to be made to get the truck into movement again.

Offer stared ahead through the shimmering air currents over the Sand Lake. As far as he could see were cairns of rocks and empty cans marking the safe pathway. He thought it was hopeless, they'd never make it. If only they hadn't an enemy at their heels and could take their time, now they'd be resting during the worst of the day's heat. But the enemy was there, hard after them.

Or was he?

R.S.M. O'Keefe, whenever conditions permitted, was taking a great interest in those distant Germans, watching them through his glasses. It was never easy to see them, visibility at its worst just after midday, solid objects seeming to break and lift above the dancing, distorted horizon, but a patient, knowledgeable man like O'Keefe could in time interpret events most accurately. Now he came to Offer with one of those interpretations, and his diagnosis was startling.

'Sir.' Offer was sitting forlornly on one of the marker cairns watching the slow, laborious efforts of his men to dig out their second truck. Here, because the 'ridge' was so narrow, if one vehicle stopped it always brought to a halt all the others behind. There was no taking chances and trying to pull round a stationary truck. Sergeant Maye had demonstrated the dangers of straying from the marked trail some time earlier.

'Watch!' he'd said, and hurled an empty metal ammo case about twenty yards from them. Fascinated they had seen it gradually disappear under the hot dry granular sand. 'And that,' Maye had pointed out grimly, 'has quite a big surface area relative to its weight. You, with legs like points, would go down faster, like an arrow.' He also told them not to struggle if they got into difficulties, for that would take them under even faster.

'Yes, R.S.M.?' Captain Offer was going through hell that day, with all those sores and bruises and this terrible sun to contend with, but now he was up and about he wouldn't yield and crawl to his blankets again.

'Sir, I think old Jerry's packed it in,' O'Keefe told him dramatically.

That brought Offer's head up with a jerk, and then a wince of pain to follow the incautious movement. 'You really think so?'

'They've been there nearly an hour, still in the same place. If they were after us, do you think they'd take such a long rest?' It was an interesting theory.

'It would be ironical if they quit just at the moment when we're stuck on the Sand Lake.' The Germans, if he knew it, could be within rifle range within an hour or two. Evidently they didn't know it. 'R.S.M., watch them. Report back to me if you see any further activity.'

Offer took a chance after that news. The men simply couldn't go on at this pace. Now he put only one detachment of men—the personnel of each truck—digging out at a time. Three-quarters of the men, then, were able to rest, crawling under their trucks to keep in the only shade hereabouts. Progress was slower—in fact they weren't doing a hundred yards in an hour now—but at least it gave the men chance to recover a little.

And R.S.M. O'Keefe kept returning with the exhilarating news that the German force was still in leaguer and hadn't resumed pursuit.

'Looks as if we're going to make it, after all,' Offer said genially, and it was as if they had triumphed, and momentarily they forgot the awful punishment they were enduring just to keep on the move, or the many days of trekking ahead, perhaps little better than this Sand Lake.

The trucks still churned up great dust clouds as frantic efforts were made to keep them moving, but the changing wind now drifted the dust haze to one side, enabling O'Keefe to maintain an almost constant watch on the distant German force.

Sergeant Maye also brought good news.

'If my memory's not slipping, sir, that marks the edge of the Sand Lake.' He pointed to a distant marker, bigger than its fellows. 'Once we reach it, it'll be a piece of cake.'

Captain Offer thought that the Great Sand Sea, even on its easier stretches, was not everyone's idea of a piece of cake. He said so, then between them they computed the time required to cover the intervening few hundred yards. Tantalisingly close, yet they reckoned, in their exhausted state, they'd still be struggling over the narrow ridge for the better part of two or three hours. Still, Maye's news was something to encourage them, and John Offer told him to go to the men and buck up their spirits with his information.

Ten minutes later O'Keefe came dragging his way through the yielding soft sand to say the Germans were after them again.

They looked at each other, knowing the implications of that news. The Germans would be refreshed, following their long halt, and could come along at a cracking pace right up to the beginning of the awful Sand Lake. The R.S.M. thought the Boche would be at the Lake within two hours at the most.

'Well, we'll not be across by then,' Offer told him, rubbing his battered nose tenderly. 'So we'll be stuck here on the Sand Lake, sitting ducks for their Mgs and rifles.' He doubted if they would be much more than half a mile from where they had started to cross this awful lake, well within range of the German weapons. 'R.S.M.,' said Offer thoughtfully, 'do you know, I think we're in a terrible mess.'

O'Keefe agreed with him, dolefully, then brightened a little, knowing his man. 'But I think, sir, you might dig up one of your better ideas and get us out of this jam.'

It was flattery, but it put John Offer—poor, bruised and pain-wracked Glasshouse John—on his mettle; yet how on earth could they escape their enemies?

Now all men were put back at the relentless digging and shoving. The heat was unbearable. Soon man after man began to collapse, white of face because of heatstroke. Progress was reduced to a snail's pace. Offer gave the men all the water they could drink, because if they didn't survive the next hour or so they wouldn't need water after that. It revived some of them, but still they progressed at pitiful speed.

Desert Marauders

Soon they did not need reports from R.S.M. O'Keefe. The advancing dust cloud was apparent even without glasses to aid vision. Morale began to disintegrate as the threat came steadily, inexorably nearer. Men who could have gone on a little longer began to quit.

So finally Captain Offer gave the order to abandon the last of their Chevs and they went on without it.

*

Hauptmann Braunschweig was a fiercely satisfied man. The killing would soon begin, of that he was now certain. The dust cloud still hung over the desert before them, but it was hanging, scarcely moving except when drifted aside by the little wind. That meant they were gaining on the enemy fast, and Braunschweig wondered at it and guessed that the desert raiding force had run into trouble with soft sand. It must be bad if it was worse than this, he thought grimly, watching truck after truck in his column being helped out of difficulties by his invaluable patrol cars. His own open staff car was less of a problem, being so light that it tended to skim the surface and anyway was easier to shove out when it did bog down.

Morale among his men, though not altogether desert warriors like some of these British raiders, was at its highest now. They had benefited by a long rest, and sight of an enemy being rapidly overhauled was an inspiration to them. They worked like maniacs to keep the vehicles going, and they were magnificently fit and the pace they made would have astounded Offer's commando. But then those four-wheel-drive patrol cars did ease the strain on ordinary muscle-power, and Offer could have done with one of them at that moment.

Even so it was about three o'clock in the hot afternoon, nearly three hours after pursuit had begun, that Braunschweig's column finally came up to the Sand Lake. Not that the Hauptmann knew it was the Sand Lake. All he realised was that where up to now there had been an occasional empty petrol can to mark the route, now the cans were more frequent and in pairs, making a little avenue across a drab grey plain of sand. Braunschweig looked at those paired cans and worked out the message for himself. He gave the order not to depart from the beaconed track.

But even as his eye fell upon those cans, they took in another sight too. Through the shimmering air currents, at their worst over the lake, the Germans began to make out an obstruction in the path some half a mile away. Vision was so distorted that it took them some time to realise what it was, then they saw it was an enemy vehicle and their hearts rejoiced.

So the British had been forced to abandon one of their precious trucks.

Hauptmann Braunschweig gave the order to resume the advance and he personally led the way between the cans. He was a bold man and a real leader of men. Deserted trucks are dangerous things, as every soldier in North Africa knew. Enemies had unpleasant little habits of booby-trapping them, leaving fiendish instruments that blew up in the faces of unwary soldiers the moment they touched the vehicles. Braunschweig could have sent some men ahead to test this forlorn and solitary British truck, but he didn't. He went himself to examine it. Anyway, he had an instinct that they had had neither the time nor the means to rig the thing, and his impatience to be at the enemy drove him on.

His staff car began to leave the more cumbersome vehicles behind, they already experiencing difficulties as the sand grew more yielding under their tyres, and the patrol cars in constant use now. His own car got stuck a few times, but still his progress was faster than the others, and he came to the abandoned Chevrolet well ahead of them.

A few hundred yards beyond the deserted vehicle the character of the ground changed. Instead of this vast flatness that stretched far in every direction, the ground resumed its grey hummocky appearance. Somewhere among these rolling dunes was Braunschweig's prey.

Their presence, though, was easy to detect. A billowing cloud of dust rose high in the air no more than a mile ahead, telling still of difficulties to progress. So near now, yet unseen.

The Hauptmann exulted. From a ten-mile lead they had reduced the race to a mere few hundred yards' difference. Within an hour they would surely be up with their enemies and then they would be brought to action, and that was what Braunschweig had been trained for, and that was all he lived for these days.

All the same, when the Hauptmann reached the Allied truck he behaved with circumspection. He stood in his car, halted behind the Chevrolet, though that meant it began to sink and would have to be dug out, and very carefully inspected the rolling country beyond the drab grey flatness. He was unable to detect anything hostile—only that more distant rolling cloud of dust, flawing the African blue sky—but Braunschweig knew how easy it would be to miss something, even so comparatively close. The distortion due to the rising of heated air above the flat sand was truly abominable. He would have to risk an enemy lying out there within gun range.

He and a sergeant descended from his staff car and came up to the Chev from the rear, interposing its bulk between them and any possible enemy lurking beyond. It was astonishing how hard it was to walk, their feet sinking nine or ten inches with every stride. The technique, in fact, was to go as fast as possible over the ground, moving quickly before sand engulfed and held down their boots.

They had to take risks and come round the side of the truck, in view of those dunes which could provide cover for an enemy, but nothing happened and no fire was opened up on them. Braunschweig relaxed at that. His enemy was probably concentrating on one thing only—keeping his vehicles moving under such appallingly bad conditions.

Braunschweig swung open the driver's door and stepped back smartly. Nothing exploded. Reassured, Braunschweig looked inside the cab but there was nothing of interest to him there and he didn't bother to climb in. He was pretty sure the vehicle would be immobilised, and consequently they would have to detour round it. It certainly wasn't worth the bother of trying to recover it. Then he turned to look back impatiently.

His column was still making heavy weather of it. Now the Germans' pace had declined astonishingly, and even with their patrol cars to aid them, they were only making a few hundred yards an hour. So this was why the desert raiders had seemed to be held in one spot for so long, Braunschweig thought. It was this awful place, holding them back.

It took an hour for the column to reach the deserted Chev (it had taken Offer's men four hours to cover the same distance), and Hauptmann Braunschweig grew more impatient at the delay. Now the enemy was making more speed than he and the dust cloud before them was becoming more distant. Still, it wasn't all that far ahead. Once across this terrible stretch of country and they'd romp after the raiders and soon put a stop to their running.

The first of the infantry carriers crept up to the Chev. Behind came the others. Now no man except the driver was aboard any truck. Manhandling the vehicles along were something like a hundred and thirty muscular, brown-backed Germans, working with masochistic fervour and achieving miracles of progress.

There was a great scene of activity as the first of the infantry carriers crawled up to the bogged-down Chev. Braunschweig's Leutnants and noncoms did a lot of bellowing of orders, and sweating, straining men did their best to obey them.

The leading German truck now swung wide of the stationary Chev. Immediately it began to sink in the sand, its off-side wheels going down more quickly, so that the vehicle lurched precariously to one side, and seemed almost to be on the point of tilting over. Men leapt to its rescue and worked frantically, digging furiously to insert sand channels under the wheels which could get no grip when in gear. It was a scene of hectic confusion.

Then a patrol car was ordered up to give the carrier a tow, and this tried to get around the bigger vehicle by driving circuitously farther still away from the beaconed track. It never even reached the infantry carrier. The front wheels began to slip under the sand, and the whole vehicle seemed to be gently sliding forward and going under.

Panic undoubtedly set in at that sight. Rescue had to be swift or never. Screaming commands brought men doubling up to haul out their precious patrol car—the steadily sinking infantry carrier could wait; it wasn't going down as fast.

At which precise moment, a machine-gun opened up on them from the distant rolling dunes—another joined it, and then some rifles started a nasty, accurate fire. The effect was devastating.

The German infantry, without command, raced for their weapons. And when they reached them and got them in their hands, many of them promptly raced on to their death.

A few ran up and took refuge behind the Chev and their own two bogged-down vehicles, but the trucks were unable to give cover to all Braunschweig's men. In any event, sound infantry training was at work.

Instinctively, most of the men began to fan out, dispersing not only to avoid being a bunched-up target for the enemy fire but also to get into a position where they could pin down the enemy marksmen and mount a counter-attack. So they began to spread out, forgetful of those grim beacons which marked the only safe way across the lake.

Those watching—paralysed by shock, for the most part—said afterwards it was the most terrible sight of the war. One moment young soldiers, weapons in hands, were running, crouching against the hail of bullets which immediately began to find targets. The next they were not running. Their feet had carried them into softer sand. They found themselves sinking. They were unable to move, and still they were sinking.

They began to shout and thresh about with their arms, weapons flung from them heedlessly, to sink with awesome swiftness into the quicksands. Some disappeared from sight screaming, all within seconds. Others, perhaps less fortunate, were slower to go under and knew the horror of what was to come for long moments before they choked and died.

Some men ran forward to try to help their comrades, and they too were caught in the treacherous quicksands. Hauptmann Braunschweig saw the danger and shouted to them to stand fast, and then men ran, more sensibly, for ropes which were thrown, to be caught and some of the victims were dragged out from death. But there were not enough ropes, and shocked Panzers had to watch while some comrades went under, the running sand filling ears and nostrils and pouring into throats that cried in agony to be saved. And then silence, the silence of death. Just one final convulsive heave of sand as the despairing eyes and then the hair went out of sight, a ripple momentarily upon the surface. And horrified comrades noted how the hair seemed to float to the surface and was the last to be dragged under.

The terror of those moments was so great, the horror of the tragedy so stunning, they almost forgot the Bren guns that were still pouring out their bursts of lead and inflicting other forms of death among them.

*

Captain Offer said, as briskly as his injuries would permit, 'There's nothing for it. They're catching up hand over fist. The thing is, can we get off the lake before they arrive? If we can't they'll have us.'

Men shoving on bogged-down vehicles were too easy as targets even for distant marksmen. That, curiously, was the thought inspiring Captain John Offer at that moment; for suddenly he realised that their weakness could be made to work in reverse against the Germans.

'We'll leave one truck—the last one. Having to man-handle only three vehicles should at least make our progress quicker.'

'But three vehicles for thirty men and all our kit?' R.S.M. O'Keefe knew the discomfort of crowded travel over hostile desert.

Offer's voice hardened. 'There won't be thirty men for three trucks if we don't do something drastic,' and then he told them his plan.

'From cover we'll site our two Brens and some riflemen while the other trucks make as much progress as possible. When the Boche reaches our Chev he'll try to get round it, and my guess is if he goes off that track he'll be in trouble.'

In any event it was a safe bet that somewhere around their Chev, which was nicely within gunshot range, those Germans must inevitably get stuck. That would mean working parties by the wheels, trying to shove the trucks forward, and those working parties would be under fire.

Offer said to his silent, exhausted men, 'Don't you see? He can't get anywhere without his trucks, and we can pin down his men until nightfall so that they don't move a yard past the old Chev. Our trucks can keep going until dark, taking it a lot easier than we've done all day, and then there's a good night's kip for us and we'll be away at daylight next morning. We ought to get a big lead tomorrow, because it will take Jerry some time to cover the last few hundred yards of the lake.'

'How do we catch up with the trucks?' It was Sibrett, a Bren gunner, a man Offer cared little for. He had been a pal of McTone, the man who had made such a painful mess of Offer only two nights before. A real villain, Sibrett, just as dirty-tempered as McTone, but more cunning with it. Now he looked his hostility towards John Offer's plan.

Offer said, curtly, 'We walk. We've all night in which to catch up.' They'd need torches; he must remember to take a couple with them.

Sibrett's unpleasantness spilled over. The strain of those agonising hours shoving trucks through soft sand told on him now. He was openly quarrelsome. 'But *you* won't do any walking.'

'Who says?' The smaller Offer squared up to the Bren gunner, though the effort sent rivers of pain coursing through his mangled body. His men all looked at him in astonishment. He was a bruised wreck, showing the ravages of brutal boot and ruthless fist. He seemed hardly able to stand erect, so destroyed by McTone's hammering. Yet he was talking of staying behind with the rear party and perhaps marching all night over soft sand.

'I shall be with the rear party, Sibrett.' In fact it hadn't occurred to Offer not to be with them. This plan was his; therefore he must be there to ensure that it went off all right. He would never make the long stumbling march back through sand little better than quicksand. He knew he would make it if the others did.

That put an end to the talk from Sibrett. Now Offer called upon his men to give him all they'd got, and they responded, spurred on by the prospect of shaking their pursuer off their tail, and somehow finally got their three vehicles across that treacherous Sand Lake. It was an experience none of them would ever forget or want to repeat.

Once they were past the last big marker, however, the going became comparatively easy, but still vehicles got into trouble and had to be dug out, though nowhere as often as before. They ground along in low gear, wheels too often spinning, bringing apprehension to the men, yet gripping most of the time and carrying them steadily away from the Lake of Sand.

A hundred yards or so into the sand dunes, Captain Offer had his rear party drop out. He allowed them plenty of water and as much food as they could carry, and they brought blankets with them and some sticks which they always carried while on the move.

Walking back to a position overlooking the Sand Lake, Offer selected a site where they could lie in ambush. There was nothing else to commend it. They struggled to the top of a dune that rolled up out of the sand plain and gave them a fair view across the lake. Here, under the torrid sun, they proposed to spend the remaining hours until darkness. It was going to be a long-drawn-out agony, especially for the injured Offer.

They made themselves as comfortable as they could, rigging their blankets on the sticks to give them shade while permitting air to circulate. Then they established a roster and those not on watch tried to sleep away their wretchedness and physical exhaustion. Offer went out, as someone said, like a light, almost collapsing into sleep again, and no one, except Sibrett, minded because they admired his pluck in even staying with them.

Time crawled. Waves of heat rolled over them, sometimes actually making them gasp, so hot was the air. All the time they kept their limbs under the shade, for without it, lying there, they would have roasted in the next hours.

Vision was awful, even from twenty feet above the lake. Nothing remained still, solids seeming to sway and to break up and float in the air. They could see their forlorn, deserted Chev out on the flatland, quite close really, yet at times it was difficult to recognise it as a truck.

Many hours later, so it seemed to the watchers, one of them became interested in some distant movement. He was a long time watching it, because it was difficult to say if it was real movement or just more dancing distortions caused by the rising air currents. Finally, simply because it seemed to be growing larger, he decided there were people out there. The Germans had arrived at last. At that he woke his officer.

Captain Offer came reluctantly back to consciousness and the agony of desert existence. But when he had drunk heavily of water that seemed cool but was as hot as bathwater, he pulled himself together and took over the glasses. In time he decided that the crawling, dancing object was a solitary car approaching their Chev. He shifted his glasses, concentrated on a greater distance and concluded that the growing dark bulk in the background was a column of vehicles. It was not easy to interpret any visual phenomenon under those conditions of light and heat.

He decided not to do anything yet awhile, out of consideration for his men. They could stay in the shade a little longer and not lie with their guns out in the open and fry. Captain Offer maintained the watch thereafter.

Sometimes vision steadied, and then Offer got the whole scene for a few seconds. In one such moment he saw a small car stationary beyond the Chev and some men standing by the cab of their old vehicle.

Time dragged along again, though the day was probably beginning to cool, and the more solid mass of vehicles came close up behind the smaller car. Finally they were all bunched together just beyond the Chev and again, several times, vision was momentarily good and they could see everything clearly.

In one such moment they saw a bulky infantry carrier come lurching round the Chev, then stop parallel with it.

'Stuck, b'God,' said Offer with satisfaction. His hunch was working.

A little later again vision steadied and they saw a turreted patrol car come round the infantry carrier and then that too came to a halt, and they guessed what was happening to it. What they also saw was men crowding around, and guessed they were trying to rescue the bogged-down vehicles. At that Captain Offer gave the order to open fire.

It was, in military terms, a logical decision to make. His plan had succeeded; their Chev had shoved enemy trucks into soft sand. Now they must delay the recovery of those vehicles as long as possible. So two Bren guns, mounted on short tripods, and six good riflemen began to hurl spinning bullets in among the enemy around the trucks.

What none of them knew was the tragedy that was being played out under their gunfire. Vision was so distorted that neither Offer nor his men realised that out there something like twenty young German soldiers were drowning horribly in the soft quicksands, and that their fire was doing injury to comrades trying frantically to save their lives.

It roused in Hauptmann Braunschweig and his surviving men a terrible hatred of the British; for they could not know that Offer's marksmen were firing almost blind, unable to identify targets accurately and certainly unable to see the victims struggling in the sand. In return the Germans put up a furious covering fire, but they too were firing blind, incapable of seeing any target.

Offer gave the order to cease fire only when it became apparent that enemy personnel had all taken cover, probably behind their trucks. His gun barrels, anyway, were getting red hot and could do with a cooling-off period. All the same, each time they saw enemy movement, men still trying to get a tow on that submerging patrol car, Offer gave the order to drive them back into cover. He wasn't interested in killing men—Offer never was, if one excepted Glasshouse screws who could be exterminated without conscience—all he wanted was to hamper pursuit as long as possible.

So they played cat and mouse until darkness, any movement by the enemy bringing swift and heavy fire from Offer's marksmen, and return fire by the Germans. Vision grew better as the day cooled a little, but it was never very good.

While the sun was still just above the horizon, Offer decided to pull out. The probability was that the enemy would go on lying behind their trucks not realising that the British had retreated. Well, let them go on lying there, Offer told his men with grim humour. Even if they rescued their vehicles in the darkness the Germans would be stuck in the Sand Lake, hardly daring to move before daylight. Meanwhile his rearguard would make as much distance as possible after the trucks while there was a bit of light by which to see.

So keeping low behind the skyline, they stumbled away, burdened with weapons, ammunition, blankets and water. After only a few yards Offer told them to drop the blankets; even if they had to sleep cold for the rest of the Sand Sea crossing it wasn't worth the effort of carrying them now. But their guns, ammo and water could not be discarded, certainly not the water. They could have drunk the whole lot within ten minutes, but on that walk Offer introduced a system of rationing—a big mouthful every half hour. It wasn't enough.

It was desperately hard going, trudging through that soft, yielding sand, and at the end of this hard day they had little enough energy left for walking even under the most favourable of conditions. In time they were so fatigued, slowly though they dragged themselves, that every ten minutes or so they had to stop and rest.

For the men it was bad enough; for Offer it was a nightmare. He started by insisting on carrying his share of weight—two water bottles—but it soon became evident that he was in no condition to help them with their burdens and good-heartedly the men relieved him of them. Even then he was a drag upon them, in spite of his fanatical determination to keep up with the party, and several times some of them were again kind and helped him when he fell, though strained and sweating faces told of their own near-exhaustion.

Night came too swiftly, not that there was any difficulty in following the deep-rutted tyre marks of their Chevs by torchlight. But somehow it seemed to slow their pace, and made them more conscious of their fatigue. They kept going, more slowly with every laboriously passing minute. It took them three hours to cover less than two miles, and now the worrying thought in all their minds was, 'How much farther do we have to go?'

In fact they would never have made it if R.S.M. O'Keefe had stuck to his orders and hadn't used his loaf. When he saw how fast the Chevs covered the ground after pulling off the Lake of Sand O'Keefe wisely decided that Offer and his men would be walking all night if they had to cover this distance on foot.

So the lean, gap-toothed O'Keefe—he'd had a tooth knocked out by a flying Arab stick and had never had time to get dental assistance since— O'Keefe ordered the first two Chevs to keep going, but halted the third and stayed with it himself.

The leading Chevs would still put up a big cloud of dust, breaking the hearts of their enemy as they watched it recede, stuck down in the middle of the Sand Lake. The third Chev would catch up with the others in the darkness, for they would have easy tracks to follow in their headlights with no prospect of wandering off the trail and coming to disaster.

O'Keefe gave the glad order to his men to rest, and they flopped out under their truck, whacked and only wanting drink and shade. The shadows were lengthening by now, and even they began to decide that the main heat had gone out of the day. The R.S.M., tireless ex-L.R.D.G. warrior as he was, just sat in the driver's seat and kept alert and listened.

Some time before sunset he began to hear the sound of firing. It was quite loud. At that he got down on to the hot sand, too impatient and anxious to remain seated. He took hold of a Tommy and walked back the way they had come for a few yards, then stood there, head on one side, listening. After a few minutes, the firing ended and then O'Keefe's nerves became jumpy, wondering what that signified. Had Captain Offer's plan failed? Had their rearguard been stormed by the enemy and put out of action? If so perhaps the Germans were coming towards them at this moment.

R.S.M. O'Keefe was a man of manic activity, yet with moments of considerable depression. Standing alone there in that heat, surrounded by grey and desolate sand and rocks, their solitary truck looking infinitely lonely in that wasteland, O'Keefe began to indulge in pessimism. After the silence had continued for a while he began to feel sure that Offer and his party had been wiped out. If so O'Keefe and his men ought to be beetling off as fast as they could go, he told himself. If they stayed and the Boche was really after them, it was only a question of time before they came into view, and what could one truck-load of men do against such military might?

O'Keefe's dilemma lasted until abruptly the firing started again. At that his depression fled; he could distinguish the sounds of their own Brens and knew both were again in action. Offer and party were still very much alive and kicking.

With that he walked back to his seat in the cab and again sat there in the shade, listening. The firing broke out intermittently over the next hour, and then there was a long silence. Darkness came with the extinction of that terrible, tormenting sun, though the world around him was still like an oven, the sand exuding the heat it had retained during the day.

The R.S.M. gave them another hour after darkness had fallen, and reckoned then that Offer's party would now be well on their way after the vehicles. At that he roused his men, and they all walked by torchlight back along the trail.

They trudged a good hour before seeing a wavering torch ahead. They had brought water with them, and Offer's party needed it; then the R.S.M.'s party took over the weapons and ammo and they all started back for the truck. It took an hour and a half to make it, even though Offer's men were assisted by their fresher comrades, but in time the dim shape of their Chev came into view and they knew that the day's travail at least was over.

Offer, who was in a state of almost total collapse for the last half-mile and had to be supported by O'Keefe and big Art Weybright, their radio operator, was lifted into the back of their vehicle and bedded down on some blankets. He passed out and didn't move until well into the next day. The other members of the rearguard were helped into the truck, and curled up and went off into noisy sleep, too. Somehow the rest of the R.S.M.'s men managed to cling on to the overladen vehicle, while O'Keefe shoved it in gear and drove off, following the tyre marks ahead. He wanted to be up with the leading trucks by daylight so as not to hold back their flight.

Defeat comes hard to men of Hauptmann Braunschweig's calibre, but next day, when light came to bring its torment again, he had to admit he had been licked. The raiders had given him the slip. He stood out by the abandoned Chev that had given them so much trouble, and looked far to the south. There was the dust cloud, betraying the presence of his now-hated enemy. He reckoned it to be ten miles away, which was a lead as great as when they had started the pursuit from Siwa. Greater, he thought gloomily, looking at their situation, still with much of this awful quicksand plain to traverse, and their patrol car hopelessly dug into the sand.

During the night, with care at first in case of hostile action from the rolling dunes, they had got to work on salvaging their vehicles, but as time wore on without trouble they had begun to work openly, even employing headlights from the second patrol car to assist them.

The big infantry carrier was finally hauled back on to sand channels and then on to firmer ground behind the Chev, but nothing they could do could shift the patrol car. By now it was nose down with sand up to the top of its bonnet.

Braunschweig had put men to work trying to dig it out, but they had to operate with ropes round their bodies, for their efforts only served to push them into the quicksands, too. Anyway, all the digging they did made no impression, as fast as they dug, loose sand tumbled into each hole their spades made. Braunschweig soon abandoned that idea, and the men, who hated being on that quicksand with a rope cutting into their bodies, were relieved when he called it off. Towing the patrol car out by use of the other car, winched also by a truck behind, both vehicles first thoughtfully run on to sand channels, did not budge the other, bogged-down patrol car by an inch. It did tear the guts out of the winching apparatus, however.

About three in the morning Hauptmann Braunschweig gave up the recovery attempt, and they all got down to rest until daybreak. At dawn the Hauptmann saw the raiders well away and gave the order to turn about and head for Siwa, abandoning their patrol car to a grave in the quicksands.

R.S.M. O'Keefe saw the dust cloud of the retreating Germans and told his men they could relax. The hunt was off.

Back in Siwa a frosty-eyed and still angry Hauptmann made out a report for his superiors. It was a report of failure, and the Braunschweigs of this world resent having to confess to such. It was an interesting report.

'The raiders who released eight P.O.W.s from the prison compound here in Siwa are an irregular force known, according to our prisoner, Private McTone, as the Glasshouse Gang Commando Unit. This unit has apparently no official status within the British Army, and appears to be the banding together of Allied army deserters, all of whom have been held for crimes in British Service Field Prisons. "Glasshouse" is another name for service prison, McTone tells us.

'The leader of this force is a former British lieutenant, John Offer, who was cashiered and served a sentence in a Glasshouse for some offence described by our prisoner as "flogging" army property for personal gain to civilians. We believe "flogging" to mean stealing and selling. Offer, sometimes known among his men as Glasshouse John, has assumed the rank of captain as an aid to disguise, but the rank is entirely unauthorised and his real rank is that of private.'

During the course of his report on the action on the Sand Lake, Braunschweig, with very great deliberation, wrote: 'When our men incautiously ran on to quicksands and began to sink to their death, the Glasshouse Gang deliberately maintained a heavy fire upon us. This considerably impeded our attempts at rescue, while at the same time caused casualties among the men trying to help their comrades who were being buried alive. If there had been no gunfire, casualties would have been smaller and more of our men might have been rescued from the soft sand. As it was, twelve men were lost in the quicksands, and three men died and nine suffered severe wounds from enemy fire.'

When this report was received at Rommel's headquarters in Derna, the field-marshal grew terribly, coldly angry, to an extent unusual in that personality. A description of John Offer and details of his Glasshouse Gang were circulated among all units in the Afrika Korps and their Italian allies, warning them of the Gang's activity in the desert. With it went the implication that at all costs this criminal unit must be brought to book, especially their leader.

The news of the horrifying death of their comrades in the Great Sand Sea quicksands spread throughout the Axis armies, and as such stories always do, it created a wave of revulsion so that if ever a Glasshouse man fell into enemy hands from then on, he would be in for a rough time. As for John

Offer, if the Germans got hold of him he would wish he had never been born.

*

The arrival of the Glasshouse Gang into Kufra Oasis, two awful weeks later, was something in the nature of a triumph. Not that the unit felt very triumphant. Even after the dreaded Lake of Sand the crossing of the Great Sand Sea had still been a gruelling experience. Tough though the men were, all except one came through in far worse shape physically than when they had set out from Siwa, some almost so far worn out as to be virtually passengers during the latter part of their journey.

The one exception was Captain Offer. He had started the journey a wreck of a man, hammered thus by the vengeful feet and fists of Private McTone. As the days passed, though, in spite of the arduous nature of the crossing, he could not fail to improve. The bruises gradually disappeared, and his various pains left him. Of course his men nursed him and for the first days after the Sand Lake he rode up front alongside a driver. So he got better, and the resilience of the tough not-very-big man was a thing to be remarked upon in some awe by his followers.

The nearer they got to Kufra, the stronger their commanding officer seemed to get. He went about remarkably cheerful, encouraging his men and bringing fresh heart to them when unusually hostile terrain knocked the stuffing out of them.

'Keep going, we'll get through,' he would tell them. 'Look how far we've got, and the worst's over.'

The worst was their time of peril on the Sand Lake. Each day Offer would pull out a sweat-stained map and show them Siwa, then estimate their position now. It did encourage them as they saw the distance back to Siwa increasing, while the route ahead to Kufra reduced accordingly.

He was a great captain, and to his devoted followers at the beginning of the journey, like Walker, O'Keefe, Weybright, Tulger and the Aussie, Lashley, now others were added to give him their unswerving loyalty. Likewise Offer's inspiration in turning the tables on their enemy on the Lake of Sand would never be forgotten.

Their signaller, Weybright, had radioed the L.R.D.G. at Kufra with a full report of their journey over the Great Sand Sea, how they had outwitted a strong German following force and done them much injury, and how they were bringing the released L.R.D.G. P.O.W.s with them. In fact, with Offer back in circulation, he and Weybright considerably improved upon fact in presenting their version of events.

'It was a very strong pursuing force,' said Offer thoughtfully, when he and Weybright sat together at a halt one evening to concoct the report.

'Sir,' agreed Weybright, 'I agree it was a very strong force.'

'It was a motorised column.'

'Indeed it was, sir,' and Weybright made a note to that effect on his grubby pad.

'I was never able to count the vehicles because of the appalling optical conditions, but it would not surprise me if there wasn't a whole German Panzer regiment on our tail.' Offer's imagination was beginning to soar.

'A thousand infantry?' Weybright brooded over the thought, then loyally supported his leader. 'I have no doubt about it, sir. There could not have been less than a whole Panzer regiment. I wouldn't even be surprised to be told we had a Panzer division after us.' Weybright could have flights of fancy, too.

'Oh, come now, Weybright,' Offer reproved. 'I think that's going a bit far, isn't it? I mean, old chap, British understatement and all that, we mustn't do it, must we?' And Weybright meekly accepted the rebuke and just wrote the word 'regiment' on his pad.

Still Offer mused over those moments by the side of the Sand Lake, while the German column had come slowly into vision through the dancing hot air currents. 'I saw gun turrets.'

'Tanks?' asked Weybright quickly, pencil eagerly poised.

Offer deliberated. Tanks? No, even G.H.Q. Cairo might find tanks crossing the Great Sand Sea too much to swallow. 'I doubt it.' Offer did not entirely close the door on Weybright's hopeful suggestion, however, 'Tracked vehicles though, they're a possibility.'

'They are indeed, sir,' said his radio operator, and the final signal that went off told of a tremendous rearguard action across the Great Sand Sea, with the heroic G.G.C.U. fighting off attack after attack from a Panzer regiment, leaving the enemy with heavy losses in men, as well as soft transport and tracked vehicles.

Before it was transmitted Offer looked at the signal admiringly. 'It's a work of art,' he told Weybright. 'You and I ought to collaborate over some literary effort when the war's over.'

'We'd be great at fiction,' was Weybright's enthusiastic contribution.

Captain Offer let the word go by without comment. After all, if it pleased that Brass Hat shower in Cairo why shouldn't he stretch truth to the point of fiction? Anyway if no one else, it did Offer and the faithful Weybright good.

Probably this time Offer's signal did stretch Cairo credulity too far, for Kufra later obligingly relayed a signal from G.H.Q., which said, simply, 'Entire German garrison at Siwa does not amount to a regiment. Check signal . . .'

Captain Offer and an unabashed Weybright did solemnly check their signal and decided after all they had overdone things. So off went a nice piece of glibness which said: 'Error in previous signal. For regiment please read column of unknown strength.' It would still make Cairo happy, they thought indulgently.

What did bring a frown to the ex-actor's face was a repeat of a Cairo injunction, following previous G.G.C.U. claims to desert victories, to reveal their identity. 'No record of any unit initialled G.G.C.U. Please identify.'

Offer, after that slight frown, though, just shrugged. 'They can find out for themselves,' he told his earnest follower. 'Hang it all, they're supposed to have an Intelligence service, aren't they?'

*

A magnificent Captain Tony Leslie was there to receive them when their battered Chevs pulled up outside the L.R.D.G. headquarters in Kufra. He was a big, bold-looking buccaneer, heavily black-bearded and still wearing that dashing headdress of the nomadic Arab, the *kefir*. Offer had met him once, at Siwa, and then for a few minutes only, but there was no forgetting this man.

Offer managed to alight with some sprightliness, his face benignly smiling. It was a much-battered face, but at least the discoloration had gone from around the eyes. The rest of his party got down from their overcrowded vehicles like a lot of old men, the impression further accentuated by the desert dust which powdered them from head to foot, their hair matted nearly white, their eyebrows and eyelashes heavy with fine sand, and it clung to their cheeks and came off their clothing in clouds when they stirred. But the L.R.D.G. were used to this, having themselves come from the desert many a time.

With Captain Leslie was an assortment of L.R.D.G. officers and other ranks, who gave a cheer when they saw their rescued comrades, not the well-drilled cheer of Germans, but that apologetic, British self-conscious raising of voices that looks to its neighbour for help but means well.

Sergeant Maye, and the other rescued P.O.W.s were delighted by the reception and there was much shaking hands and buffeting of each other, then finally all went to a canteen, taking the Glasshouse boys with them. When the rescued L.R.D.G. told of their daring rescue and escape nothing was too good for the Glasshouse Gang. The drinks were on the L.R.D.G. It proved a costly night for the desert marauders, for the Glasshouse Gang had formidable thirsts even without crossing a Great Sand Sea. By midnight the G.G.C.U. were beginning to feel it had all been worthwhile, even the Lake of Sand, an impression departing next morning when the inevitable hangover reminded them that alcohol is not entirely a blessing to humanity.

Captain Offer was given the freedom of the officers' mess. Clean uniform was laid out for him, a tent devoted to his needs behind the L.R.D.G. H.Q., an old but comfortable Arab house with a walled garden, and then a happy feast was held in his honour. John Offer ate the delicious native-cooked food like a hog, but drank like a gentleman, and that was exactly what that mess expected of him. Later they talked for hours, sitting out in the moonlight in the garden, a native servant bringing cold drinks whenever they were needed. If this was war, Offer thought more than once, he could suffer quite a lot of it.

Very politely no one there asked any direct questions that evening. No 'Who are you?'; 'What's your unit?'; 'What are you up to?' Cloak-and-dagger outfits keep themselves very much to themselves.

Even so, next day, after the most marvellous night's sleep Offer could ever remember, followed by a check-up by a medical officer with a detachment of S.A.S., also in Kufra, Captain Leslie did reveal interest in the G.G.C.U. Offer wondered if there wasn't some long-range prompting from Cairo radio behind a delicate approach for enlightenment.

It began in the evening. Offer had taken one look at Kufra and decided it wasn't up to Siwa—too crowded with military, for one thing, but also somehow lacking in Siwa's serenity. So he had taken himself into the cool L.R.D.G. mess and was prepared to stay there until circumstances made the Glasshouse Gang move.

Captain Leslie took over later that night, and Offer thought that other officers had been tipped off to leave them together so that Leslie could talk. John Offer smiled to himself indulgently. He was quite prepared to talk, and looked forward to an evening where his histrionic talent could have full play.

Leslie took a long time to work round to his subject, because of course a fellow couldn't ask outright or display curiosity about the other chap and his business. There was that code to be followed. A man could get as much information as possible, but the getting must be done decently, no blunt and awkward questions. The form, in fact, was to leave the door open and if the other fellow wished to put a verbal foot through it, that was acceptable. But one's guests must never, never be embarrassed by direct enquiry. It just wasn't done.

The L.R.D.G. captain carefully opened wide an inviting door. The technique of door-opening is simple. You sit and talk about yourself, and if the other fellow follows the form he will contribute something, as much as he wishes, about what he is up to. Of course deep military secrets must be maintained, and no officer and gentleman expects confidence that would be in breach of top army secrecy. They all knew the rules of the game, and most played them well.

So Captain Leslie talked about L.R.D.G. adventures in the desert, and the special missions they had gone on. It was exciting stuff, even though underplayed by Leslie—that also was the form, never talk big and show off; that was for cads. John Offer thought, 'I'm going to be a cad tonight,' and the thought tickled him. He'd get away with it because with his acting ability and control over words he'd shoot monstrous lines while giving the appearance of modesty. John Offer was going to enjoy himself.

When he had done quite a lot of talking, Leslie sat back with his drink and left it to Offer to do his turn. 'He's aching to know what G.G.C.U. means,' Offer thought, and decided to tell him—well, something.

John Offer set down his drink very carefully, then gave a quick glance round, like a man does when he wants to make sure he isn't going to be overheard. It was cleverly done, a most unobtrusive glance round, suggesting in fact that the action was a reflex and involuntary and one not to be noticed by his host. Leslie, of course, saw it and his heart warmed, knowing that the game of confidence was to be properly played by this genial, sophisticated even if broken-nosed man. But one could always recognise a pukka wallah, and flattened noses were no demerit in their hierarchy.

'You know, Les—' Captain Leslie was Les to all his fellow officers— 'I'm a bit huffed over this Siwa do.' Offer allowed the worry to creep on to his face, the smile momentarily gone, the tight lines of anxiety for an instant showing around the eyes. Those eyes lifted and looked levelly at the big black-bearded officer hanging so intently, yet without seeming to do so, on his words. 'Knocked my plans for a Burton, y'know,' he murmured, and he was playing it beautifully.

The smile of good humour switched on again, and the effect was of a man who has shown himself off guard for a second but has now pulled himself together.

'You were——' Captain Leslie held up his glass to the light, an electric lamp bulb which was proving the death of some very interesting African moths. He was picking his words delicately. 'You were on to something?'

'A bit of a show.'

'Based on Siwa.' A statement, nothing so crude as a question.

A shrug. Offer had his man and knew how to play him. A great game, being an officer and a gentleman. The lowest of murmurs in reply, a murmur because it suggests the height of confidence: 'Well, not really . . . Just passing through, you know.' A pause, Offer swishing the drink round in his glass, knowing he had Leslie waiting on his words. Still that murmur, but softer than ever. 'Derna's the real place.'

Why Derna? Offer didn't know. He had to say something, and Derna just came to mind, that was all.

'Derna.' Leslie stopped playing with his own glass, his eyes swinging almost startled to meet Offer's, then instantly pulling away. 'Warm place this time of the year, Derna.' And very carefully he added, 'I mean, with Rommel there and all that, y'know.' His glance swept Offer's face for reaction.

'Rommel?' Offer repeated the word with the same elaborate care that Leslie had said it. John Offer had forgotten that Derna was now Rommel's H.Q. Well, if Captain Leslie thought there was significance in that, Offer would play upon it. 'Rommel in Derna? Now, I think somebody did mention that fact——' An actor's pause. How those pauses carried an audience along! '——when I was in Cairo.'

'Ah!' Leslie thought he was being told something, something very discreet. Rommel, Derna and someone talking to Offer in Cairo. Captain Leslie thought it was he who was doing the fishing, and with great cunning threw out ground bait. 'Poor old Keyes!'

Keyes? Offer thought, 'Who's Keyes? What's he got to do with this conversation?' But he played up to the line. 'Yes, poor old Keyes,' he said softly, and lifted his glass and drank solemnly, and it looked like a toast to someone, perhaps some poor old someone who had cashed in his chips in regrettable circumstances. Captain John Offer was inspired that evening; everything he did struck exactly the right note.

'Wonder how the war would have turned if Keyes had got Rommel that night in Derna?' Captain Leslie mused, and something clicked in Offer's mind at that. Colonel Keyes, son of Zeebrugge Keyes. Killed on a commando raid on Rommel's H.Q. near Derna. It had happened while he was in the Glasshouse, but he'd heard of it later. Now Offer knew what was going on in Leslie's mind.

He stared over the high wall to the palm tree silhouetted against the starlit sky. He spoke very thoughtfully, and let Leslie see that he chose his words with care.

'Could have changed the course of war in North Africa, y'know, Les. He's the biggest prize. I mean, if anyone'—he laid slight emphasis on the word—'if anyone topped Rommel it would be as good as winning a battle, if not the desert war.'

'True . . . And you're off to Derna?' Captain Leslie now did look directly at Offer, and Glasshouse John did look directly at his prey.

'It's Derna for us,' and Offer allowed a look of hard ruthlessness to appear in his eyes. That was all. No more to be said. Captain Leslie gave another sigh and relaxed. He thought he knew everything now.

That engaging smile back on Offer's battered, good-humoured face. That voice still murmuring, as if giving confidences. 'Just one thing, old chap. If any silly sods in Cairo start asking questions about us, head 'em off, would you? Doesn't do to let too many people in on the act.' He drank again, humour brimming in his voice once more. 'I find it all very droll. I mean, this hush-hush stuff. Not much different from play-acting, you know. But we have to go along with it.'

'Yes . . .' said Leslie with manly tolerance for such frivolities, but later, with his L.R.D.G. officers around him, he spoke very quietly about Offer.

'Just had a talk with him. Good bloke. Absolutely first-class.' He switched his eyes to the far darkness and kept them there fixedly while he continued. Again he selected his words carefully. 'They're on to something, these chaps. Something deuced big, I can tell you.' He could feel them hanging on to his words and he had to hold the drama of the moment even longer. 'By God it *is* big!' He allowed his breath to seep out in admiration, and his fellow officers were dying to know but too gentlemanly to ask.

Very briskly, suddenly, changing the mood. 'Can't tell you about it, of course. Too much at stake to have this going the rounds of gossip. Which reminds me, anybody asking awkward questions about Offer, just head them off. Even G.H.Q. Cairo isn't supposed to know.' And John Offer would have been delighted to have heard him, for that was all he wanted from his play-acting that evening.

One question from his respectful audience. 'I say, Les, you didn't find out what G.G.C.U. means? Cairo doesn't seem to know.'

'Cairo isn't supposed to know. Never trust the Top Brass with secrets, you know.' They all laughed, captains and lieutenants, a laugh which said it was unaccountable how military inepts somehow rose to top rank while dashing young competence was so slowly rewarded.

A bright young L.R.D.G. lieutenant, Jack Edwardes, very clean shaven in the midst of this hirsute mess, made them all laugh. 'G.G.C.U.? Got Gutsy Come-Uppance,' he said and they all agreed solemnly that it did describe the flat-nosed John Offer.

Offer returned to his tent to find Weybright waiting for him. It was only to ask if Offer had any radio messages to transmit; Weybright soon got bored and liked to play with his set. But who was there to transmit messages to? Both agreed they had no friends beyond Kufra, so it didn't make sense to transmit any message, even the loveliest of fiction, to the world outside.

'The quieter we are here in Kufra, the longer we'll enjoy life,' Offer said wisely. 'Forget your wireless set, my good friend.' He liked the big shapeless Weybright. The more he saw of him the more he respected the signaller. A most intelligent man, though his hatred of the upper hierarchy of the British army was at times pathological.

Weybright was departing when Offer held him back. 'I'm afraid, old chap, I must go back on a half-promise I made back up in the Blue.'

Art Weybright looked puzzled. 'Promise?'

'We almost decided to go into literary collaboration, remember, though you were incautious enough to refer to it as fiction.'

'Oh, that.' Weybright wondered what was coming.

'No, my friend, I'm not cut out to be a writer. I'm going back to my old job, acting!'

Weybright walked away slowly, puzzled. There had been an almost dreamy, ecstatic expression on his officer's face when he'd spoken of acting. Weybright shook his head and forgot the moment.

But Captain John Offer didn't. He had just put on one of his best acting performances, restrained, true, but that was why it was so pleasing. All that quietness, those subtleties of tone and facial expression, everything balanced delicately to carry a man into a mood of believing. And it had come off, come off magnificently, Offer was sure.

'By God, I'm an actor,' he told himself, reclining on a camp bed thoughtfully provided by his respectful hosts. 'I will not waste my talent on writing – I'll give it to a deserving world!' The world of the theatre, of course.

He was a little drunk. His last, sweet thought before he went off to sleep was that Leslie had persuaded himself that the Glasshouse Gang were on yet another mission either to capture or kill Field-Marshal Erwin Rommel in Derna. Well, if Leslie wanted to believe that, he was welcome. Poor old Keyes, indeed. A fine, brave man. He'd landed from a submarine off Derna and had stormed Rommel's H.Q. but had been shot dead himself. Rommel, anyway, hadn't been there at the time. Roger Keyes had got a V.C. posthumously. John Offer didn't want a V.C., posthumously or even alive. Give him a quiet life for the duration here in Kufra . . . better still, Siwa . . .

John Offer slept the even sleep of a man without fear or concern to his conscience. If he had known, though, what was going through Captain Tony Leslie's mind at that moment he would have had a nightmare.

*

It was several days after their quiet, intimate conversation under the stars that Captain Leslie told Offer what he had in mind. Glasshouse John was really enjoying himself, though he felt a bit of a humbug. It was all this respect the tough L.R.D.G. officers gave him with their eyes. They'd accepted the hint that Offer was up to something extraordinary, something so big that even the experienced Captain Leslie was reduced to respectful awe, and they followed suit and sought Offer's company and couldn't do too much for him.

Offer was amused but took it all with the modesty necessary for the rôle of intrepid hero-adventurer.

They'd driven over to the landing strip to await the arrival of a plane from Cairo. It was usually a Bombay, and it didn't come every day, so when it did drop in it was something of an occasion. Some of the officers always went to meet it, just in case there was someone aboard they knew and could welcome. Whatever John Offer thought of it in those first days, Kufra was a deadly hole, still too much heat and too many smells and flies, and too little to do. Action up the Blue, in fact, was welcomed by most as an excuse to get away from Kufra. So new faces, with tantalising stories of the delights of Cairo and Alex, were greeted with enthusiasm.

The Bombay also brought fresh supplies of beer and short stuff, cigarettes and canned luxuries that helped to make rest periods in Kufra just supportable. Sometimes it brought unexpected luxuries: some happy chairbound warrior in Cairo once came out of his pink gins long enough to think that their mess could do with a piano and had shoved one aboard the next Bombay. And once some nursing sisters were given a swift trip across the desert and spent the night in the mess, and no one there would forget that event.

So hopefully they trekked out to the dusty landing strip and watched the plane emerge out of the blue sky to land bumpily, dust-jets like hissing steam billowing pale yellow where the wheels had touched down. But this day there was nothing to come off the old freight carrier that would excite them.

The pilot came down and talked affably to them, and invited them to fly back with him. John Offer learned that this was sometimes done, L.R.D.G. and other personnel quietly slipping back to Cairo for a night's junketing, to return, no one of importance any the wiser, by Bombay later.

'A bit traumatic,' Leslie murmured, 'the fleshpots of Cairo, then coming back to this.' Kufra was dismissed with a slight wave of the hand.

'I was never more glad to see it,' Offer said simply, and that was true. He did not yet quite share Captain Leslie's aversion to the place.

'True.' They fell into slow step back to their Jeep. 'It's a sight for sore eyes, after weeks in the Blue. But a few days of it and I'm restless. You know, beginning to crave to go back and see some action.'

Offer said he understood, and let Leslie see that he too was a craver for action. Bloody hypocrite, he told himself but without rancour. Action was for the birds. He'd stand boredom ...

'Just another week of it, then we're off, thank God,' Leslie told him. They got into the Jeep. 'It's the Road Watch.' The Road Watch was possibly the L.R.D.G.'s most magnificent contribution to the Allied war effort. They ferried their men sometimes a thousand miles up the desert to places behind the enemy lines where, with binoculars to their eyes, they could keep watch on Axis troop movements along the Mediterranean coast road. So British generals in Cairo had valuable up-to-the-minute information of enemy concentrations of strength right down to the last tank and armoured car.

They started off on a leisurely journey back to the mess. Once they came off the bare air-strip and ran under the palms the day became bearable, in spite of Arabs and their animals who obstinately insisted on their rights to the centre of the track up to the last half-second.

'Where is it this time?' It was a question Offer could ask because the Road Watch had been going too long for it to be a secret in the mess. 'Benghazi?'

Leslie neatly avoided a suicidal old patriarch who stepped into their track. 'Too far behind to be useful now. No . . . Derna.'

Glasshouse John, sensitive man, experienced a little shock at the word. Somehow, in context with their earlier conversation, the name this morning acquired a slightly ominous sound. 'Derna?' He repeated the word in a flat tone, to give nothing away.

'Derna. Your next port of call,' Leslie said slyly. 'I'm sure you're just busting to get cracking on your job.'

Offer agreed heartily. He had to. His rôle of fire-eater must be maintained yet he had a feeling he was going to regret it.

'Can't wait too long—Rommel won't stay in Derna forever.' That was incautious of Leslie, to let drop that name and the word Derna coupled with it.

'No. I must say that's quite a bother to me.' Offer allowed a frown of anxiety to cross his face. 'God, it would be just too awful if the war moved on while we're sitting it out here.'

Leslie, good chap, showed his concern. 'I know how worrying it must be to you, old fellow. *Well, why don't you come with us?*'

That was when the balloon went up. Leave Kufra and go with the L.R.D.G. to Derna? What for? asked Offer of himself ungrammatically. What the heck did he want with Rommel and Derna? It was all in Captain Leslie's mind. Just leave him here in Kufra in peace, that was all he asked. But now he had a rôle to play, damn it. Why had he ever allowed this stupid Rommel business to become a thing with Leslie!

'Why don't I?' He allowed enthusiasm to grow in his voice. 'Nothing would suit me better. When do you say you leave?' His mind was seeking a way out.

'In seven days exactly.'

'Ah,' said Offer, letting the regret gild his voice, 'I just wonder if that isn't a little too swift. Some of my key men were badly knocked up with all that fighting and the Lake of Sand, you know.'

'I know how you feel, but my betting is within a week all your bods will be fit and raring to go. Tough-looking mob you've got there, John.'

'Yes, I suppose you're right.' Offer let it sound as if he wanted to be persuaded out of his pessimism, but to himself he was saying grimly, 'Like bloody hell we're going with you, mate!' At the end of that week he'd have some damned good excuse to hang on to the comforts of Kufra and leave Rommel to be shot by some other brave bloody hero. Glasshouse John was all for a quiet life and intended to get it . . . The odd thought came to him that if he hung on in Kufra he could wangle the odd trip to Cairo and have the best of all worlds.

In a way Offer did not take Captain Leslie seriously. He couldn't—after all, he wasn't planning to kill anyone, much less Rommel, so why on earth should they all go off to Derna as if they were? A thousand miles over that desert? And then where? John Offer's mind entertained the illogical feeling that even Leslie couldn't mean it.

But he did.

As the days went by, Offer began to be increasingly perturbed. Leslie was too damned serious and went out of his way to help the Glasshouse Gang to take to the trail. He rustled up two more Chevs for them—the L.R.D.G. was going over to Jeeps—and every day came over with some offerings in the way of rations or new jerricans and bits and pieces that he thought they might need. It was embarrassingly friendly of the fellow, and Captain Offer showed his appreciation with many courteously expressed thanks.

What was particularly hard for Offer, though, was to maintain this subtle rôle of his. With Leslie he had to show impatience to be off, to let the L.R.D.G. officer feel that he couldn't get at the enemy quickly enough, while at the same time trying to pave a way to an excuse for not departing with him.

Once Offer tried it on by saying he thought he'd need just a little bit more time, so why didn't Leslie set off and he and his men would catch up with them? Leslie merely smiled tolerantly. No one caught up with the masters of the desert once they got going. 'We'll hang on a couple of extra days, John,' he said obligingly, shooting down that kite. 'We can always make up two days on a journey as long as that to Derna.'

Then once again Offer tried to make out that his men were still languishing, following their ordeal, but when Captain Leslie walked with him through their lines his ruffianly crew looked embarrassingly healthy, and that excuse had quickly to be abandoned.

In fact, the nearer they got to the time of departure the more certain it was that the Glasshouse mob would have to move out with the L.R.D.G.—they had nothing left in the way of excuses. Offer began to feel decidedly blue.

Even so, they weren't going to Derna! All that way—well over a thousand awful miles only to shove their heads into the lion's mouth? That was too ridiculous to contemplate. Right at the last he would find some excuse not to trek off with Leslie, he vowed. Kufra for him! Yet all at once circumstances came to change his mind and he went off gladly with the L.R.D.G. Gladly? Well, perhaps not quite gladly . . .

There was a lot of stir suddenly in Kufra before Leslie's patrol took to the desert. Part of it was rumour, though all felt it was based on fact. Word came that the Free French had recaptured Jalo, a far distant oasis north of Kufra, from the Italians; and a mixed force, including some S.A.S. who had recently left Kufra, were mounting an expedition against the German garrison in Siwa. Word was also coming through that Allied forces were making a spirited attack on Rommel and it looked as if the tide of battle might once again have reversed along the Mediterranean coast. That news was exhilarating to an army which had felt defeated and inferior far too long.

Part of the stir, however, was news of a Brass Hat inspection of Kufra very shortly. Leslie told him about it.

'They swan in occasionally, John. Don't stay long because Cairo messes are much more comfortable.'

'But why are they coming?' Offer was alert to danger. He knew he couldn't meet Top Brass and get away with it.

'Usual business. Keep up the morale of the troops, you know. See that discipline isn't lax and we blanco our gaiters regularly. A bit of bullshit, in other words. Thank God we'll be away before they arrive.'

'Yes,' said Offer, allowing his own voice to sound fervent, too. 'Thank God for that.'

He returned to his own lines a very thoughtful man. Whatever young L.R.D.G. captains and lieutenants said about Cairo Top Brass there were some very sharp minds under those red-banded hats.

By the end of the day Offer knew they had no alternative—like it or not, they had to depart from Kufra very soon. Blast the Brass! But Derna? That most definitely wasn't on.

Well, if not Derna, where? And then an idea came to him from the other griff they'd heard, that Siwa was going to be recaptured.

Siwa was a long way, true, but not a two-thousand-mile round-trip like going on the Derna lark. If Siwa was recaptured that would do for him. In spite of the beating up he'd received while in Siwa, Offer had a pleasant memory of that place of cool, bubbling springs in the vast oasis. The few more months until war in Africa was over—John Offer was sure it couldn't last much longer—would pass pleasantly under those graceful palm trees. He'd rig up some plausible excuse for their presence in Siwa, he assured himself, and determined eventually to head for that oasis.

He had to tell the men what was in the wind, of course, so he called them together in their dining tent and addressed them. Looking at them sprawling in unmilitary fashion over the scrubbed trestle tables, happily smoking and seeming without a care in the world, he thought he had never seen such a collection of cut-throats and villains. They were a right, rotten shower of jailhouse birds, and that's where they would all end up if he didn't look after them . . .

Yet John Offer had real affection for some of the men there. A few had loyalty to him, he knew, and for them he now had loyalty, too. He was no sentimentalist, however, and had no illusions about many of his army deserters. Quite a few were poisonous, and if he could get rid of them he would. Sibrett, Dodge and Skipper—they were the worst.

Sibrett was the one John Offer particularly loathed. He hadn't much real intelligence, but there was cunning about him that could make him dangerous. He looked unpleasant and never tried to be anything but unpleasant—a man who scowled and sneered, showing nicotine-browned teeth, and wasn't fastidious about his toilet and everyone was sure he nicked things when his mates weren't around. But there it was, he was saddled with the fellow, him and his uncouth mates.

'Now, men, we're in a bit of a spot.' That was how Captain Offer began his address, and he didn't waste any time about telling them to keep their mouths shut. At least they'd learned that lesson after one unfortunate bit of line-shooting along the Sweet Water Canal.

They became silent and tense at his words. Men on the run sober at the merest hint of danger, and none of them wanted another brutal spell in the Glasshouse.

'Personally, though I prefer Siwa, I could linger on in Kufra for a long time, but there's a war on out there.' His head jerked towards a distant Mediterranean. 'Now, wars are run by Brass Hats, and I'm not fond of Brass Hats, and one of them has decided to take it into his head to drop in on Kufra in a few days' time.'

He saw they did not comprehend, so he enlarged on the theme. 'I'm afraid that means we've got to pull out of Kufra in a hurry. I can pull the wool over the eyes of men of my own rank, but don't let us kid ourselves I could bluff a visiting brigadier. Generals are direct men, and *they'd* ask awkward questions, and——' He shrugged.

'Now, my good friends, the L.R.D.G. captain's got it into his head that we're on a top-secret mission to try to top Rommel in his H.Q. in Derna.' Everyone roared at that. 'And he's got it all planned that we go up the Blue with him. Hanged if I'm going anywhere near Rommel. Instead, when we go through the Qattara gap I intend to make some excuse and beetle off to Siwa, which should be in Allied hands any day now.' That is, if they could believe the griff.

He explained about the big push up the coast which ought to send Jerry back once again beyond Benghazi, and a simultaneous attempt to regain various enemy-held oases in the Libyan desert. Then he announced that all must prepare to move off with the L.R.D.G. in two days' time.

The news had a mixed reception, of course. Some of the more comfortable fellows like himself groaned at the thought of further desert travail, but to his surprise most of the men seemed to welcome a move.

'You're a lot of bloody masochists,' he told them. 'Good grief, wasn't the Sand Sea enough for you?'

Apparently not. They were all young and restless, and a few days in Kufra were enough to recover their strength and then after that there was only boredom. It was as R.S.M. O'Keefe had prophesied some weeks back, once men got used to desert travelling they were always drawn back to it.

'I must be odd,' thought Offer, and then found he wasn't all that disturbed by a move, not if they ended by the sweet water springs of Siwa. But definitely he drew the line at heroics.

They moved from Kufra just on sunset two evenings later. To the L.R.D.G. the route round the south of the Great Sand Sea presented no problems, and night travel was infinitely more comfortable than moving by day. For most of that night, anyway, they had a good moon, and the ground was firm and they made very steady progress. One hour after dawn they made camp for that day. There was breakfast, a pint of hot sweet tea per man, then tarpaulins were stretched from their trucks and everyone except the sentries got their heads down and kipped all during the heat of the day. The Glasshouse Gang found it stickily hot but no real hardship.

A late afternoon meal, then the trek was resumed before darkness quite fell. And so the long journey went on, day after day, and because they were with the L.R.D.G. everything seemed almost comfortable and easy. Anyway, the Glasshouse Gang were fit men and hardened to desert travel now, and after that Sand Sea crossing anything was a picnic.

The picnic lost some of its charm as they neared the gap between the Great Sand Sea and the Qattara Depression. They ran into a series of terrible dust storms. For the whole of one day they were unable to move, crouching miserably under their tarpaulins, blankets over their heads, trying to keep the driving sand out of their faces. Next day started well, but by midday the wind was howling again, and driving the sand at them, so there was another halt. And next day was a repeat of the first day. It brought a shortness to tempers, and there was some trouble as a consequence with some of the men—Glasshouse men.

After the third day of sandstorms, when all within half an hour the wind simply died away, the dust fell to the desert again and a brilliant blue sky appeared, Captain Leslie came striding over to where Offer was chatting with O'Kcefe and Weybright.

Leslie caught Offer's eye, jerked his head a little and Glasshouse John accepted it as an invitation to a confidential tête-a-tête. Instantly Offer had a feeling that something was wrong. They moved away from the men and then Leslie spoke. There was a note of indignation in his voice.

'I say, old chap, your fellows are a bit easy on discipline, aren't they?'

John looked him straight in the eye. 'Come on, Les, tell me about it.'

So Captain Leslie, whose own men were notoriously easy on discipline, told him. Several incidents, which he did not detail, had occurred during the trip which had set the L.R.D.G. officer's back up. But a few minutes ago something had happened which Leslie was not prepared to overlook.

'They're your men, John, and I don't want to interfere, but I think you ought to know.'

'I'm sure you're doing it for the best. Must have discipline or we become a rabble.' Offer was saying the right things and soothing the ruffled officer. 'What did my ruffianly bastards do to put you in this paddy?'

It came out, Captain Leslie seething about it. 'Just now one of your men told me to go and stuff myself.'

'Did he, b'God!' Offer wasn't play-acting now. What bloody fool was stirring up trouble with the L.R.D.G.? Must be stopped immediately. Anyway, this Captain Leslie was as good an officer as any man could hope to serve with, and he wasn't having one of his shower telling him what to do, not in that manner, anyway.

Captain Leslie had merely told a Glasshouse man, in passing, to sling some stuff, half-buried following the dust storm, on to a truck right away or it might get overlooked when they moved out. 'Some first aid kit, and a box of tools. Shouldn't have been put down in the first place.'

Leslie then added that he'd had no trouble with most of Offer's men, and his brushes were always with the same group. It also turned out that when he'd been told to go and do things to himself by Offer's ruffian, the said ruffian's companions had burst into most unpleasant laughter, not so much a laugh as a jeer at him. Plainly it was that which now brought the indignant Leslie to Offer with his protest.

John Offer dusted his shorts with slow slaps of his hand. 'I have a tough mob, Les, a very tough mob. I let them get away with a lot, but I won't have this sort of conduct. I want you to point out the miscreant so that I can deal with him right away.'

He meant it. He knew without being told who was causing trouble, and you don't go out of your way to create trouble when you're an army deserter on the run. Inside, he too was furiously angry. Christ, he spent half his life buttering people up, and then some thick bastard went and got someone all het up and prickly.

Leslie said, 'They're watching us now. They know what I'm talking about.' He nodded towards one of the vehicles.

The fairground bullies were there, Busker and Cruiser, lolling against the van. Sibrett was sitting on the step, Skipper standing alongside him; the lumpy coal-heaver, Dodge, with them, too. The same old vicious, troublesome gang, though Busker and Cruiser could be handled if they didn't have that evil bastard Sibrett to lead them on.

'Les, I'll just go and slap their wrists for five minutes.' Offer shook his head sadly. 'They're bad boys, that lot. Very bad. You see, they'll all end up in the Glasshouse.'

He walked over to the group. The group saw his approach and their grins broadened. They were in truculent mood, made nasty by the trying days of dust storms, looking for trouble, Offer saw, but he was in no mood to try to be placatory. Anyway, you don't get anywhere placating bully-boys.

Offer halted before them. He stood there, head forward, slightly stooping, but for a few seconds he said nothing. It is hard for men to maintain grins—in a while it becomes uncomfortable and they begin to slide off. Offer gave them those seconds. In fact he gave them a minute during which time he was quite silent. At the end of that time they had stopped smiling, though they looked no less unpleasant. Captain Offer had won the first round.

Now he turned his attention to Sibrett, Woodbine-puffing on the Chev step. Sibrett had made no attempt to rise when his officer came before him. John Offer let his brooding glance take in Sibrett. Never tackle a group of thugs, he'd once heard a wise drill sergeant on O.C.T.U. say. Pick on one. Destroy him. The others are easy after that.

Offer picked on Sibrett. In the distance, Captain Leslie saw Offer's lips moving and thought, irritated, 'He's too soft a chap, Offer. It's no good gently slapping their wrists, these hooligans want a bloody great rocket up their jaxies!' He felt dissatisfied. Good kind John couldn't handle these toughs . . .

Good kind John said, so quietly, 'Private Sibrett, if you think you can sit on your arse when I come to speak to you, you're making a mistake that's going to prove painful. Get on to your feet or I'll smash your bloody jaw just as I smashed McTone's in Siwa.'

It was the quietness of that voice that did it, making the threat far more terrible than if it had been shouted. But perhaps equally intimidating was the way John Offer slowly withdrew his hands from his shorts pockets, just as he'd done that time in Siwa Oasis, they all remembered. Now he gently thumped his right fist into the palm of his left hand—that right fist that had whipped in a swift arc and all in one blow had smashed the jaw of six-foot-two McTone, a professional boxer.

Only that time, Offer thought, unknown to all he'd had that steel knuckleduster on his fist. This day he had nothing but his own soft skin, and if Sibrett called his bluff the villain wouldn't suffer much damage. But

Offer would. Offer, in fact, would be finished in the eyes of all those men. Sibrett would finish *him* off.

All the same, Offer knew that he wasn't going to be finished. John Offer knew men and their limitations, and he knew he could outbluff a maggot brain like Sibrett, dangerous ruffian though he was.

Busker and Cruiser, now they were different. If he'd threatened to break the jaw of either of the fairground bullies they'd have leapt at the challenge and he'd have been on his back in a second. But Sibrett had a devious mind, one that quickly examined situations for gain or for unsuspected peril. He could hardly have forgotten the terrible way this smallish captain had chopped down the big McTone.

'Do I have to remind you,' Offer continued, his voice no more than a murmur, 'that I am a master of the Japanese art of——' He had to think hard. What the devil were those words he had invented? '—*Hui tsui!* Jaw-breaking!'

What a bluff he had put up that morning in the palm grove outside Siwa, and now he was using the bluff again. For all the hardness of his face at that moment, inwardly John Offer was laughing. Christ, they were swallowing that story again.

Sibrett was. Doubt leapt into his mind. Offer saw it on the lowering unpleasant face. Sibrett's confidence fled. McTone had copped it awfully, and suddenly Sibrett didn't want to take the risk of having this ferocious man smash his jaw, too. He came swiftly off his perch and instinctively stood to attention. Surprisingly, some sort of reflex action, it brought the others to attention, too.

Offer did not relax. 'You're a thick and stupid shower, and a horrible lot of men.' Few officers in His Majesty's forces would ever consider addressing O.R.s in such a manner, but John Offer had no real commission and held his leadership by plain force of personality . . . and one chopping blow to a man's jaw, a most impressive performance.

'Don't ever step out of line again with Captain Leslie, you hear me?'— very sharply. And finally, a real rasper, *'Now scram, you bastards, and get on to your truck!'*

Sibrett, now thoroughly shaken, turned and started to climb over the side. Dodge and the nasty-squashed-up-faced Skipper were with him instantly. The big rogues, Busker and Cruiser, slower to react, followed them half a second later. Busker and Cruiser needed others to think things out for them, and if Sibrett or the others had made a stand they would have joined them. Offer, for all his confidence, did emit a sigh of relief when he saw the rubber-limbed fairground pugs finally heave themselves into the Chev.

Captain John Offer strolled slowly back to an approving but surprised Leslie. Offer said in that gentle, good-humoured way he had, 'Les, my boy, you will never have any more trouble with my plug-uglies.'

Captain Leslie said, 'I must say you handled those fellows well, John. My crew aren't angels, but your men . . .'

'Oh, it was easy.' Then Offer, the old hypocrite, had to look very apologetic and say, 'I'm afraid I didn't exactly handle the situation according to King's Regulations. Do you know, Les, I actually used a swear word at them!' and he looked shocked at his own unmilitary indiscretion.

Leslie went off, hilarious, to tell the tale to his sergeant. 'You know what, sergeant, Captain Offer's just used a swear word against his naughty men!'

That incident became one of the choice myths of the L.R.D.G., and for a long time officers and N.C.O.s, faced with minor refractory behaviour, would say in the soft voice of John Offer, 'You'd better do as I tell you or I shall use a swear word against you.'

But all agreed that Captain Offer was a top-liner in his ability to handle the toughest mob of irregulars roaming the desert.

*

The L.R.D.G. had a lot of trouble with radio reception at that time, especially in those several days of dust storm. They were all anxious to know what was happening along the coast, where the big battles were being fought, and Offer was also extremely concerned to know who now were masters of Siwa Oasis. No good turning up there hoping it to be in Allied hands only to find themselves a target for German guns.

The good Captain Leslie, black beard permanently grey with dust now they had moved into the Libyan desert again, was most concerned for the success of Offer's mission.

'I wish we could get more news,' he said time after time, indeed a very worried man, but not for himself. His own rôle in the desert was simple and he'd performed it often—just drop the new Road Watch and bring back the old.

'How awful for you, John, if we drove Rommel out of Derna before you could get at him.'

John Offer solemnly agreed that it was too ghastly to contemplate.

'All this would simply be a waste of time.' A gesture over the desert. 'It must make you feel very anxious, old boy,' and old boy said, he, Leslie, had no idea how he felt inside.

John Offer couldn't care less about events up the coast; all he listened for was news about Siwa. Whatever the relieving force was up to, however, it was plain they were maintaining radio silence.

'That means they haven't gone in on the place yet,' interpreted Captain Leslie, gloomily.

'Well, they'd better be slippy about it, for we're not coming much further with you, mate,' said John Offer, but he did not utter the words aloud. As their convoy of vehicles came up through the gap he was indeed a very anxious man. Why on earth didn't Kufra come through with some news about Siwa! If he were to follow his plan, next day they must make their excuses and split up from the L.R.D.G.

Offer had told Captain Leslie that the last time they'd been in Siwa, the Germans had set up a patrol across the gap. 'By Arab account there were two patrol cars keeping watch. We'd better keep our eyes skinned for them.'

Captain Leslie nodded. 'If they're *Kubelwagens* we'd better steer clear of them.'

The L.R.D.G. would tackle any enemy if put to it, but it was Group policy never to start a fight if they could avoid it. Their rôle in desert warfare was much too important to wage minor battles, for the one thing they could not afford was to be deflected from missions by damage to their precious vehicles and injury or death to their highly trained personnel.

The dust storm which blew up as they came into the gap was of assistance to them, for if they did run into the patrol they could quickly slip away under cover of the murk. The storm, however, wasn't continuous and in between lulls they proceeded with caution.

Finally Captain Leslie decided there weren't any patrol cars, though they still moved with care. 'Looks like they got tired of patrolling once you got out by the back door, John.'

Quite probably, thought Offer, but perhaps they had been withdrawn from patrol by urgent need for them in Siwa Oasis. Did this mean that the German garrison there was now under attack? The thought was a comfort during the miserable times when the wind came swirling up and assailed them, driving sand that hurt their exposed skin and got in their eyes and choked up their nostrils so that they had to breathe through their mouths and that lost them moisture which they could ill afford to lose.

They were now travelling by day as well as sometimes at night—it all depended on circumstances. If the going was easy, they would travel after dark but at times when there was no moon, or if there were storms blowing or the ground was too treacherous to negotiate without good light, they drove by day.

They came through the stormy gap in daylight, then, and made camp before dark because of the wicked weather conditions. With evening, again the storm blew out, though Leslie gloomily prophesied further unsettled days ahead. They were in the *khamsin* period, when storms blew for a reputed fifty days on end.

At eight o'clock that evening the L.R.D.G. radio operator set up his aerial and stood by for news. He hadn't expected to raise Kufra because previous nights' reception hadn't been good, but this night, by a freak of radio conditions, reception was quite good and the operator came up with a number of signals for their party.

One of them reported a successful attack on Siwa Oasis by the S.A.S.

Everyone was jubilant at that news, none more so than John Offer. His heart sang when Leslie gave him the griff, for Siwa had made Offer a worried man for the past few days. If Siwa were now in Allied hands, his problems were over. All he had to do was put up some acceptable excuse, leave the L.R.D.G. and head for Siwa with all its pleasant possibilities remote from war. But what sort of a story would pass with Captain Leslie?

John Offer had an inventive brain, yet the present circumstances quite stymied his imagination. Idea after idea came to him, yet each time he rejected them. 'Too thin,' he kept saying to himself. Leslie, shrewd man, wouldn't fall for any lame excuse.

These thoughts ran in Offer's mind that night as he sat with Captain Leslie against the wheel of an L.R.D.G. truck. What the devil was he going to say to Leslie? The longer he delayed making his excuses the more convincing they would have to be. John Offer, normally a blithe and sanguine man, was somewhat depressed that evening, though it is doubtful if Leslie noticed anything wrong with him. When Offer put on an act he put on a good one.

They were talking about Shepheard's and Groppi's and other delectable haunts in Cairo, a conversation that went round and round among men with nothing else to think and talk about in the isolation of that vast desert.

Offer contributed his share of the talk, while his brain grappled with his problem.

At intervals the L.R.D.G. wireless op came over with signals he had picked up. Some were for other L.R.D.G. patrols, some were general information about the state of the war. One of these reported a major battle around Bardia, with Axis forces being driven back beyond Tobruk and Gazala.

'Good news,' said Captain Leslie cheerfully. 'But you'd better hurry, John, or your bird will have flown.' By now he had so accepted that Rommel was Offer's target that without thinking he spoke of it openly.

'Yes,' said Offer, and the way he said it could have meant anything.

Soon after that message the operator came over with another one. It was to tell Leslie to keep in radio touch, as far as possible, for the Road Watch might have to be moved west along the coast to a point beyond Agheila. 'This means they think we're going to overrun Derna and even Benghazi,' said Leslie with satisfaction. The wireless op was still standing there. 'Anything else?'

'Nothing for us, sir, I think. They keep putting out a signal, though, as if it's very important. All it says is, "Topdog using another tree. Return to base."'

The operator looked hopefully at Captain Leslie. Every night the air was full of mysterious messages radioed to the many guerrilla groups and friendly agents operating in the desert. It was always tantalising to hear them, and to wonder what they meant. Topdog certainly sounded intriguing.

'Topdog using another tree,' mused Leslie. 'Now, that's a good one. Wonder who Topdog is?'

But it was the latter part of the signal which had made John Offer sit up. 'Return to base.' That was exactly the sort of instruction he wanted.

John Offer's imagination clicked into gear. In that fraction of a second it worked overtime.

'Topdog?' he asked incredulously. 'Would you mind repeating that message?' That gave him another second or so in which to think. The radio op repeated his signal.

'Oh, God!' John Offer snapped his fingers in well-simulated exasperation. Captain Leslie looked at him, startled. 'Topdog!' said Offer, making his voice even more exasperated. 'Topdog!' and each time he repeated the word it gave his fluent imagination chance to put his thoughts together.

Dramatically he exclaimed, 'Well, I'm Topdog! At any rate, we're on Operation Topdog.'

'Topdog?' Leslie did some finger-snapping, too. 'Topdog's Rommel, hey?' He looked so pleased with himself for having guessed right, back in Kufra.

Offer hauled himself to his feet as if annoyance was too great to keep him seated. 'Oh, Hell's teeth, all this way to be told it isn't on! Rommel's pulled out from Derna, by the sound of it, and now I'm told to return to base! Can you imagine how I feel?'

Captain Leslie could; at any rate, he said he could. 'That's the way war is, I'm afraid. I'd hate it, myself, getting so near and then Topdog shoves off to another tree.' He was tickled by the message and said someone had a sense of humour back in G.H.Q. Cairo.

'Well, it's all off.' And Siwa, lovely Siwa, was in Allied hands. John Offer had difficulty in maintaining his air of exasperation because of the elation within. That signal could not have been better worded if it had been intended for him. He wondered who Topdog really was and who was getting the message and what was he doing about it? It would be quite a coincidence if Topdog *was* Rommel and somewhere in the Sahara there was a real assassination party now thwarted in their plans.

He looked down at Captain Leslie. ''Fraid, old chap, this means the parting of the ways. Hanged, though, if I'm going all that way back to Kufra—no need to, anyway.'

'No . . . Where will you go? Mersa?' That was the nearest point on the Mediterranean.

'Perhaps, but later. Siwa's little more than a day away. I think we'll try that first.' Cool springs and green shade. 'Maybe I'll be contacted there with a new mission.' How smoothly it all came out. Yet Offer suddenly wondered if he oughtn't to have kept quiet about Siwa.

They parted soon after dawn, with the wind already blowing ominously, making life grittily unpleasant. There was a lot of handshaking all round, and a couple of bottles of rum went circulating, then Captain Leslie left them, still heading north-east for Derna. He had had no orders to change plans.

Offer and the Gang watched them roll away into the gathering murk, then turned to mount their own trucks. As he moved down the line Offer noticed that one truck driver this morning was Private Sibrett. For some reason he wished it wasn't the fellow's turn to drive. A curious thought, or perhaps a premonition.

He gave a last warning before they moved. 'We'll be heading into this storm, and by the look of it we're going to have a beauty.' He was having to shout to be heard. 'For Christ's sake maintain contact. If anyone gets lost in this it's hard lines on 'em.' O'Keefe would lead them, O'Keefe who alone knew how to navigate in the desert.

He watched O'Keefe's truck, Walker driving, pull out and drive into the howling wind, then he mounted his own and followed. Weybright was doing his turn at the wheel. Without windscreens it wasn't going to be a comfortable ride to Siwa.

Conditions worsened, and increasingly they were forced to stop so as not to lose each other. Several times Offer was on the point of calling a halt and camping until the storm blew out, but everyone was impatient to get inside Siwa and who was to know how long this storm would rage, anyway? While they could see to move, they moved.

There were times, even so, when the wind died completely, so that the Glasshouse men thought hopefully, 'That's the end of it. Siwa, here we come!' But always the clear skies became obscured again as a fresh wind came howling across the desert. What was particularly trying was when the dust storm blew and it wasn't really bad enough to stop, but with visibility limited to thirty or forty yards they had to crawl at snail's pace. They drove in a cocoon of space within the dust storm, and only the thought of Siwa kept them going through that miserable weather.

Two hours passed. They halted for a brew-up, somehow managing to get the firecans burning in spite of the gale-force wind. Again the storm subsided and for a few minutes they could see for miles in every direction. Then the dust cloud rolled on them once more, but before that happened they had taken advantage of the moment to board their trucks and made a quick mile before settling down to the old crawl . . .

In Truck No. 3, Jimmy Wilborn, who had a most useful talent for cracking open safes, said suddenly, just as the storm closed on them again, 'Hey, I just saw Siwa!'

Neither Offer nor his R.S.M. would have agreed with that statement, not unless O'Keefe's navigating had become suddenly wildly out. Siwa was still many hours journey across the desert; Wilborn could not possibly have seen those distant palm trees, even on the clearest of days.

Blissfully unaware of this geographical contradiction, the men on No. 3 Chev were happy. Siwa was closer than they thought. Soon there'd be vegetation to protect them from the worst of the *khamsin*, and anyway there'd be tents for certain, and a damned sight more comfort around those pools than crawling here in the hot desert.

But Jimmy Wilborn *had* seen something, and it was no mirage or figment of the imagination. It was a black line along the summit of a great sand ridge ahead and slightly north of their course.

R.S.M. O'Keefe drove towards it, though unknowingly. The wind howled and vision became bad, but doggedly they kept going, making as much progress as possible. Offer, peering against the storm, saw O'Keefe's truck making all speed in a temporary lull while Weybright accelerated and bumped along after him. Then O'Keefe's Chev disappeared, dust swirling round him all in seconds.

Something bright and flashing raced before Offer's eyes, several of them. Then something hit the side of their Chev with a mighty bang. Someone started to hammer frantically on the cab roof, then there was an explosion as their petrol tank went up, and before Offer realised what was happening their truck was burning furiously.

Weybright shouted, 'Jerry! Bail out!'

He shoved Offer and came tumbling out with him through the door on the near side. They fell into the sand, the stink of furiously burning petrol hitting them, an awful heat singeing their hair.

Both rolled away from the blazing truck, keeping down and scrambling off as hard as they could go. Offer had a momentary impression of other men rolling on the sand and then racing into the dust storm. He also saw tracer skipping round their vehicle and ran from it, keeping their truck between him and the unseen enemy. He lost Weybright in the murk, then found him again and the two ran together.

A brief dropping of the wind, vision better. Offer, in panic because he wanted cover from the dust storm, turned. Silhouetted along a ridge was a column of vehicles. From several of them machine-gun fire was being directed around their blazing Chev.

Offer lost Weybright again in turning, the dust cloud rolling over so thick for the moment that Offer couldn't see much more than the proverbial hand in front of him. Still he stumbled on, falling over tufty grass and hooking himself on nasty thorn bushes. All he could think of was putting as much distance as possible between him and men who were trying to kill them.

He heard a truck approaching. It all happened in seconds. Out from the murk burst a Chev, and the way it was being driven told Offer that the driver was in a panic, trying to escape those flying bullets.

Offer signalled frantically to be picked up. He thought he heard the beat of the engine falter, as if decelerating. The cab came level with him. Offer saw the driver. It was Private Sibrett.

Sibrett was peering out, eyes half-closed against the flying sand. Offer was within five yards of him, and undoubtedly he recognised him. Then Sibrett drove on, accelerating, and his head turned slightly to follow Offer and his captain saw a grin on the face, an unpleasant grin, a grin that was laced with malicious triumph, and then the Chev disappeared in the dust.

John Offer came to a halt, shaken by the moment. Sibrett had seen him, had recognised him and had just driven by. 'You sod!' said Offer to himself. 'You absolute, rotten bastard!' Sibrett was getting his own back on him; yet though Offer had no greater love for Sibrett than Sibrett had for him, he knew he, Offer, would have halted in similar circumstances to pick up the other fellow.

A few seconds later Offer heard another straining engine, but this time it passed by on the edge of vision, a shape only dimly discerned in the distance, and certainly the driver would not see him in that fog.

All at once John Offer realised that he was alone in the desert, alone unless he could find Weybright and the others. It had all happened so quickly that he was still unable to reorientate his thoughts, and now he could only stand and wonder what next to do.

He settled it by walking steadily, as he thought, away from that enemy-occupied ridge. He didn't know where he was going, and he didn't know what good walking would do him. Without food and water his prospects of survival if he did escape the enemy were minimal. Yet a man keeps walking when he thinks that if he doesn't someone will start shooting at him again.

The wind began to die down, and the dust settled with it. All at once, as had happened before, visibility so improved that he could see quite clearly for several hundred yards around him.

It was a depressing picture. There was Art Weybright about eighty yards away, but no other human being in sight. There were some forms lying beside the furiously burning Chev, and Offer knew that his men hadn't kept the truck between them and the machine-gunners when they ran for it.

There was no sign of any of the other Chevs, which suggested that at least the rest of the Gang had got away.

But coming down the long grey, coarse-grassed ridge were literally dozens of assorted military vehicles. The situation was hopeless. Weybright was trudging towards him. Offer yelled, 'Get your hands up!' and his own hands shot up above his head and he turned to watch the approaching vehicles. Weybright halted and put up his hands, too.

They were Germans. Some nippy scout cars came racing across towards them, the big infantry carriers wallowing more slowly in the rear. Offer, frozen into complete immobility, expected any moment to be shot down, but it didn't happen. One of the scout cars scudded across to where Weybright was standing, while another halted alongside Offer. All at once Captain Offer found himself surrounded by vehicles, engines making the devil of a din, and men were clambering down, men in the green-tinged KD that marked the difference between German and Allied desert uniforms.

John Offer was a man who had remarkable control over his emotions. In fact in Civvy Street his fellow actors had said that old John never flapped and was completely imperturbable.

This moment, though, surrounded by hundreds of tough-looking young Germans, all carrying guns as if they intended to use them, John Offer knew what horror meant, and probably showed a little of it on his face. He was aghast at his position. Never in all his nightmares had he imagined himself being taken prisoner-of-war. Dazed by the swiftness of events, he could only stand, hands aloft, and sweat with fear.

An *Oberst*—colonel—got out of a scout car and came towards them. For a moment Offer thought it was Rommel himself, then decided that like Chinese all German senior officers looked alike. He was a solid man, treading the ground in his knee-length laced-up boots in a way that suggested ruthless power. He came right up to Offer, and behind him marched other officers of lesser rank. Offer looked into a roughened face, into hard grey eyes set in a broad-cheekboned face, and his heart quailed. The Oberst looked formidable.

'You speak German?' a harsh voice asked, in English that appeared rudimentary.

Offer jerked himself out of his frozen fear. 'No.' The word came out hurriedly. 'Sorry, not a word.' And then, to cover his confusion and fright, he began to turn to Weybright at his side, and was about to say, 'But my driver does. He speaks excellent German.' Then he stopped. Weybright was not saying anything. All right, then Offer wouldn't, either; but he wondered why Weybright didn't jump at a chance to please, even slightly, their captors by interpreting for them.

There was a tall, hard-looking Hauptmann standing just behind the Oberst. Offer became conscious of his presence because in some way he projected profound hostility, eyes mere slits of suspicion as they surveyed the British officer.

The Oberst said, 'All right. What is your name? You are a captain, *ja*?'

'My rank is captain. My name is Offer, Captain John Offer.' That was all the information a prisoner should give to an enemy.

At that the tall Hauptmann came stepping forward. Offer saw implacable enmity on that lean, brown face. Startled, Offer heard him say, 'You are Glasshouse John, *ja*?'

Hauptmann Kurt Braunschweig had got his wish. John Offer had fallen into his hands.

*

In Siwa Oasis only twenty-four hours earlier, the German garrison commander, Oberst Franz Schiller, had received marching orders. A signal from the Afrika Korps H.Q. in Derna had spoken of an Allied push along the Mediterranean coast, and of Axis armies falling back before it. The garrison occupying Siwa could no longer remain there in case it was cut off behind the advancing enemy lines.

They were almost ready to move out when a mixed Allied force, including Free French and S.A.S., suddenly appeared over the horizon and mounted an attack on them. The German commander sensibly decided not to have it out with the fierce intruders—why fight over an oasis when you were leaving it, anyway?—and made an orderly retreat, reducing his own casualties to a minimum.

Under cover of darkness the Oberst finally withdrew all his forces from the oasis and took to the Mersa caravan trail, travelling east. He had a strong force at his disposal, and had no fears of being out-fought if it came to a battle in the desert, so two hours after leaving Siwa he called a halt for the night.

Next morning they moved on again. The day was a shocker, their pace considerably reduced by the dust storm. Finally it became too much for the German commander who called a halt, intending to remain where they were until conditions improved. So they were settled down in the lee of a long sandy ridge when one of those moments of better visibility occurred and their sentries spotted five trucks heading towards them. Instantly an alert was sounded, and all men stood to their posts.

The dust storm blew up again, obscuring the five trucks. The Oberst did not commit the folly of going off hunting for them—that way could lead to disaster for his own men, for they could easily lose touch with each other. Instead he stood there, goggles protecting his eyes, waiting and hoping that the tiny force would emerge close to, near enough for the Germans to sweep into action.

Hauptmann Braunschweig came to consult with his Oberst on the matter. Both agreed that the trucks must be enemy; German or Italian patrols would not be operating so far from the coast. And both were pleased at the thought of wiping up an Allied guerrilla force, some consolation for being chased out of Siwa the previous day.

So they waited and prayed in good German for the enemy to be delivered into their hands; and that day He must have been merciful, to the Germans, anyway.

Things could hardly have turned out better for Oberst Schiller. There was a moment when the wind sighed away and visibility improved, and only two hundred yards off—perhaps less—dimly through the dusty air they glimpsed the little convoy passing.

Oberst Schiller had the impression that one or more vehicles had already passed by—there was just a feeling of a dark shape dissolving into the sandy murk—but right before them one vehicle trundled along.

Immediately fire was brought to bear on it, and their Spandaus and other machine-guns could hardly miss at that range. Almost immediately they registered a direct hit, as evidenced by an explosion of the vehicle's petrol tank. They saw figures leaping off the truck and some jumped over the tailboard and were exposed to fire and his highly-trained machine-gunners again could hardly miss. The Oberst saw them stop running after only a few strides.

But there had been five vehicles. Another emerged from the dust haze but this could hardly be seen and within a second it was lost to sight, as if it had fled from that burning vehicle. And that was all they saw of Offer's party.

It put the Oberst in a benign mood, all the same. He wasn't after scalps this day, but to have one enemy truck as target practice for his gunners was a pleasing diversion. His men had acquitted themselves well, and he sent a compliment down the line to them.

He and the Hauptmann rejoined their *Kubelwagens* and led the way closer to where the truck burned. There were corpses to examine in case they carried some minor military secrets, and perhaps the truck mightn't burn completely out and there might be something of worth to salvage from it.

The dust storm had closed in on them once more, but within a couple of minutes, before they quite reached the burning vehicle, it swirled off again. The Germans saw two figures alone in the desert, and very forlorn they looked, too. Both immediately shot up their hands above their heads.

The Oberst shouted to his men and the command stopped them just as fingers were tightening on triggers. Neither Offer nor Weybright realised that they continued to live by a half a second's grace—that fraction of time between a command to hold fire and the triggering off of a hail of lead.

So the scout cars led a race past the burning truck—there was no hope of salvaging anything from that wreck, they all saw as they came up to it— and surrounded two very startled and apprehensive Britishers. The Oberst, shoving his goggles above the peak of his cap, got out and stalked over to the pair. He saw that one was a British Panzergrenadier and the other a Hauptmann.

Just as Offer took in the personality of the Oberst, so the Oberst surveyed John Offer critically. The private didn't count. He saw a not very big man, a man with a flattened nose as if he'd been in some accident, yet in spite of his battered appearance the Oberst gained an impression of a soft man, a genial man playing at soldiers. The Oberst, being a professional, was contemptuous of amateur soldiers in any army, though Field-Marshal Rommel was forever warning them not to underrate the British amateur.

Oberst Schiller could speak English, having, like so many of Hitler's army, been ordered to take a holiday in the United Kingdom before the inevitable war broke out between the two nations. The Oberst had also thoughtfully toured France and the Low Countries, in all cases mentally noting anything which might come in useful if they were to try to occupy them.

He first asked if either of them could speak German, being not so sure of his own English. Neither admitted to German, so the Oberst asked the usual first question. 'What is your name?'

And when the British captain said it was John Offer, the Oberst was startled by his Hauptmann's reaction. Braunschweig stepped forward at that, bristling with hatred, so much so that his Oberst felt it, further astonishing him.

'You are Glasshouse John, *ja*?'

The Oberst recovered immediately and turned brusquely upon his Hauptmann. In German he asked, 'What is all this? Do you know this man?'

A slight shake of the head, the Hauptmann still focusing his glowering attention upon the British captain. Braunschweig answered in German.

Offer, listening to the harsh German speech did not know what they were saying, but saw the reaction to this tall Hauptmann's words upon his colonel and men within earshot. Where before there had been an almost politely neutral attitude towards the prisoners, now there was a great stir. All heads were turned upon Offer, and they were glaring hatred like the Hauptmann. Offer could feel their sudden anger, and he was bewildered by it.

The Oberst's expression grew thunderous. His rage was so apparent that Offer was sure he was going to be despatched out of hand, a feeling almost confirmed when the Oberst's hand rested on his holstered automatic pistol. The two German officers still continued to talk in German, swift jerky sentences filling in the details of knowledge about Offer.

In that moment they were oblivious to the storm once more raging around them. Their passions had been caught up by the memory of that terrible tragedy on the Lake of Sand. In their power now they had the author of it, and both were determined that the English captain should suffer for the crime he had committed against good German soldiers.

The Oberst rapped, 'Guard them! These men must not be allowed to escape. They will be taken to Agheila, where we will hand them over to the S.S. for trial.'

Like most German officers Schiller detested the S.S., Hitler's private and ruthless army, but for once they could come in useful. If Glasshouse John, as his Hauptmann called him, was placed in S.S. hands they would see that he paid terribly for his crime. Anyway, Glasshouse John was masquerading as an officer, and that was another offence in the eyes of the Oberst, a terrible offence. He said so, before going off to look at the burning vehicle and the corpses close by it.

For perhaps one minute before they were detected and stopped, Weybright got in an interpretation of the Hauptmann's speech. 'Sir.' Offer heard the soft voice beside him and had the sense not to turn his head. It sounded as if Weybright was speaking without opening his lips. 'They're on to us. They know we're army deserters, and they know you're not a real captain.'

'Why did they change, as if they could kill us?' Offer spoke softly, too, head averted from Weybright.

'Remember the Sand Lake? Remember opening fire on the Germans when they were crossing? Some German soldiers got caught in the quicksands, and they couldn't be rescued because you pinned them down with Bren fire. The German captain swears you did it on purpose and even shot at the men who were caught in the sand.'

Offer wanted to say, 'It's not true. In that heat haze we hardly saw what we were firing at.' Certainly they hadn't known of men being trapped in the quicksands or they might have eased on their fire, illogical though that would have been in terms of warfare.

Then Weybright got in a whisper about their being handed over to the S.S. when they reached Agheila. At this moment, a young Leutnant barked sharply, in English, 'Be quiet! Talking is not permitted.'

So they shut up, and now Offer, head bowed against the driving sand, knew the full depths of fear. It was bad enough being taken prisoner, but to know one was going to be put into the hands of the terrible Hitler S.S. shook his morale to the core. Panic rose within him, and he looked round quickly, desperately, for some chance of escape, but there was none. They were ringed by too many unpleasant young soldiers all with weapons ready for use.

Then John Offer, Offer the unflappable, pulled himself together, forced his brain to think logically, and in the process shoved his fears into the background.

'We've got to escape; we mustn't be taken to the S.S.!' But how and when? He answered the second part of his question first. 'It's got to be now, quickly.' Once they were taken out of the desert and behind the Axis lines escape would be too late. But now—how? And if they got away from the Germans here in this storm-swept desert, how long would they last without water?

Offer's brain concentrated for a moment on that thought. Escaping from their captors only to die in an agony of thirst here in the desert seemed no

Desert Marauders

better than dying after torture in the hands of the hated S.S. Offer was thirsty already and could have done with a gallon of water for his fear-dried mouth. Some of the Germans were drinking from their bottles.

Then Offer thought, 'I know O'Keefe. I think I know how he will react.'

O'Keefe mightn't have been aware of the attack but he wouldn't have gone far without stopping, for his men in the rear would shout when they lost contact with the second truck. Perhaps Sibrett's truck and the others, who must have seen his Chev blazing, had run on to O'Keefe's vehicle and reported what had happened. What would O'Keefe, very sensible man, do?

'He'll drive off to a safe distance, perhaps a mile or two, then halt and wait for the storm to die down.' When it subsided, as most days it did after a few hours, O'Keefe would come back to the scene of the attack to pick up any survivors. Certainly they would return to identify any dead and bury them, if the Germans hadn't done so.

If they were to escape at all, the attempt must be made here, so that O'Keefe could pick them up when conditions grew more favourable.

'Here they come,' he heard Weybright whisper, but the Leutnant detected it and once more shouted ferociously, 'Be quiet! No talking!' The Oberst and his Hauptmann were returning from the wrecked truck.

At that moment a Feldwebel came up with a water bottle in his hands. Plainly he thought the prisoners should have water, too, and the Leutnant did not object, but the tall Hauptmann did. He saw the German sergeant offering drink to the prisoners and immediately barked an order. The Feldwebel withdrew very quickly, taking the water with him.

Offer licked lips that seemed even drier now. Was this part of their punishment, that they should be made to go thirsty? Well, all the more reason for making a quick escape.

The Hauptmann gave another order, and the same Feldwebel stepped forward and with a piece of thin but strong cord bound Offer's right wrist to Weybright's left one. That really depressed Offer. Shackled together like this, how could they coincide any movement to make a swift escape? And not being able to talk, even whisper, put out of question a co-ordinated plan. Yet, God in Heaven, Offer thought desperately, it's got to be now or never!

The Oberst gave an order which sent everybody running to their vehicles. The Feldwebel appeared to have been put in charge of the prisoners, and the way the Hauptmann spoke, so severely at him, standing stiffly there at attention, Offer guessed he was promising hell if the prisoners got away.

'He's going to get hell,' Offer told himself, fervently. That was his hard luck. A pity, after the way he had been prepared to give water to them.

The prisoners were hoisted up the side of a big infantry carrier, an awkward proceeding with their wrists tightly bound together, but in the end they managed it. They found themselves in a big truck, very high off the ground. Down each side ran slatted wood seats, so that the Panzergrenadiers sat facing each other across a pile of kit that lay down the middle. The Feldwebel took a seat opposite the prisoners, the better to keep an eye on them, Offer thought. On either side and on the seats opposite, German soldiers sat almost at attention, their rifles between their knees, ready for action.

The dust storm was pretty bad again, but the Oberst was in a hurry to rejoin his comrades on the coast and get away from this awful desert, and the column began to move off.

Panic once again assailed Offer with the movement. Even at this pace, if they left escape for an hour they would never be able to find O'Keefe.

'It's got to be now!' Offer kept telling himself, and he thought his desperation might be showing on his face, for the Feldwebel was regarding him very closely. *Now, now, it had to be now!* But how? God, wasn't he looked up to as a man with a fertile imagination!

Then he told himself it was his panic that was reducing his ability to think, so once again he took hold of his tattered nerves and calmed down and began to work on the problem. And the way he finally worked it out was in terms of the simplest of logic.

'We've got to get out of this truck if we are to escape into the desert. That means jumping off it before anyone realises what we are up to.'

Once they hit the dirt they had just a chance of dodging bullets in the dust storm, raging more fiercely than ever, and threatening to bring the column to a halt at any time. So the attempt, Offer told himself, must be made when the dust cloud came rolling up at its thickest, reducing visibility to twenty or thirty yards.

The truck was bumping over rough ground, and Offer thought, 'The ground's in our favour.' Men trying to fire from a bouncing truck wouldn't be accurate in their aim. Also, the way the German infantry sat was to the prisoners' advantage if they did make a break for it. The soldiers facing him, including the Feldwebel, could not open fire because of their comrades sitting opposite, and the infantrymen on either side would have to get to their feet, and turn before being able to fire. What with the bumpy nature of the ground and the awkward positioning of the German infantry, Offer felt they might have a few seconds' chance to get safely lost in the storm before bullets flew.

The sand pattered into the crowded infantry carrier, and all bent their heads against the painful blast. Visibility was very bad, yet still the column kept going, closed up so that trucks were no more than five yards from each other. Offer doubted if they were travelling more than eight or ten miles an hour, something else in their favour.

'All right,' he told himself, 'but we're not down on the desert yet. *How do we get out of the truck?*' Oh, what a handicap, this cord around their wrists! Even more so, not being able to whisper his plans to Weybright.

They must have travelled close on a mile, when suddenly Offer saw one slight way out for them. Even then he held the escape bid for a few minutes longer, until coincidentally with a particularly bumpy bit of ground, the dust storm swirled up in as thick a cloud as they had experienced to date. John Offer promptly went into action.

He leapt to his feet, dragging a startled Weybright up with him. At the same time he was shouting and pointing as if something terrible was out there in the fog. 'Look!'

The startled infantry lifted their heads and stared wonderingly in the direction of that pointing finger. Offer swung his arm, that arm fastened to Weybright's. He swung it with desperate force as hard as he could right across Weybright's throat, at the same time throwing himself backwards. Both went head over heels over the side of the slow-moving vehicle. By the law of averages one or the other should have broken his neck, but the sand was soft hereabouts, and neither did.

The moment they hit the ground, Offer grabbed Weybright and started to roll frantically over and over, and then using their momentum he came to his feet, dragging on Weybright's wrist, and Weybright, responding now, came up with him and they began to run. Ten paces and they couldn't be seen from the truck. Offer went flat on his face then, Weybright, not able to think things out for himself, tumbling down beside him. He was making gasping noises as if that crack across the throat hadn't done him any good. They heard bullets fly overhead. The German infantry were firing blind.

Offer began to scramble frantically away on hands and knees as fast as he could go. It was a handicap, being tied together, but Weybright caught on and they moved their locked arms in unison and made good progress.

They felt themselves going downhill, and after a moment or so, Offer climbed to his feet. They could hear bullets screaming above them, but the slope momentarily put them out of danger, so they began to run.

Now Offer turned and raced into the wind. It wasn't the most comfortable way to go, but it held an advantage—for certain the Germans would be leaping from their trucks to get after them, though they wouldn't come far in case they got lost; and if they followed the prisoners' tracks they would have to face into this driving, sandladen wind that would be against accurate shooting. Another thing, this wind was their compass. It had been blowing directly in their faces when they were heading for Siwa; therefore heading into it now they would be on course and with a bit of luck they might run into the R.S.M. and his boys.

Running was hard going, with the soft sand holding them back and tufty coarse grass threatening to send them tumbling. Within fifty yards they couldn't run any more, and they dropped into a shambling walk. Even this pace couldn't be maintained for long.

Behind them was a lot of noise. They heard harsh shouting voices, then automatic weapons began to spray bullets into the murk. At that, Offer and Weybright tumbled to their faces again, but continued to crawl frantically as fast as possible. The big dread in their minds was that this storm might go through one of its periods of abatement and they would be revealed to their enemies. If they were spotted at some distance from the vehicles, too far to justify recapture, Offer was certain the Germans would open fire on them, and he didn't expect to survive if they did.

They were sobbing now as they crawled head into the stinging wind, their lungs gasping for breath, fear adding to their laboured breathing. How slowly they seemed to progress, and how near those shouting voices and rattling guns sounded. And all the while they listened to the moaning wind and were sure it was dropping and visibility was improving. For the first time in his life John Offer prayed for the *khamsin* to blow at its worst.

Finally, they could crawl no more, both simply stretching flat on their faces, chests heaving and aching and noisily sucking in air. It was Weybright who collapsed first, big, heavy Weybright who wasn't designed for running, and he dragged Offer down with him. Not that Offer could have gone on much further. Only a second or so lying there, though, then Offer rolled over and began to work on the knotted cord that bound his wrist to Weybright's. It took some doing, but in time he succeeded and he was free though the cord still dangled from Weybright's wrist. When it was done they had recovered sufficiently to set them again scuttling along on all fours.

'Don't get lost,' Offer managed to pant. 'Got to keep together.'

Still those harsh voices and the guns occasionally rattling off, and they seemed as loud as ever. Perhaps the Germans were following their footmarks. If so, going uncomfortably on all-fours wasn't much good; the Germans would be running and catching up with them. So Offer took a chance on being shot, clambered to his feet and started to run again. Weybright came up with him.

They ran and walked, ran and walked, and the storm kept blowing, giving them cover. Finally it dawned on them both that no longer did they hear German voices or guns. Instead came the distant sound of engines being started, then of gears meshing noisily. It was surprising how sound travelled in spite of the moaning wind.

'Take it easy,' Offer gasped, holding his side because he had an excruciating stitch. 'They've called off the chase. Hear them? They're moving off.'

Still they did not trust their own interpretation of those sounds. It might be an example of German cunning, Offer thought, pretending to move off but leaving a party to run silently after them. So they kept walking, still apprehensive, still forever looking back over their shoulders and watching the driving dust cloud, expecting it to part and they would see their enemies closing upon them.

They walked, and that was easier and they got their breath back and calmed down, and now exhilaration slowly mounted within them. By Jove, Offer kept saying to himself, we did it! We got away!

Quarter of an hour later they were sure they were completely safe. No longer did they hear the sounds of German trucks departing, no voices, and no gunfire. God, they must feel narked, Offer thought, and chuckled to himself at the thought of the German's annoyance. Losing their prisoners so soon after capturing them would set that Oberst and Hauptmann—especially the Hauptmann—dancing. Poor bloody Feldwebel, but one man's penance was worth two men's luck.

Now that their panic had subsided Offer began to think of the next move ahead. He was still confident that his R.S.M. wouldn't drive out of the area until he knew what had happened to the second truck. That meant waiting around until the storm dropped and O'Keefe could make sure there was no lurking enemy to ambush him if he started back exploring.

When he was satisfied there was no danger he would return as far as the burnt-out Chev, but he wasn't likely to go much further than that. He'd probably stay there a while, burying the dead, and surveying the desert around him for signs of human life. If he didn't see any, then he would turn about and head for Siwa. It would be tragic if he and Weybright were hidden in some fold of ground when O'Keefe started to look for them, or if they were too far away to be seen. Too far? Offer pulled himself together once more, beating down the fears that rose too frequently in the last few hours. He didn't think they were much more than a mile from the Chev. But he could be mistaken. Suppose it was two miles? Or more. So difficult to judge when your thoughts were concentrated on planning a hazardous escape.

Offer halted. He had almost to shout to be heard. 'We've got to find the Chev.' No good just sitting down and waiting for the storm to settle. They couldn't take risks on not being seen if R.S.M. O'Keefe was back there looking for them.

Weybright, whose steel-rimmed glasses had somehow survived all the tumbling, said, 'How do we do that? In this muck?'

'We must find the tyre marks of the German column.' So Offer began to move across the face of the wind because somewhere to their right must be the tracks of the German vehicles.

They trudged on. After a time, without coming to the tracks, doubts began to assail them. Perhaps the driving sand had already smoothed them over and they had crossed them without knowing they had done so. If that was the case they might be heading miles away from the Chev.

It was an awful, ghastly thought, and finally it brought them to an irresolute halt. They seemed to have been walking for hours, yet their watches said only twenty minutes. Offer said, 'What do we do now?' He was so thirsty he thought even the S.S. might be preferable to this torture, and all the time now he had to fight down panic.

Weybright simply said, 'I leave it to you, sir.' A great compliment but one Offer could have done without. It was at times like this that he wished someone else would make the decisions.

'All right.' That was the thing men liked about Captain John Offer. When the time came he could always rise to the occasion. He did so sensibly now. 'Tell you what we'll do. We'll risk another five minutes' walk in this direction. If we don't come across the tyre marks in that time we'll just squat down in the sand and hope the storm will soon blow over.'

Weybright agreed, and said they didn't seem to have much alternative. So once more they set off, heads bent against the sand-laden wind that stung as it showered them with tiny needle-like missiles. They trudged along, elation at their escape dying swiftly, the old adage strongly in Offer's mind about frying pans and fires.

Five minutes went by and there was no sign of the elusive vehicle tracks. Offer cheated then, without telling Weybright. 'I'll give it another minute,' he told himself, and for another uncomfortable minute they battled across the wind. At the end of that minute and still no tracks, Offer cheated yet again and decided on one more minute's search, and this time he meant it.

Weybright called, 'It's a long five minutes.'

Offer looked at his watch. 'Fifteen seconds to go.' They walked on. Offer glanced at his watch. The fifteen seconds had gone by. He halted wearily. It was no good.

Weybright said, in a surprised sort of voice, 'Why, there they are,' and there they were, quite plain for them to see. Literally at the last second they had come within a few yards of the tracks.

'Oh, great stuff!' gasped Offer, and for a second time in half an hour he knew elation. Suddenly in spite of their thirst and the discomfort of the sandstorm they felt as if they had come out into safety. These tracks would lead them back to the Chev. O'Keefe was bound to return when this blasted storm subsided. It was a comforting thought, and they set off at an easy pace now, and once again the wind blew hard against their bowed heads and filled their hair with sand.

In time they came to the Chev. They found the bodies there of four of Offer's men. They removed their identity tags and went through their pockets for any valuables, but apart from a little money there was nothing for grieving relatives back home to break their hearts over. Ex-Glasshouse men don't run to much accumulation of objects of sentiment.

They buried them, quite an easy job even though they only had their hands to scoop out shallow trenches to take the bodies. It was a bloody, gruesome task, because these had been their comrades until a couple of hours ago. It put paid to any feeling of well-being and they were glad when it was over and they could retire away from the still smouldering ruin of a Chev.

'Now, what do we do?' Weybright asked.

'We lie down, wait patiently for this storm to blow out, and hope my hunch is correct, and the R.S.M. does come ferreting back to find us.'

'And if he doesn't?'

'Just too bad, isn't it?' Without water they'd never make Siwa on foot. 'But he'll turn up, you see.'

Offer's confidence began to evaporate, though, as the hours passed and the storm refused to subside. By late afternoon their thirst wracked them so that speech became virtually impossible, and pessimism took over and both wished they were dead and were sure the end wouldn't be long now. The wind was a hot blast that dried their flesh as well as showering them with flying particles that hurt increasingly when they hit bare skin. Yet they had had one brief conversation in those minutes after they had dug a hole in the ground and crawled in to crouch in discomfort together.

Weybright started it by saying, 'Next time you hit me across the throat, do you mind letting me know beforehand? It still aches, sod it!'

Offer said, 'I'll do just that, next time. It might interest Jerry if he knows what I'm up to.'

They talked in desultory manner for a few moments, and Weybright was in high praise of Offer's resource. 'I thought we were goners, sir. Couldn't see how we were to get away from the Hun. And when he said we'd be handed over to the S.S., God, did I get scared!'

'You didn't let on you understood German.' Offer remembered being puzzled at the time. 'Why?'

'I told you once, my father was a German.' Offer nodded. Weybright's father had been captured in World War I and had been brought as prisoner to serve out the war in England. Afterwards he had stayed on, marrying an English girl. 'In some eyes that makes me a German, and I've heard that Germans are harder on people like me if they get their hands on us. We shouldn't be fighting against the Fatherland, they say. Anyway, I thought I'd take no risks of drawing attention to myself.'

'Good job, too.'

'A good job,' agreed Weybright. If he hadn't understood the talk about their being handed over to the German S.S. they might have gone innocently into captivity.

After that they hardly spoke a word but crouched together, arms over their heads, dying of thirst and praying for the storm to lift as it usually did some time during the day. But that sandstorm kept on blowing and finally night came, and now they knew that their misery must continue for at least another ten hours until dawn.

As the dark hours slowly passed the torture of their desiccated bodies continued. They knew they couldn't last much longer. Sometime in the night Offer came out of a doze and realised that the wind had settled at last. It should have brought joy to him, but he was too wretched for anything except pessimism. The wind had settled. So what? Often the *khamsin* settled at night, only to spring up with the first rays of sunlight. This calm could only be kidding them, and he refused to rejoice prematurely. Then as more hours passed pessimism took complete control of him and he knew that O'Keefe wouldn't turn back. He and Weybright were alone in the desert. Better to die quickly than to endure much more of this agony, but how does one kill oneself without any means to hand?

So his thoughts flitted disjointedly through his brain in between merciful snatches of sleep that were close to delirium. A grey light began to appear to the east. *And again the wind began to sigh over the desert.*

Weybright stirred. 'I was dreaming I was making char.' Big, lumpy Weybright was far gone.

Offer hadn't the energy to speak, but he thought, 'I can smell char.' The strong acrid smell of desert brew boiling over a fire. He'd heard that men dying of thirst conjured up mental mirages of water and fountains while he, British to the last, dreamt of tea on the boil.

Light came swiftly, grey, then yellow, then orange, then flaming red and hot with the first rays to come over the horizon. The wind was blowing up and the dust already beginning to fly. Offer couldn't even be bothered to stand erect. There seemed no strength left in him. What a place in which to die.

He was still dreaming of hot sweet tea, so vividly again he could smell it. It made him moan and stir at last, and finally he got on all fours and then came unsteadily to full height in their hole. He looked round, and not eighty yards away were four trucks—Chevs—and O'Keefe with his men having breakfast.

*

Offer said, 'I want to speak to Private Sibrett.' That was after a rest and a frantic time drinking all the water that their dry, sponge-like bodies could absorb.

R.S.M. O'Keefe had been delighted to see them, and so were others of his men. When he could speak easily again, Captain Offer said, 'I thought you'd have gone on.'

O'Keefe said, 'It was touch and go.' The men had thought that if Offer's party weren't all killed the Germans would have taken them off to the bag. 'We almost tossed up, whether to keep going or hang around.'

But you didn't toss, and you did stay. R.S.M. O'Keefe was a first-class man even if he did go berserk at the sight of a Military Policeman. 'We'll move on to Siwa when you're ready, R.S.M.' But first he wanted words with Sibrett.

They brought Sibrett to him, and he came with guilt obvious in his slouching walk and lowering gaze. He halted before his captain, and Offer wanted to strike him, so incensed was he by this man's conduct.

He kept his temper, though, O'Keefe standing there, watching. He said, 'You didn't stop to pick me up.'

Sibrett opened his eyes in simulated astonishment, but he couldn't hold John Offer's gaze. 'Me, sir? Didn't stop? I don't know what you're talking about.'

'You do, Private Sibrett. You do know what I'm talking about. You had chance to pick me up when Jerry strafed my Chev. You passed within feet of me, but you wouldn't stop.' And he'd bet that other cronies of Sibrett, who always travelled together, must have been aware of the incident.

Sibrett said, 'I never did!' He tried to make his voice sound indignant. 'I never saw you.'

Offer knew he was wasting his time. He was making a most serious charge but it was only his word against Sibrett's. All Sibrett need do was keep on denying that he had seen Offer by the blazing Chev, and there was nothing his captain could do about it. And plainly Sibrett wasn't going to admit he had left John Offer to the mercies of the Germans.

So Captain Offer said, 'I won't forget it,' and his voice was grim. Sibrett turned away. What stung Offer then was to see the tiny grin of triumph on the fellow's face. Sibrett knew he had won. 'But I'll get the bastard!' Offer told himself, and though officers aren't supposed to come to such decisions, many do. Given a chance, Glasshouse John would put the knife in Sibrett for what he had done.

Offer didn't bother to explain to the puzzled R.S.M. what was behind his brief conversation with Sibrett. Time was against delay, the wind—blast it!—was rising, and the sooner they made ground towards Siwa, the better.

But it wasn't a bad day, after all, and before nightfall they were trundling through the familiar oasis, intent on stripping off and wallowing in the freshwater pool behind the battered concrete buildings so recently occupied by German enemies.

They stayed there for close on a month, and for the first week everyone declared that nothing on earth would move them from this heavenly spot. In the second week it was all right but beginning to be a bore. After three weeks Captain Offer knew he'd have to do something because his Gang was getting right proper browned orf—Private Charley Crookshank's appreciation of the situation.

John Offer tried his best to keep them all in Siwa, to cope with his men's restlessness, but just over three weeks after coming wearily into the oasis, circumstances dictated a very hurried packing and movement out again. Almost to the day Hauptmann Kurt Braunschweig was also given a commission which could bring him into conflict with Captain Offer.

*

In Cairo there was a major-general who did not conform to the stereotype set for Top Brass by envious junior officers. This man was a sharp fellow, always wanting to know and insistent on getting at the truth. To him had come this matter of the G.G.C.U., and he was very vitriolic about it.

'It's bloody nonsense,' he declared one day to his Staff. In World War II generals had begun to talk like human beings, a big advance on the ponderous verbosity of World War I Brass. This one never missed an opportunity to lard his sentences with the earthy words his men used, and they liked him all the better for it.

'Here we have some sort of unit swanning around in the desert, maintaining a most successful guerrilla rôle, if their reports are to be believed, yet we don't know a damned thing about them. You can't have those goings on in an army.'

His Staff dutifully agreed. They'd done their best to trace any unit responsible for the G.G.C.U.—what the devil did those initials signify? the major-general kept asking—but nobody seemed anxious to own them.

'Perhaps they're not British.' That was a Staff captain, Tansley, coming up with an idea. 'I wonder if they'll turn out to be Free French or Poles or even Greeks?'

The thought was debated, then shot down. 'The L.R.D.G. would have reported them as being foreign.'

'Oh, yes, the L.R.D.G., the cloak-and-dagger boys—they've met the G.G.C.U. and must know something about them.' The major-general pondered for a moment. He had his suspicions about those radio reports from the G.G.C.U. concerning their operations against the German enemy. There was something about them that did not ring true, yet the evidence from the L.R.D.G. in Kufra did at least confirm one of their claims—they had indeed rescued four L.R.D.G. P.O.W.s in German hands and brought them through the Great Sand Sea to safety.

'Kufra,' said the major-general, snapping his fingers. He was a great finger-snapper, having found early in his career that finger-snapping projected an image of energy. 'That's where we'll learn something about this mob. Roger,'—to Captain Tansley—'you will take the next plane to Kufra and start asking questions. Right?'

'Right, sir,' said Tansley, well-pleased to be offered such a trip, and two days later he went off as a passenger in a Bombay and duly landed in the oasis. There he had a long and startling conversation with an L.R.D.G. captain who had also been in Kufra when the G.G.C.U. came suddenly out of the blue. Yes, he'd met the officer commanding that unit.

'His name?'

'Captain John Offer. Awfully decent bloke, you know.'

Captain Tansley made notes. 'A good bloke?'

'They don't come better.' This L.R.D.G. patrol commander retained the highest opinion of John Offer. 'Very keen to get at the Boche, I remember. He just couldn't hang around Kufra but had to be off on some mission.'

'Do you know what that was?'

The patrol commander shook his head. 'Tony Leslie might, though.' Tansley raised an enquiring eyebrow. 'Captain Leslie, one of our patrol commanders. He went off with Offer's mob. Leslie took a relief for the Road Watch.'

'Where's Leslie now? I'd like to talk with him.'

The L.R.D.G. had a consultation which involved their wireless operator, then came up with an answer. 'Our last report said Leslie was heading for Derna. He shouldn't be far off the place by now.'

'Can you raise him on the radio?' Tansley turned to the wireless op.

A nod. 'Yes, sir. I think conditions are pretty good and he'll be in touch at eight tonight.'

'I'll be back at eight. Get him for me, will you?'

Radio conditions were favourable that evening, and the radio op did raise Captain Leslie and there was a very interesting exchange of signals. Yes, Offer had been with him travelling north, but they'd parted when Offer's mission had been called off.

Desert Marauders

'Oh?' said Tansley at that, controlling his eagerness, and wrote down a signal, asking, 'Do you know the nature of Offer's mission?' He waited anxiously for Leslie's distant operator to tap out a reply.

It came. 'Yes. He was off to Derna to do something about Rommel. Uncertain whether aim was to kill or capture him.'

Tansley was incredulous, almost stunned by the news. At G.H.Q. they had no plans for such an operation. Back went his signal. 'Who called off the mission? Where?'

'No idea. Passing through the Qattara Gap Offer received a wireless signal calling off the op. Offer seemed cut up about it.'

Next signal. 'When you parted did he tell you his destination?'

The answer. 'Siwa.' And gratuitously the far-distant black-bearded L.R.D.G. patrol commander threw in, 'First-class desert officer, Offer.'

'Everybody seems to like Captain John Offer,' Captain Tansley said, turning to the other L.R.D.G. officer at his elbow. 'First-rate, eh?'

'First-rate.' There seemed common agreement about Offer within the L.R.D.G., and that meant John Offer had passed the highest test. 'He has to be. Never met such a gang of cut-throats as his mob.'

'A rough lot?'

'I never saw the likes of them.' And that was saying something, in the desert. 'But Offer has 'em eating out of his hand.'

Tansley rose. 'Most interesting.' But baffling. An operation to top Rommel and they knew nothing about it in Cairo? 'I'd like to meet the bloke. Looks like a trip to Siwa for me.' But first he must return to Cairo before his commanding officer blew a gasket. Tansley gave a little snort to himself. The old boy was going to blow a gasket, anyway, when he heard the news. Rommel . . . Ye gods!

'They were off to top old Rommel?' The major-general could scarcely believe his ears. 'Good grief, who put them up to that? We ought to know when something as important as assassination is mounted. We can't have people taking it into their heads to go off and do in enemy generals.' He was appalled at the idea. 'We must find out what's back of this shower.'

For a start they got on to Records and asked for information about any officers bearing the name of John Offer. Records eventually came back with the news that no officer of that name held rank in the Middle East.

The major-general was growing increasingly exasperated. 'God damnit, here we have a mob roaming round the desert and we don't know what it is, and it's commanded by an officer who apparently doesn't exist.'

They got on to Records in the War House in London's Whitehall, and learned that in the whole of the British army there were only three commissioned men with the name of Offer. None of the three was named John. Only one of them was a captain, and he was doing his bit to win the war with the Army Post Office.

The major-general had had enough by now. He said so to Captain Tansley. 'This Offer chappie, if he's at Siwa he doesn't answer our radio calls. Surprise him. When a plane goes off to Siwa, get passage aboard, right?'

'Right, sir,' and a few days later a plane was taking off for that distant oasis and Captain Tansley had got himself a seat aboard it. It was a very bumpy ride over the desert, but Tansley didn't mind. He was quite looking forward to meeting this guerrilla outfit which appeared to lack legitimate military parentage.

*

Captain Leslie's black beard came shoving into Siwa early one morning after a long night's trek. He found John Offer genially quaffing cold liquor in the mess. They liked each other and were glad to meet again, and both settled down to swop stories.

Quite soon, though, Leslie said, 'John, Cairo is very interested in you.'

'Are they?' Offer looked his surprise, though it wasn't as great as he put on. Offer had a feeling that events were closing in on them, for in the past two nights Cairo radio had tried to contact him, addressing him by name. So now they knew his name, he thought, when Weybright came quietly in with the news. Offer had been shaken by that knowledge, and bewildered, for he couldn't understand how they had got on to him.

'Very interested. G.H.Q. Cairo had a talk with me two or three nights ago. They wanted to know all about you.'

'And you told them?' So that was it.

'Why, certainly. I mean, why shouldn't I?' Captain Leslie was looking most curiously at this officer in whom Cairo expressed so much interest. 'John, you *were* on a mission to collar Rommel, weren't you?'

'Well, you were there when it was called off. Your wireless op took the signal, didn't he?'

'Yes.' That did seem to settle the point. 'John, in Cairo nobody seems to know anything about you. Don't you think you ought to do something about it?'

'Of course. I can't understand what all the fuss is about. I'll give them a call on the wireless tonight.'

'I'm sure they'd appreciate it.' He remembered something. 'Anyway, Cairo's sending a Staff officer by plane to talk to you. He should be in any day now.' That had come in a chatty signal from Kufra after Tansley had left for Cairo.

'What a waste of time.' John Offer rose with great leisure. 'If they'd asked I'd have given them their information without all this nonsense.' A remark which puzzled Leslie. Hadn't Cairo tried to contact Offer by radio? 'I'll see you later, Tony.'

*

Field-Marshal Rommel, back once again at El Agheila on the Bay of Benghazi, was a man somewhat out of sorts. His lines of communication had been too long with the forces at his disposal, and with half his supplies failing to reach him via Italy, because of the R.A.F. and the Royal Navy, he could not continue to hold out when the Allies struck back beyond Sollum. Rommel was not a general to enjoy retreat.

Another thing was rousing his wrath. This was the activities of the British S.A.S., who were hurting him more than he could hear. Here they were, bands of them impudently roaming far behind the German front line and doing terrible damage, especially to his aircraft. Time after time now the S.A.S. came out of the desert to strike at his airfields after dark. In the past ten days alone they had set fire to over sixty precious aircraft parked on three of his desert air-strips. That was millions of marks worth of planes gone up in smoke, just when he needed all the aircraft possible. Not content with that, the S.A.S. sometimes ambushed and shot up his soft transport, and raided isolated repair depots and gun positions, and Rommel simply could not go on incurring such heavy losses.

'We must put a stop to their activities,' Rommel told his officers. 'They do more damage than an enemy division in battle. For too long they've been allowed to get away with their depredations. They are masters of the desert and we are not. When they've done their damage they go off into the desert to hide, and we give up the chase too easily.

'Gentlemen, all that's going to be changed. From now on we must be relentless in our pursuit of these raiders. At all costs they must be taught that they cannot raid our airfields and supply columns and get away with it. They will be pursued until they are caught, and then they must be destroyed.'

Next time the S.A.S. came raiding, Luftwaffe aircraft, as many as were available, would immediately take off and make a most intensive search to spot the fleeing raiders. If nothing else, intense air activity would retard their movements across the desert, for undoubtedly it would mean they would have to hide up during daylight hours.

'I am also going to create a special task force to go into the desert after them. This force will be air-lifted, if need be, into the area where the S.A.S. has been active. If the aircraft spot the enemy they will direct the task force on to them. If not, the task force will try to follow the S.A.S. tracks across the desert. One way or another these raiders must be wiped out as a lesson to others.'

Field-Marshal Rommel made his determination very clear. A Staff officer was deputed to raise this task force. This officer, an Oberst, looked first for an officer with experience of the desert, and they were very few, he soon realised. In the end his choice alighted on an infantry Hauptmann who had recently penetrated farther into the Sahara than any other German officer. The man seemed particularly keen to go in pursuit of their Will o' the Wisp enemies, as if he held some special grudge or hatred against them. He was a tall, hard-looking man and the Staff officer felt he had made a good choice.

So Hauptmann Braunschweig became officer commanding the punitive task force. Within a week he had got the volunteers he needed, as well as all the equipment he required. Then he took up his post at an airfield south of Agheila and waited for the mouse to come creeping into the trap.

*

Captain John Offer came at leisurely pace out of the officers' mess, into the bright hot sunshine of that morning, though it took him all his time not to go running off to find his men.

'That's torn it,' he was saying to himself, his nerves jumping. 'Christ, we can't stay here now!'

He continued, without any appearance of haste, towards the Glasshouse Gang's lines, but the dominant thought in his mind was, 'Where the devil can we go?' The Sahara was getting smaller for them. The Nile Valley was out. They had had to scarper out of Kufra and could hardly reappear there, and now Siwa was proving untenable. True, there were other oases like Kharga and Farafra, but these were regularly visited by S.A.S., L.R.D.G. and other desert roamers.

Offer had no illusions about the future. When he and his men sloped off from Siwa, as clearly they'd have to, something like a hue-and-cry would be raised. Honest men don't slide away when they are told that G.H.Q. Cairo want a word with them.

When he reached the lines he headed straight for his tent. His batman-driver, universally known as Pomegranate Face because of his mouthful of tiny teeth, was there, doing something to Offer's spare bush jacket. Nasty little squirt, Pom. Still, they had shared the same cell in Sharafim, and that put a bond upon them.

He said, 'Get the R.S.M., jildy!'

Pom went off at the double. In no time the lean red sweating face of R.S.M. Angus O'Keefe came stooping in through the doorway. 'You want me, sir?'

'By God I do. If you haven't some nice retreat up your sleeve, we're goners, old chap. Goners, d'you hear me?'

O'Keefe heard the story. 'We're going to move out?' The thought was pleasing. He showed his pleasure with a big hungry grin that was marred by an absence of a front tooth. R.S.M. O'Keefe was of that mad brigade which was in love with the desert, and masochistically sought it whenever possible.

'If we don't we're for the Glasshouse quite soon, my friend.'

'Then we're going to scarper, sir.' O'Keefe, an unruly prisoner, wasn't going back to the dreaded Glasshouse again if he could help it. The screws at Sharafim had given him a painful time in the punishment cells on two never-to-be-forgotten occasions.

'There's a Staff officer on his way from Cairo just to have a talk with me. He may drop in at any time, and we mustn't be here when he arrives. The question is, where do we go from here?'

O'Keefe was the expert. He had never let them down before. Offer spread a map on a tea chest that served as a desk and waited hopefully.

'Egypt's out. And we can't stay in this part of Libya. So there—that's the only place we can head for now.' The R.S.M.'s finger stubbed at a point on the map. Offer peered down and thought he was indicating the Mediterranean coast near to Circe. When O'Keefe lifted his finger, however, Offer saw it had been covering the words Jebel el Akhdar.

'The Jebel?' Jebel meant mountain, didn't it? Everyone referred to that area merely as 'the Jebel'. And Akhdar was Arabic for green.

'This morning's radio says that Allied troops entered Benghazi yesterday, and Rommel is digging in at his old line at Agheila. That means the Jebel's in our hands now, so it will be safe for us to shoot off up there.'

It sounded all right. 'What's it like, the Jebel?'

'Beautiful. In parts you'd think you were back in England. High mountains, cold enough at nights to warrant a fire. Some villages, a lot of fruit-growing, and plenty of springs and streams.'

'You make it sound as attractive as Siwa.' O'Keefe shook his head. He was a desert man, and while he could describe the Jebel as beautiful it did not have the attraction for him of the Sahara.

'We'd be behind our own lines, R.S.M.' Where would they get food or equipment that needed replacing? The R.S.M. dismissed the question almost as if unworthy of answer. 'Knock it off,' he said abruptly. 'Forward food dumps have no proper guard. We could help ourselves without much trouble.'

John Offer was convinced. Anyway, what other solution to their problem was there? It was the Jebel or nowhere.

'Get the men together. We'll have a talk.'

So the men were recalled from their places of leisure and came crowding together, some still wet-bodied from lying in the refreshingly cold pool. Offer explained very carefully the position they were in and his decision to head for the distant mountains. Everyone seemed highly enthusiastic. Movement for these restless souls was as important as intervals of doing damn all. Probably the prospect of cool days on mountain sides lured them more than anything.

'So you all like the idea?' There was a general chorus of approval. 'Well, before we pack up and clear off, any further questions?'

One came. It was from Private Charley Crookshank, one of the several ex-pugs who adorned their outfit. Offer wondered if there wasn't some connecting reason for so many boxers ending up in jug.

'Sir, couldn't we have a go at an airfield or soft convoy, like the S.A.S.?'

Offer could see that their neighbours within the oasis, the redoubtable S.A.S., had been passing some beery hours recounting to his men their adventures behind the enemy lines. Plainly his followers were thrilled by the stories and were keen to emulate the swashbuckling S.A.S.

He sighed. His fire-eaters craved for action, and never saw themselves lying dreadfully wounded or being hauled off to an enemy prison camp or getting killed. It was time he told them what they were up against.

'Let me come clean with you. We're now going to be chased by our own side, but don't kid yourselves that falling into the hands of the enemy will be a cushy way out for the duration of the war.'

For the first time he told them clearly of their special position as No. 1 targets for Afrika Korps' hostility. 'They think we behaved inhumanly, out on the Lake of Sand. If we fall into their hands it's God help us, and He won't have much power over the S.S., I can assure you. Now do you still want to go raiding?'

Offer would go if they wanted him to lead them, but any enthusiasm he had for guerrilla warfare was tempered by memory of the time when he had found himself caught by the enemy. He still woke up out of bad dreams in which he found himself tortured by the S.S., though the faces that leered over his sleep were those of the Glasshouse screws at Sharafim.

There was the briefest hesitation and then his villains said unmistakably they wanted action. Offer looked at them benevolently. 'Stupid sods,' he said. 'All right, shove off and pack. We're moving out jildy.'

So the men all raced off to pack their meagre kit. Jerricans were filled with water and petrol, and all stores were packed aboard their vehicles. O'Keefe did his usual scrounging and came back driving a big 3-ton Dodge, the same Allied Dodge that the German M.T. section had repaired following the evacuation of Siwa by the L.R.D.G. six or more weeks earlier. It was an asset, that truck, though slower and clumsier than the Chevs. It meant that Offer's men could spread themselves more thinly among the wagons, a decided advantage with so much equipment and stores to carry.

They slipped out of Siwa quietly, while the S.A.S. and others were having siesta, not wishing to advertise their departure, and they rode off in a picnic mood, thrilling to the adventure, however hard it turned out to be, of another desert foray.

When Captain Leslie rose from a much-needed sleep he was astonished to learn that Offer and his men had abruptly folded their tents and departed. 'Where's he gone?' He was incredulous.

'I gather his mission's on again, though not at Derna.' An S.A.S. officer had run into Offer on the point of moving and Glasshouse John had been swiftly glib in explaining their hurried departure.

Leslie opened his mouth to say, 'But isn't there some Brass-bound bod flying in from Cairo specially to see him?' Then closed it. He wasn't going to get tangled with special missions and G.H.Q. Keep out of other people's affairs was a solid army maxim, but he did feel the whole thing was rather odd.

*

Though the heat of the afternoon sun assailed the Gang as they came out of the shady oasis, the light-hearted mood continued. The news picked up by Weybright on the wireless that evening was also something to keep up their spirits. The port of Benghazi had been opened to Allied shipping, they heard, and reinforcements and stores were pouring into the town.

Talking among themselves over the evening mug of char there was general agreement that it was the beginning of the end for Axis forces in North Africa. Even John Offer, who ought to have known better, accepted this opinion and made his own prophecies as to how long it would be before the desert war was over. He thought, though, it might be six more months, though everyone else talked in terms of weeks.

For a few nights they travelled by moonlight, resting up during the day, but when they hit some rugged ground, needing all the light they could get to negotiate it without accident, they reverted to daytime travelling.

Then came a day when over the far distant horizon they saw a thin layer of white.

'Clouds,' said O'Keefe, who had seen it all before. 'That's the coast, and it's probably raining.'

As they travelled steadily north, the white mass seemed to climb into the sky, and they saw that they were indeed rain clouds. Parched as they were from the arid desert travel, the sight filled them with joy. They day-dreamed of being able to stand naked while cool rain pelted down upon them, and could talk of almost nothing else.

They camped that night somewhere east of Agedabia, the Jebel a mere hundred miles ahead. They would do it in two days, O'Keefe was pretty sure, though he seemed to remember some pretty rough ground ahead of them.

But R.S.M. O'Keefe had other things on his mind. He spoke of them to his captain that same evening. He was very casual about his approach, and it was some time before the shrewd John Offer realised he was leading up to something.

'It's great news, this push into Benghazi.' Offer agreed it was. O'Keefe drank rather elaborately, then said, 'Great place, Benghazi. Big city, very civilised.' Now he waxed enthusiastic. 'It's got fine big shops and big broad boulevards. Some lovely bars, too, and you should see the Italian crumpet! Cor, the bints are smashers! Never seen juicier crumpet anywhere!'

He went on and on, extolling the delights of Benghazi and its maidenry, until finally the penny dropped, and John Offer eyed him coldly. Having run out of cunning at last, O'Keefe shut up and waited hopefully.

Offer said, crudely, 'You're up to something, sergeant-major. Now, what?'

Abashed, O'Keefe hesitated a moment then came out with it. 'Let's get to the Jebel via Benghazi. A night on the town would do the boys good. What do you say, sir? Just one night. It'll be safe enough, full of Eighth Army, and no one will have time to wonder who we are.'

'True,' said Offer, and Benghazi was suddenly tempting. For one thing, it was nearer than the Jebel. Perhaps he could find a bed in an hotel and have the luxury of a bath and clean cool sheets. He agreed with O'Keefe; no one would look twice at his band of ruffians. The place would be overrun with tens of thousands of troops, probably no smarter than his own men. Yes, Benghazi would be safe for a brief halt.

'I think you've got an idea there, old chap. A night on the town in Benghazi can't do us much harm.' His voice hardened. 'But it's got to be one night only.'

His R.S.M. agreed enthusiastically, then went off to give the good news to the men. Offer heard raucous cheering and then crude voices competed to give intimately detailed forecasts of how they would spend that one glorious night in Benghazi. Offer thought, 'The women will have to be tough to satisfy these randy sods.'

With this change of plan, it meant an alteration to their course across the desert. O'Keefe drew a line on a map showing Offer where they would hit the coast, somewhere near an Arab hamlet called Soluch. 'There's a good road round the bay, and once we're on it we'll make Benghazi in no time.'

Late that afternoon they were still a long way from the coast—twenty miles at least—for they ran into warped and chasm-rent ground which time after time had them doubling back on their tracks to try to find an easier way around. It was disheartening.

Still, one good thing was that they were moving towards rain. The cloud mass over the coast grew until it filled the farther sky, and a few times stray clouds drifted far enough over the desert to sprinkle their bare bodies with light rain.

Finally, about four in the afternoon they ran into continuous rain. It was quite heavy, and for a time was welcome. Then it didn't seem all that good, after all, for they began to shiver, their extremities numb with cold, and everything in the back of the vehicles awash with water. No one would sleep very comfortably in those blankets that night.

The worst of it was that the red earth turned to mud and the trucks kept skidding and indulging in wheel-spins. Still, the ground wasn't rough and broken here, and they were able to keep going. But why keep going, Offer began to ask himself, as the rain showed no sign of abating. He decided that if they could find some shelter—a cave, for instance—they would not travel further that day. Be damned to the fleshpots of Benghazi; they could wait for another night.

They drove on now looking for suitable shelter, but could find none. The trouble was, the rain acted almost like a curtain, so that visibility was restricted to little more than fifty yards. Safe enough for driving, but not much help when they were looking for caves.

When nightfall was approaching everyone began to get anxious. The ground was monotonously level here, giving them no prospect of shelter. Everyone was cold and fed up and in need of a meal, but there was nothing here to stop for. They had to keep grinding on through the red mud, and Offer hated the thought of having to make camp after dark.

Finally there was a break in the flat monotony. A dark mass began to show to their right through the rain, and there was a hint of another such mass a little farther along. Offer thought it was an outcrop of rock. Deciding it held more prospects than this level plain, he told Gunner Wilborn, his driver at the time, to head towards it.

The truck turned a little, and almost immediately the dark mass took on shape. It was an aeroplane.

'Christ, sir!' he heard Wilborn exclaim. 'Look at that!' But Offer's mind was registering equal astonishment.

They came up to the bomber, the other trucks following. In everyone's heart hope was rising. They had stumbled on an Allied airfield, and shelter and hot food would soon be theirs . . .

Wilborn gave tongue again, but this time it was shocked. 'God Almighty, a swastika!'

His remark was unnecessary. Captain Offer too could see the swastika on the tail of the parked aircraft, and the cross of Germany on the fuselage. Behind him he heard his men talking, voices rising in excitement. He swung the door open and hung outside. 'Shut up, you clots, d'you want us all killed!'

They were innocents abroad in a warring world. They had listened to radio reports of Axis armies being driven back along the coast, of the occupation of Benghazi and the setting up of Rommel's headquarters at El Agheila. Blithe inexperience had caused them to translate this into meaning that Agheila was now the Axis front line. What neither Offer nor his R.S.M. considered was the trend of modern generals to direct strategy from far in the rear of the fighting zone. True, good generals like Rommel also drove to the front and often directed battles from the thick of the fighting, but once the fuss was over, back they went to where their Staffs worked to feed, supply and re-equip their fighting men.

As some excuse, John Offer had been trained and commissioned in the Royal Army Service Corps, which didn't bother much about warring generals and their behaviour. Later, a bit of smooth talk and a little wangling had landed him the job of entertainments officer for the Jerusalem area, which again was somewhat removed from the details of war. Still, he was an intelligent man and should never have fallen into such an erroneous assumption.

R.S.M. O'Keefe had more fighting experience but of a limited nature— guerrilla warfare with the L.R.D.G. This hardly equipped a man, even a sergeant as he was at that time, to ponder much on deployment of essential non-fighting Staff far behind the front line where they were in no danger of being over-run and captured by the enemy. And generals have to confer with such Staff, and so set up their H.Q.s with them.

They had been driving for days behind the enemy front line, though happily unaware of that fact. Even now they were not up to the Axis fighting front, that being a mere ten miles west of Benghazi. In their ignorance they had wandered on to a desert air-strip, one of several in that vicinity, and only this steadily pouring rain was keeping them from sight by the enemy.

It was an Italian airfield, though with some Ju88s operating from it and some German maintenance staff to attend to their own aircraft. The officer commanding this improvised dirt landing ground knew all about the S.A.S. and their devastating raids on airfields, but didn't take their threat very seriously. The S.A.S. tended to commit their outrages on airfields well to the rear of the front line, and the Italian commander perhaps thought their closeness to the fighting zone therefore provided them with some protection.

In fact his only worry was one of being suddenly overrun if the Allied armies made a further swift advance. His sentries, then, were posted in machine-gun pits in a line on the Benghazi side of the air-strip, but there was no such guard around the airfield perimeter. Instead he relied upon wandering patrols, two Italian sentries armed with rifles who were supposed to make the rounds of the parked aircraft continuously. This night both had quietly slipped back to the guard tent, where a good-hearted guard commander cheered them with some Chianti and said who would come and do anything to their aircraft in this heavy rain?

Quarter of a mile from this tented area a group of astonished commandos brought their vehicles close together. Night wasn't far away, but still the light was quite good, and they all gazed in awe at the powerful-looking German bomber. Every man had his hand on his weapon, safety catches off and ready for action.

Offer was the only man to alight from his truck. He stood there, the rain pelting steadily upon him, and he was going to say, rendered helpless by this astonishing situation, 'What are we going to do now?' when a hoarse whisper from one of the trucks posed him with that question.

Offer's answer was a simple, 'Christ knows!'

That same hoarse whisper said, 'Let's shoot the bastards up!'

There was a chorus of approval from the men. John Offer was constantly surprised at the way his villains wanted to get at the Axis. Here they were, again asking to be turned loose with their guns, though it would for certain bring the wrath of a formidable enemy upon them.

He made up his mind, briskly. He thought, 'In for a penny, in for a pound.' They were perhaps almost as likely to run into trouble trying to sneak away undetected as inviting it with a surprise attack on these aircraft.

'Okay. We'll earn our pay tonight.' But if they were to shoot up this airfield they must know what they were doing. Now he studied the light with concern. They needed twenty minutes or-so of daylight to get them away from this area; afterwards darkness would be their ally. When he thought of it, if they had planned it they could not have arrived at this airfield at a better time or under better conditions of weather. Beginners' luck, he told himself.

'This must be a three-minute operation,' he told them. 'Go for the petrol tanks.' That's what the S.A.S. always said. 'If they don't fire first time, don't linger. When you see me turn off, follow me, understand? We've got to keep together, and after dark that's going to be difficult. Anything to say, sergeant-major?'

O'Keefe had; this was right up his street. 'We'd better head back into the desert, sir. If we go forward we're bound to run into enemy posts. This rain's blowing in from the sea. If we keep it on our backs we'll be heading deeper into the desert. When it's dark we can use our lights—they won't follow far in this weather.'

The R.S.M. made it sound easy. Everyone was cheered by his nonchalance, and nobody now moaned because they wouldn't get to Benghazi that night. They had all tomorrow in which to round the enemy lines and descend on Benghazi.

Perhaps because they had listened so attentively to those experts, the S.A.S., they went into action like veterans. Offer's truck led the way. Behind him the cover had been removed from their Vickers. Thirty yards from the Junkers, Offer's machine-gun let it have it.

The night's silence was shattered by the harsh roar of their rapid-firing gun. It was devastatingly loud, making them jump almost out of their skins in shock, but if it was startling to them, how much more so to the enemy, shrouded somewhere in this steadily pouring rain.

Captain Offer leaned forward and watched the tracer hurtle in to the belly of the aircraft. It did not ignite. But there were other gunners behind him to rake it with fire, and they might find the petrol tanks. Offer drove on and another Junkers loomed up and again their Vickers raked it, and again it did not take fire. Behind him he heard other Vickers coming into action, and almost immediately the darkening night began to brighten. The first Junkers had responded to his other gunners' tracer and was going up in great roaring petrol flames.

John Offer heard cheers, and he cheered a little himself, but he was looking ahead for trouble. Gunner Wilborn was racing the truck as fast as it would go, and they were doing a lot of bumping and lurching, not exactly helping the aim of their gunner behind.

A third aircraft—it didn't look like a Junkers this time, but Offer didn't stop to investigate. The tracer flitted out and Offer could imagine it tearing through the fragile hull. Suddenly it began to glow. Within a second a great tongue of oily flame leapt from the flat belly of the plane. Offer saw the interior of the fuselage light up, and he took alarm and shouted, 'Pull away! Quick!'

Gunner Wilborn hauled on the wheel and they began to put distance between them and the blazing aircraft. Just as well. It exploded. The blast rocked their truck and sent everyone in the back flat on their faces.

Suddenly everything was noise and light. Another explosion, a plane they'd passed also going up. Flames were now climbing hundreds of feet into the sky, black oily smoke rising with them. They felt a mighty draught as the hungry petrol fires sucked air towards them, and felt the heat and it was so great it curled the hair of their beards and eyebrows, and they could smell the singeing on their heads.

They had gone into this sabotage recklessly and almost lightly, certainly on the spur of the moment, but none of them had expected it would be like this. It was, for most of them, one of the most terrifying moments in their lives and they were lucky some of them didn't get killed right there.

Offer's truck went circling away from the heat and light but debris from the explosions showered down around them. In the back men had to kick debris frantically over the sides or quickly grab flaming pieces and hurl them away before their truck took fire.

The place was so light now. There was so much brightness that it penetrated the steadily falling rain, and they could see more aircraft. Without any order Wilborn dragged on the steering wheel and brought the truck parallel with the dispersed line of bombers. All the same he maintained a good distance away from the next plane under attack.

Again without orders Offer's machine-gunners opened up their Vickers on a fourth target, and tracer got that going almost at once though not with such immediate, spectacular results. It took fire, though, and they knew it would spread and destroy the plane and that was all that mattered.

Captain Offer leaned out of his cab and looked back. His other trucks had pulled away from the flaming wreckage and were in line behind him. They were merrily hosing lead into anything they passed, whether it was on fire or not. Offer counted—all four aircraft were now on fire. One of them—the first—blew up while he was looking, and fascinated he saw great flaming pieces of aircraft go sailing into the sky.

He brought his attention round to the front. Another plane. No sound from their Vickers, though—probably a jam. The other trucks would attend to this aircraft, he thought. Their Vickers was still out of action when they went roaring past the next couple of planes, again bombers, but it opened fire as they approached their eighth victim though it didn't get that one burning like the others.

The ninth took fire. Behind him his other gunners were dealing with the aircraft they'd missed.

Tents ahead. They came looming up in the bright light from the burning planes, and Offer saw figures running and they knew they had lingered enough. A glance round made him think all nine planes were now on fire. In fact there were eight burning, but the ninth had suffered considerable damage. Not bad, if they got out of here with whole skins.

Fire was being directed upon them from somewhere among the tents. 'Left, left!' shouted Offer, and Wilborn hauled hard on the wheel and they went alongside the ninth aircraft, swiftly brewing-up. That put other aircraft between them and the men with the guns. Offer saw his other trucks follow suit, coming hard round and racing between the fiercely blazing aircraft. It must have been hot work for them, Offer thought, and not without danger. Another plane did in fact blow up shortly after their rear truck had scuttled by.

They kept running, charging almost line abreast over the flat land, trying to put as much distance between them and the enemy air-strip as possible. Some Italians behind did manage to get a machine-gun going, and tracer sped disconcertingly close to Offer's truck, but before it could range upon them it stopped firing. Perhaps another gun was playing up that night.

Still they drove as hard as they could go, and as they put distance between them and the blazing aircraft the bright light from the flames gradually diminished. Quite soon, while it was light enough behind, it seemed to be very dark ahead. Offer saw headlights go on and guessed that O'Keefe had decided to risk travelling by them. Wilborn now switched on without telling. Distance was their objective now; it would not be healthy in this area soon.

So they trundled through the dark, and it seemed that the farther they travelled away from the coast the lighter the rain became.

They kept going all night, having the usual stoppages, twice for punctures, and several times getting stuck in the mud and having to use other trucks to haul out the unlucky ones. They also lost a lot of time on occasions when impossible ground caused them to make wide detours.

Finally, about two in the morning they ran out of the rain and came on to ground which clearly had suffered no wetting in a long time. The sky cleared and the stars came out, and back they were in the familiar dry desert again.

By dawn Offer guessed they had put thirty or forty miles between them and the airfield. He gave the order to halt just before the sun was up, and his cold and weary men clambered down and got the firecans going.

O'Keefe immediately came up to his captain. Offer knew he was coming, ostensibly for orders, but in fact intent on giving him advice. So he just said, 'Now what do we do?'

They squatted together on the cold ground and watched the sun inch its way over the horizon. The first rays of warmth upon them were like a blessing. They felt at last they could relax; soon they would feel all right.

The R.S.M. said, 'We'd better hole up during daylight.'

'You think they'll have aircraft out searching for us?'

'I'm damned sure they will, sir. Anyway, we don't need to take risks. We're all shagged and could do with a lay-up.'

Offer nodded agreement. 'Wish we could have put more distance between us and the airfield, though, sergeant-major. They're going to feel very mean this morning when they see what we've done.'

He was still dazed by how easy it had all turned out to be. It was incredible that with so little effort such a few men could create so much destruction in a mere matter of minutes. All night his mind had retained those pictures of wild incendiarism, of the heat and roar as aircraft exploded into fragments high into the sky. So easy to destroy, but then wasn't that war?

During the bumpy ride through the night, John Offer had done quite a lot of useful thinking, as a result of which he called Weybright over to him.

'If you've a chance, get a signal off while we're here. If not, shove it out tonight.' Then he dictated the signal, which was: 'Successful raid on enemy air-strip SE Soluch. 9 bombers destroyed on the ground.'

Deliberately he signed it 'Captain John Offer, o/c G.G.C.U.'

John Offer was never quite sure why he did it. Probably at the back of his mind was the idea of piling up some credit in case he was unlucky enough ever to be picked up and charged with desertion and dozens of other military offences. One never knew when something like this could be hauled out and posed as a mitigating factor.

After a brief break for breakfast of hard tack and tea, with a cloudless sky overhead once more, the small convoy took off again, but not very far. Within a mile R.S.M. O'Keefe saw hard ground and led them on to it. No need to wipe out tyre marks here; none showed. Another couple of bumpy miles, heading north this time, brought them to some evilly rough country, all chasms and fissures in tumbled rocks. It was ideal for their purpose. Within five minutes, with their camouflage nets stretched out, no one more than fifty feet away would have detected their trucks.

A great many aircraft crossed overhead that day but did not linger. Then sometime early in the afternoon, an Italian spotter aircraft came over and seemed to take a great interest in their locale. It failed to see them, but the Breda buzzed around, at first in random fashion, then finally systematically, apparently searching the ground below.

'Looking for our tracks,' said O'Keefe complacently, watching it through the netting. 'Well, he's looking in the wrong place.'

Finally the Breda fled away. About four in the afternoon the R.S.M. suggested they should take a risk and move off while there was plenty of daylight. This country was too rough to negotiate after dark. Besides, he was pretty sure they wouldn't be troubled by aerial searchers again. 'They give up pretty quickly,' he said, as Offer had sometimes heard him say before.

So the convoy, still filled with satisfaction from their successful exploit the night before, happy in the thought of booze and bints ahead, continued north until they were sure they had rounded the enemy front line, then struck out west for the coast and Benghazi.

*

The first call for action for Hauptmann Braunschweig's Special Task Force came that rainy night from Soluch. It proved to be a frustrating experience.

The Hauptmann roused his men and got them going at top speed up the coast road to Soluch. The road round the great bay was quite good, but progress was made slow by the heavy traffic on it, as German and Italian troops retreated on Agheila. The heavy rain did not help progress, either, and in several places the road was flooded and German Military Police with their little batons were directing them over diversionary routes, remarkable for their mud and lack of tyre grip.

It was well after midnight when the Task Force found the Soluch airstrip, and only then because of the fires still burning. The rain was easing off and finally stopped altogether, and for a few hours the sky cleared and they had hopes of putting up some spotter aircraft at first light.

However, frustratingly, with dawn heavy clouds once more rolled in from the sea and deluged the coastal plain. It was no good sending up aircraft in this weather, Hauptmann Braunschweig was told, because they wouldn't be able to see anything on the ground. So the Hauptmann and his Task Force had to hang around some quite inadequate tents, smelly with damp clothing, as hour after hour passed and nothing could be done to pursue their foes.

For Braunschweig it was particularly galling. He wanted to make a good show of this first call-out, but instead it had all the appearance of a damp squib. There was another reason for his barely concealed impatience, which betrayed itself in irritation and little bouts of anger as the wet day dragged on. While everyone referred to the raid as being by the S.A.S., the Hauptmann could only picture in his mind the battered face of the pseudo-captain, John Offer. This was to be the pattern for the German captain on every call-out thereafter—he identified all of them with the man he had once met outside Siwa, never with the S.A.S.

Hauptmann Braunschweig had built up an almost obsessional hatred of the man they had captured but who had so neatly outwitted them and got away. He would never rest until he had got his hands on the criminal who had caused his men to die so horribly in those quicksands, he kept telling himself, and his temper grew viler as the rain came down and held them helpless on that muddy air-strip.

Some time after midday quite suddenly the clouds rolled away and the sun shone on them. Immediately there was intense activity around the air-strip. Every available aircraft was sent up to try to find traces of the saboteurs. Back at the air-strip all waited in various degrees of tension for news from them, but the hours kept going by and still nothing about the last night's raiders.

All at once excitement. The Station Commander, a handsome Italian, came up to Braunschweig with a signal. 'Herr Hauptmann, tracks have been picked up on the desert by one of our aircraft. They may have nothing to do with last night's raiders, but my pilot is following them.'

Quickly they plotted the position on a map, while Braunschweig's Task Force clambered on to their vehicles. The column lumbered off, again making all possible speed and maintaining radio communication with the air-strip. Within ten minutes a message was relayed to them which brought disappointment. The trail had been lost on some hard ground. The pilot would continue to search the area, though, but was not optimistic of success. He reported that the ground below was ideal for the enemy to hide away, and really it needed a ground search to rout them out.

That put more heart into the Task Force and at reckless speed they went roaring out into the desert. It took them some time to find the tracks, but when he saw them Braunschweig's heart leapt. The tyre patterns were undoubtedly British. These were indeed the tracks of the impudent raiders, and again in his mind's eye he saw John Offer's face and the fury and hatred built up within him.

He drove as fast as he could keep the column moving but the big infantry carriers were clumsy and held down their pace. Even so they came to the hard terrain where the British tracks ended not much after four in the afternoon, while there was still plenty of daylight for a search. Looking ahead at the broken ground, Braunschweig thought grimly, 'They are there, somewhere in there. I'm going to find them.'

But he didn't. They never found any tracks again, though his Panzergrenadiers, advancing on foot, did find a place where obviously their quarry had rested up during that day. But by now they had departed.

O'Keefe's impatience had saved them by little more than an hour. Blissfully unconscious of their narrow escape, the Glasshouse Gang rolled on into the night.

Braunschweig called off the search when darkness fell. Next day they returned to El Agheila where a very bitter Hauptmann wrote a report sufficiently interesting to warrant it being presented to Field-Marshal Rommel.

'The S.A.S., or whoever the raiders are, will not always be able to choose rainy weather to screen their operations and assist them to escape into the desert afterwards. But clearly to be of any success against these clever raiders, my Task Force must have the maximum of mobility. I therefore recommend that it be made smaller, though not lacking in firepower, and it should be provided with its own air transport to the point where tracks are first found.'

Braunschweig then went on to detail the type of personnel and vehicles he wanted. For him lumbering infantry carriers were out. They had a number of *Kubelwagens* at the base and he requested the use of six of them. He picked on the *Kubelwagen* (a product of the Volkswagen company) because it was an excellent patrol vehicle, sufficiently armoured against light machine-gun fire, and very rugged. It could cruise at over fifty miles an hour, was armed with twin machine-guns, and did not set a weight problem for Ju52s. Braunschweig was careful in his calculations and finally worked out that for a short range operation—up to one hundred miles—two Ju52s would be sufficient to carry his Task Force.

Rommel, ferocious because of the loss of nine valuable aircraft that night, gave Braunschweig all he asked for. He got the *Kubelwagens* standing by within an hour, out at the nearest air-strip, and instructions were given that two Ju52s be placed at Hauptmann Braunschweig's immediate disposal if there was a callout.

When that was done, Braunschweig sat back grimly to wait for the next mouse to put its nose into the trap. He was confident that next time the daring raiders behind the enemy lines would regret their destructive activities.

*

Captain Roger Tansley returned to Cairo from Siwa in that comfortable mood which young officers enjoy when they have news which will upset their superior. He came to his major-general's office and was immediately greeted with a barked, 'Well? Everything go off all right?' Very sharp, to show he was a general and a busy man.

''Fraid not, sir,' said Tansley cheerfully. 'Someone tipped the beggar off and he cleared out of Siwa only a few hours ahead of my arrival.'

'Well, sod me,' said the down-to-earth general. 'What's this we're running, a bloody Fred Karno's army? What d'you mean, somebody tipped him off? And where's the fellow gone, eh?'

'It was not intentional, sir, the tipping off. The L.R.D.G. chap I went to see let drop to Offer that I was on my way to meet him. Leslie—that's the L.R.D.G. type—said within two or three hours, while everyone else was having siesta, Offer and his mob moved out, and they haven't heard anything about him since.'

The general could only stare in shocked incredulity at Captain Tansley. Finally he roused himself to say, 'If this doesn't beat everything! What's the fellow think he's up to, mucking around the bloody desert apparently not under any military control!'

'We don't know that, sir. We might find, after all, he's on some highly secret mission for someone . . .'

'Come off it, Roger! We've tried every corps and unit and nobody wants to own Offer and his mob. I tell you, the fellow's on his own, conducting his own private war, by the sound of it. Well, we can't have it. Just can't have this sort of nonsense. What if everyone decided to fight the war their own way? Where would we be, generals without armies?'

Desert Marauders

He had a sense of humour, this major-general, and it came peeping through now. In fact he was beginning to see the comical side to the situation, and it would make excellent talk in the mess at dinner. Still, this did not cause him to reduce his efforts to bring the mysterious bogus Captain Offer to heel.

'What do you suggest, sir?'

'Suppose we try a new tack. We can't trace any commissioned officer by the name of John Offer——'

'That might not be his real name, sir.'

'For the moment, because we can't do anything else, let us assume it is. Let us make another search but widen it. I want to trace all men by the name of Offer, John or any other name, here in the Middle East. Go to it, lad, pull your bloody digit out and let me see results by tomorrow.'

He gave Tansley a time that was impossibly short, which was one reason why he had risen to be a general, and Tansley was two days on the hunt. He put out a signal to all units, as well as attacking Records. That signal brought the quickest and most unexpected result.

Out at H.M. Field Prison along the Sweet Water Canal, the commandant, Major Adam Tulloch, read it and nearly passed it over for filing, when something about the name struck a chord. His R.S.M., Fry, was with him, still showing signs of wear and tear from the prison riot nearly three months ago. Tulloch passed the message across.

'Offer?' said Tulloch, who enjoyed the soubriquet of Himmler within the Glasshouse, and did his best to earn the title. 'Didn't we have some git called Offer not long ago?'

Fry remembered him well. 'Yes . . . bit of a ponce, he was. Actor in Civvy Street, wasn't he?' So he had to be a ponce or a homosexual, in Fry's mind. 'Did up Staff Milkin in the Punishment Block, remember?'

'Of course.' Tulloch remembered clearly now. 'Old Milky kicked his face in for it.' They both smiled in satisfaction because Right must always prevail in a Glasshouse and screws were always right. 'Wonder what they want the bastard for?' He put a call through to Captain Tansley at G.H.Q. Cairo.

Tansley was immediately interested and shot out along the Canal without delay. When he had introduced himself to the prison commandant, Captain Tansley said, 'Tell me everything about this former prisoner of yours, Private John Offer. What's he look like, for a start?'

Major Tulloch sent for R.S.M. Fry to assist him, Fry having more day-to-day contact with the prisoners. Between them they supplied Tansley with all the answers

'What's he look like?' Tulloch and Fry looked thoughtful. 'Medium-sized, dark-haired——' Fry said no, brown-haired but not black. 'Walks like a puff,' Fry contributed, but Tulloch spoke of a more distinguishing feature. 'He's got a broken nose, pretty flat it is. He had an accident while he was here. Fell down some steps or something.'

Captain Tansley thought, 'This is getting hot.' The description tallied with that given him by the black-bearded L.R.D.G. Captain Leslie out at Siwa. 'Do you know anything else about him?'

They didn't need to send for records, R.S.M. Fry having a mind that retained most information. He it was who said, 'Before the army he'd been an actor. He'd also had a commission, but got shopped for something, flogging Government property, I seem to remember.'

Tansley said abruptly, 'What was that? Offer had held a commission? Was he a captain, by any chance?'

But Fry shook his head. 'No, sir. I think he was a first-lieutenant.'

Slightly disappointing until Tansley thought, 'But if he's given himself a commission he might have promoted himself in the process.' He was pretty sure this was his man now.

'When he left Sharafim, where was he posted?'

That did mean a call to the clerk in the next room to bring in 'the book'. Running his finger down the columns, Major Tulloch found John Offer's name and date of release. It also contained the signature of the sergeant-escort who had taken Offer back to his new unit. Even more important at that moment, it gave the number of the regiment to which he had been posted.

Tansley rose, feeling pleased. Things were certainly dropping into place. This was their man—so long as they didn't find John Offer spud-bashing in his new unit.

He wasn't. More enquiry revealed that John Offer had quickly tired of his new friends and had gone A.W.O.L. Captain Tansley returned to his major-general with an impressive amount of information. The general blew a few gaskets and bellowed. 'The cheeky bugger! Goes on the run, forms his own cloak-and-dagger outfit and starts a war with Rommel! A Glasshouse boy, too. Jesus, now I've heard everything!' Then he did start to laugh, because the situation was too outrageous to be contained in solemnity.

Tansley said, 'By all accounts, sir, he makes a damn' good officer.'

'Does he? Well, he did have some experience, only two pips, though. Who said he was good?' The general had stopped laughing now.

'Everyone who'd met him,' said Tansley simply. 'Captain Leslie—the L.R.D.G. wallah, you know—said he'd never seen a bigger shower of cut-throats than Offer's outfit. He said he would have hated to have had to command them, yet Offer seemed able to control them perfectly. One word from him and even the toughest jumped to it. Leslie told me a very droll story about Offer swearing at a man and being upset because he'd done so——' But the general didn't want to hear funny stories.

Unexpectedly more information fell into their lap. The general had said, 'Where has this fellow picked up his mob? A lot of men, thirty, you know.'

On an inspiration Tansley did a lot of phoning, which included Major Tulloch at Sharafim. What he wanted from Tulloch was a list of the names of men who had been released from the Glasshouse around the time that Offer had ended his sentence. When the list was dictated back over the phone, a now very curious Tulloch asked, 'What's it all about? Why this interest in the little bastard?'

So Tansley told him. 'There's a fellow calling himself Captain John Offer who's got himself a commando outfit and is waging a private war against Rommel. As we don't approve of private wars we're trying to catch the blighter.'

'Oh, I see,' said Major Tulloch and it was not for several hours that the penny dropped.

Tansley, during that time, was phoning the Military Police. They confirmed that several of the ex-Glasshouse inmates listed were also on the run. What was puzzling was the way they had seemed to disappear. Usually when a man went A.W.O.L. in the Nile Valley he didn't stay free very long. 'Not many places where they can go,' the M.P. told him. 'Just a few bars and canteens and we keep a close watch on all of them.'

Captain Tansley rejoined his general and gave him his latest theories. 'Sir, I think Offer's outfit consists of former cell-mates at the Glasshouse.'

The general said, 'If you tell me more I shall end up liking the sod.'

Within an hour Tansley was back in a position to tell his general much more.

Some time after Tansley had spoken about Offer's rôle in desert warfare, Major Tulloch took a drink in the sergeants' canteen. He usually dropped in for a stiff whisky with his staff-sergeants after they'd put their prisoners into their cells for the night. This evening R.S.M. Fry joined him in his drink, and while they were knocking them back, Tulloch told Fry about Offer and his ex-Glasshouse Gang.

He was still explaining when all at once he stopped speaking, too startled by a random thought to go on. When he resumed, his voice was choking. 'Christ-all-bloody mighty, Jack, why didn't I think of it before!'

R.S.M. Fry quite reasonably asked, 'What?'

'This Offer bugger. He's got some sort of commando going. Jack, remember the riot? Those black-faced commandos making a raid on us?'

R.S.M. Fry would never forget it. That was the day prison history was made, when a gang of armed commandos stormed the place, turned the prisoners on to the screws, beat up everyone in Staff uniform, then vanished into the Blue taking some of the long-serving prisoners with them.

From that day on Sharafim had never heard anything about the commandos nor of any of the escaping prisoners, and never a lead to their identity. It had been a bruising experience, in more senses than one, for Major Tulloch and his staff. Some had had to go into hospital for treatment; Tulloch, the iron Scotsman, had taken a ferocious beating but despising weakness hadn't even seen the prison M.O. All the same, memory of that terrible day still seared his soul, for again the affair was a blot against his record. In the enquiry that followed he was severely censured for the inadequacies of the Gate Guard who had so easily allowed themselves to be over-powered.

'As if anyone in their right senses would ever imagine men trying to break into a Glasshouse,' Tulloch had fumed to his R.S.M. after the enquiry. Still, he'd taken a physical beating, and a ticking-off from his superiors that rankled. All he hoped was that some day he'd have all those bastards out there on the parade ground at his mercy. And Major Adam Tulloch had no mercy.

All those months since the affair Tulloch had hoped that someone somehow would be able to identify the miscreants. Now, all in one moment it was Major Tulloch himself who guessed it.

'Jack, it was him, that bloody little ponce, Offer! Don't you see?'

R.S.M. Fry did see, and he had taken one of the worst hammerings from that commando, so now he could only sit and mouth every foul word that came to mind, close to insanity at that moment. Two violent men then planned what they would do if ever the gang came into their hands. Now they knew their identity it was more than likely.

Major Tulloch rang Captain Tansley with his news. Tansley shot round to the major-general's office. The general, staggered, said, 'Offer raided Sharafim?'

Tansley nodded. 'Then took off after Rommel, sir,' as if sportingly trying to put Offer in a more favourable light.

The general ignored the interruption. 'That fellow's a menace. He's got to be picked up. You know what to do. Start a hunt for the bugger, though where the heck do we start?'

Obligingly the bogus Captain Offer sent him his address. When the general read the message he said, 'Good grief, how those boys do get around! Nine aircraft destroyed? Wonder how good the claim is?'

A few hours later Allied aircraft reconnaissance confirmed that eight aircraft were indeed burnt out on an air-strip near Soluch and a ninth had some appearance of being badly damaged.

But before that news came to Cairo the major-general had said, 'I'll lay you ten to one Offer's mob are in Benghazi, living it up. After a long desert journey all they'll think of is crumpet and ale, and Benghazi's the place for that. Tip them off, Roger; tell them to concentrate on Benghazi. We'll nail the little sod, you see.'

But he was chuckling when Tansley left the office, rubbing his chin and thinking, admiringly, 'We could do with more of Offer's enterprise in the army,' and he began to think for the first time that they mightn't be handling the situation to best advantage.

*

In happy ignorance of the two-pronged attack that was being mounted for them, the Glasshouse Gang came trundling into Benghazi shortly after ten o'clock that morning. It was a sight for sore eyes—for eyes, anyway, which might love a desert yet pine for fresh vistas after a while.

The vista that was Benghazi that day was infinitely satisfying. There was little sign of bomb damage—that was down by the harbour—and everything looked bright and busy and pleasing. At first there were fine houses and boulevards with much greenery, then came a shopping centre with big stores and inviting bars, cinemas and restaurants.

Walking the streets were civilians, many of them in Arab attire, a lot in European clothing, and some of these set the men in the backs of the trucks wolf-whistling and calling invitingly. These were the summery-attired girls, and there seemed thousands of them, Italian, French, Greek and many other nationalities in this cosmopolitan city. Ripe, round-hipped creatures, mostly with dark lustrous hair, but even here with the occasional blonde. The men felt they couldn't wait—these were the first women they had seen, apart from the veiled creatures in the oasis, for nearly three months.

John Offer sat beside his driver and took it all in no less avidly than his men. Perhaps more so. He was more a creature of comfort than most of his followers, perhaps because he was that much older, and while he could cope with the desert and its physical demands upon him, he was not all that enraptured by it. Give him Benghazi every time! His eye rejoiced, then, at sight of civilised company, and he too eyed the local talent and made plans to strive for bed-wifery that night.

The noise his men made, all that whistling and catcalling, did not disturb him. Benghazi had its civilians but they were completely outnumbered by fighting men of the Eighth Army. If his own men looked wild and unshaven, so did those happy warriors thronging the sidewalks of the Arab port that morning. They were already out on the town in their tens of thousands, men given leave which they deserved after months of desperate fighting. Like the Glasshouse Gang, most were there for a good nosh, a change from army food, to be followed by a great swilling down of beer, and then, hopefully, having it off with some obliging lady, preferably not in one of the Arab brothels.

The businessmen of Benghazi looked cheerful, with an army of new customers, pockets full of back pay, buying everything on sight even at war-inflated prices. The local girls, too, didn't seem altogether displeased to be the centre of so much loudly voiced appreciation.

No, John Offer decided, no one would notice the Glasshouse Gang here in crowded Benghazi. As O'Keefe had said, this was a place where they could hide and no one would be any the wiser. He even began to think of dallying longer than one night, then pulled himself together firmly. He knew his men. Lingering much longer in this city with all its temptations would put too great a strain on his gang of ruffians, and they'd soon bring trouble upon themselves. Perhaps even one night would prove too much.

They came to a big square where the Town Hall was. Here they parked among dozens of other army vehicles, and here John Offer held a pay parade, though it was very informal, ten pounds shoved into every man's hands, quite enough for a one-night binge. They were told not to get into trouble—a waste of breath—and to be here by the vehicles at ten o'clock next morning preparatory to moving on to the Jebel.

'We'll be able to have many nights out in Benghazi while we're there,' Offer promised them, and off they shot to sample the joys of the town even at that quite early hour.

That left O'Keefe with his captain. Offer gave him thirty pounds, that being some compensation for the responsibility of the rank he bore. 'You're all right on your own, sergeant-major?'

The gap in O'Keefe's front teeth showed in a wolfish smile. 'I've been here before, sir. If she's been a good girl, there's a little Eyetie bint warming it up for me right now. Very athletic, sir, most nimble in bed.'

'I envy you, R.S.M.,' and the R.S.M. looked modest, as if he had achieved something notable in the field of love. John Offer fingered the last notes from the £2,000 they had robbed from a Canal Pay Corps office. 'Keep your eyes skinned, will you? We're running short. We'll have to knock off another Pay Office soon or no one will get any more money.'

They parted. John Offer went to find an hotel. Of course he started at the top—the celebrated Hotel Berenice—but there was no room for him there. In the end he found an hotel that could accommodate him, small but efficient and clean, with a youngish French lady owner who seemed promisingly without male encumbrance like a husband. Offer decided to talk winningly with her later that night.

Just now he wanted a shower, then a few hours recuperating from the night's slog in that bed with the fresh white sheets. After that he would give Benghazi the accolade of his approval if it deserved it, and he had an idea it would.

So sleep it was during the heat of the day, then another shower, and the chic lady-proprietor herself brought him coffee, fresh rolls and salt butter, and stood in the doorway quite a time, very animated, laughing a lot and mangling her English enchantingly.

'We're in,' Offer told himself, dressing, very complacent. There had been a promise in those delightful French eyes. Now he could view the town at ease, enjoying himself, not having to compete with the Eighth Army for talent.

So he went out, delighted to see neon signs again, and buses running, even to hear juke boxes pounding away in the bare-looking cafes, all well patronised by Desert Rats. He solemnly inspected the cathedral, looked into a few banks to see if they could be knocked over instead of tapping His Majesty's pocket via a Pay Corps office, then strolled down to the harbour and saw the bombed buildings and wrecked shipping there.

In a succession of cafes—good ones—he sipped iced orange and soda from a tall cooling glass, or had good French coffee filtered in a highly chromed device at his very table, and he ate cakes galore—always a hog for creamed and sugary things. He thoroughly enjoyed that day, and he had no need of companionship until night and then it seemed he was to be well provided for. Deliberately he kept off alcohol until after sundown.

When evening came, a breeze from the sea making life extremely bearable, he dined at an excellent, if rather expensive, restaurant on a broad verandah overlooking a pleasant tree-lined square. All round, seen entrancingly through the leaves of the trees, were awninged pavement cafes, very busy with smartly attired girls and often surprisingly smart soldiers. Not far away, from a garden-restaurant rose the strains of a tiny three-piece orchestra, dominantly French with its accordion, and a clear male tenor singing songs of love in many languages.

At peace with the world, Captain John Offer partook of an excellent five-course dinner, assisted by a Pernod as an *aperitif*, a bottle of good local red wine, and finally a glass of cognac to send him on his way rejoicing.

John Offer decided not to be too late turning in to his hotel. He would take a bottle of cognac with him and invite the French lady to his room for a sip, and if he and the cognac between them couldn't get her willingly into bed within ten minutes, it would be surprising.

It was still a little early to make his return, however—the good lady would certainly have duties to perform until much later in the evening—so before buying his bottle, Offer decided to make a tour of the best bars in the town.

He went back to the Berenice. The bar was crowded with officers of all ranks and many nationalities. There were few ladies there, and Offer would have preferred a place less military, but he took a seat at a small table, absent-mindedly ordered a whisky and soda, and was surprised to get it without demur.

About fifteen minutes later, Offer saw a Military Police officer step into the room. He was a lieutenant, and on duty because he made no attempt to remove his hat.

There were men of far higher rank than the lieutenant in that bar, yet sight of the Military Police uniform had an effect on all of them. Most turned to watch the lieutenant, though it was discreetly done, without it being obvious.

'Nobody's friend,' quoted Offer to himself. When M.P.s were around, everyone seemed to become a little thoughtful.

That uniform lifted the young lieutenant above rank; he need be subservient to nobody, and he wasn't. Offer watched him stalk slowly round the room, looking every officer there full in the face, not a bit abashed by the affront it roused in some of higher rank. All at once it came to John Offer that this fellow was very intently looking for someone, and suddenly he wished he had chosen another bar for his drink. Too late to move now, and with a curious tightening of nerves he watched the lieutenant make his slow tour of the bar.

Finally the M.P. came and stood before his table. Offer looked into a face from which all trace of human feeling seemed to have been drained—a neutral face, a face that was the official mask of the lieutenant's calling. The hard grey eyes just looked at him. They continued to look at him, perhaps for half a minute, so long that John Offer could feel people beginning to turn and covertly regard him.

Offer should have been at ease, as he normally was, should have waved a welcoming hand and said humorously, 'Do take a seat. Be my guest. What would you like to drink?' But that expressionless face, those unswerving eyes and that smart uniform for once had a paralysing effect on his tongue. He could only sit there and stare and know that he looked guilty . . . of what?

Abruptly, and it was a shock: 'Captain Offer?'

Offer came out of his stupor like greased lightning. A Military Police officer knew his name! The bells of danger clanged horribly in his mind, yet now he rose to the occasion magnificently.

'Pardon?' Sharply, moving his head forward in a quick little motion that was at once surprise and interrogation. The eyes seemed to be resting on his flattened nose.

'You're Captain John Offer.' It was a flat, uncompromising statement, no beating about the bush with this M.P.

Offer relaxed. He put on a perfect act. 'Sorry, old chap, wrong number.'

The M.P. cut in. 'Your name?' Hard and sharp, to give a victim no chance to think and throw him off his mental stride.

'Raeburn.' Offer was as quick with his wits as this chap. 'Robin Raeburn.' His tone was suddenly edged with annoyance, like a man who has had enough of this nonsense already. Robin Raeburn, his old stage name. 'Field Salvage.'

The M.P. wasn't a man to accept any story uncritically. 'May I see some proof of identity?'

Promptly Offer's hand went to his left tunic pocket. Left was Raeburn and Field Salvage (Forward Area) Coy documents, thoughtfully forged in Cairo months ago; right pocket was John Offer's identity and the Glasshouse Gang Commando Unit papers, all now convincingly grubby and sweat-stained. He handed them across, face very tight-lipped to show he was indignant at this public humiliation. The lieutenant took the Field Salvage (Forward Area) Coy papers. When first he had gone on the run, that had been Offer's bright idea. So far as he knew there wasn't such a unit as Field Salvage, but it had a nice ring and would have a familiar sound in anyone's ears. Only when it had outstayed its usefulness did Offer create the G.G.C.U. and the documents appropriate to such an outfit.

The lieutenant's expression didn't change as he glanced at the papers. Then he handed them back, just saying, 'Thank you.' No apology for annoyance; that wasn't the M.P. way.

Offer replaced the papers in his tunic pocket and looked coldly round the room. All eyes were instantly averted from him. With every appearance of composure and leisure Offer slowly sipped his drink, but out of the corner of his eye he watched the M.P.

The lieutenant finished his inspection of the room, but Offer noticed that in the doorway, leaving, he turned and looked back at him, and the M.P.'s face seemed to brood as if not entirely satisfied.

'I'm getting out of here,' and five minutes later Offer rose and departed and had the good sense to use a side entrance in case the awkward fellow was waiting in front to have another suspicious chat.

He was sweating, wanting to break into a run. Christ, that had been a shaker, a cop standing before him and coming out with his name. Bewildered, he thought, 'How did they do it?' How could Cairo have traced him right to that very hotel on his first night in Benghazi? John Offer had an awful picture of a long arm remorselessly stretching close on a thousand miles across the desert to reach down and pluck him up. It was a chilling thought, quite a terrifying feeling. Offer's mouth was dry and it wasn't desert dryness this time.

It took him all his time to keep from panicking, yet once more he talked himself into calmness. 'If I lose my head now it won't do me any good,' he told himself, but he wouldn't go into any other public place that night.

He thought, 'The safest place now is my hotel,' and even that wouldn't be safe for long if the suspicious lieutenant sent his men round examining hotel registers. In future he must sign in under some other name, but never again as Offer. And tomorrow they must get the hell out of Benghazi and into the Jebel until the heat died down. He only hoped to God his men didn't invite trouble or talk too much so that at ten next morning there would be no posse of M.P.s watching their trucks in the big square.

In a small bar he bought a good bottle of cognac. By the time he reached his hotel, though, his nerves were under control again. The very smart, entrancingly smiling hotel-owner welcomed him with a lot of cooing sounds. Had M'sieur enjoyed himself in Benghazi? Had M'sieur dined, or would he like a drink?

M'sieur played gallantly up to the lady, paying her compliments and assuring her that he had dined well but it would have been better in company, leaving her in no doubt as to whose company he meant. She grew roguish and fluttered her eyes and threw out every come-on signal known to Woman.

When Offer told her he would have a shower, and yes, he was thirsty, she was immediately there offering to prepare coffee and no, it was no trouble, she would personally bring it to M'sieur's room.

Fifteen minutes later when there came that discreet tap on the door, Offer was bathed and clad only in a bathrobe. In his hand was a glass of cognac and what more natural than that he should offer the lady a glass to accompany him. So she closed the door behind her and they had their cognac, and very soon they were romping happily in bed together, the coffee forgotten and going cold.

*

Captain Offer reccied the square from a safe distance long before ten o'clock next morning. He was not a man to create unnecessary nightmares, and when his eyes told him no Military Police lurked within quarter of a mile of the Town Hall, he lost his fears and strolled up to his trucks and waited for his men.

Before the hour of ten his men began to gather there, the brighter ones first, the bleary-eyed and with hangovers staggering in at the last minute. Some of them, in fact, were a bit late on parade, but John Offer was now so far recovered from the previous night's shock that he did not worry and waited patiently.

Among the late arrivals were Sibrett, Dodge, Bannister, Skipper and a few other less pleasant of his flock. If they had been the only ones late, Offer would have been tempted to move out without them, and be glad to get rid of the trouble-mongers, but unhappily some of his good men— Walker and even his R.S.M.—were also tardy in arriving.

Eventually they drove out of town, a subdued but satisfied R.S.M. O'Keefe leading the way. Not long afterwards they ran into the foothills of the Jebel, and it was as O'Keefe had promised, a sweet and pleasant land.

Here again the invaluable O'Keefe knew his way around. Once when he was with the L.R.D.G. they had to hole up in the Jebel for several weeks, and he was a mine of information about the place. Increasingly Captain Offer grew respectful of the former L.R.D.G. man's knowledge; without him his commando simply could not have existed in the desert.

They travelled for hours along rich and fruitful valleys, everywhere citrus and pomegranate fruits, lush greenery and tall trees, passing the neat white new houses of the Italian *colonizzatore*, much more prosperous than the Arabs' shacks, and though they were supposed to be enemies the civilian Italians greeted them with smiles. Even when they ran out of the valleys and came into the cool, bare mountains, still everywhere was green and soft to the eyes. They did not keep on climbing, however. The R.S.M. found his way down a track to a well-remembered pocket of trees, thick vegetation and a bubbling spring, and that was far enough for them. They all got down and looked around. At this height, the sun beaming upon them but the air invitingly cool, they had a sense of well-being. As camp sites went, this could hardly be bettered.

So they camped, a process which took little time, for they had no tents to put up, and little in the way of equipment or comforts. O'Keefe later got them cutting branches from trees, and showed them how to stick them into the ground, tie the tops together like a haystack, then cover them with groundsheets and tarpaulins.

'Rains like hell up here,' he told them. 'You'll need these shelters, you'll see.'

It was when they were finishing tiffin—a poor sort of a meal after the previous day's luxuries—that the natives found them. Someone looked up, saw three Arabs staring down at them from a nearby knoll, and immediately leapt for his rifle. O'Keefe caught the movement, grasped the situation at once, and snatched the weapon from the startled man's hands.

'You don't need that, mate. You make friends with the locals, not shoot at 'em.'

He waved friendlily towards the Arabs and trudged towards them holding aloft a packet of cigarettes. They saw him join the group and there seemed great amity, and after some talk and sign language the three Arabs went away rather hurriedly. O'Keefe returned, looking pleased with himself.

'We'll have eggs by the dozen within an hour and as much fruit as we can eat. I've asked for a few chickens, too, and they'll be here every day to look after us, just so long as we have cigarettes for barter.'

Everyone brightened at the idea of chicken meals, though some seemed a bit apprehensive. 'Is it safe to stay here with the local Arabs knowing where we are?' John Offer asked the question later.

'Safe?' O'Keefe looked surprised. 'You only hide from talkative natives when you're lying up in enemy-occupied country. That's from fear of someone giving you away. But here, our army's in occupation. If we behave naturally, fraternising with the locals, they'll just think we're on some army exercise in the mountains, and no one will bother to talk about us being here.'

It all made good sense. Happily they lay back to read some newspapers picked up in Benghazi. They were all from England and weeks old, but none the less welcome for that.

Later in the afternoon quite a number of Arabs, this time including children, walked over the hill. R.S.M. O'Keefe waved encouragingly and finally, highly delighted, they came right into the camp to sell their produce. Captain Offer saw the sense of the manoeuvre. It was all so open, no one would suspect anything untoward.

Soon everyone was gorging on fresh fruit, everything from melons to grapes, and the camp cooks were plucking a dozen smallish chickens preparatory to making their evening meal. Good food would keep the men happy for a while, Offer thought, but for how long?

He turned his mind to the idea of returning to the desert on an occasional raid of the enemy in the manner of the S.A.S. His men wanted action, especially after the success of their incendiaries on the Soluch air-strip. It was all very hazardous, but he supposed they'd have to do something about it.

Weybright was trudging up the slope to the little bivvy Offer had made for himself, and he seemed quite excited. In his hand was a newspaper, one of London's quality Press, Offer could see.

'Take a look at this, sir!' exclaimed Weybright, beaming in delight through his steel-rimmed glasses. 'We've made the Sundays!'

It was the London *Observer*. The article which had got Weybright going was headlined EX-PRISONERS TAKE OVER M.E. GLASSHOUSE. Startled, Offer read on.

'With outrageous impudence a small commando, presumed British, recently stormed Sharafim, the services Field Prison on the Sweet Water Canal, and completely turned the tables on the prison staff. You won't find any reference to the incident in the heavily censored English-language *Egyptian Mail*, and G.H.Q. Cairo is extraordinarily tight-lipped about it, but making all allowance for exaggeration it does seem that one of the most daring commando raids of the war has been successfully undertaken—against British military authority.

'The griff, as it is known in the Middle East, tells of a lightning action by about a dozen black-faced commandos early one morning, when the Gate Guard was surprised and disarmed, and the prison over-run.

'The commando, which was armed with Thompson sub-machine-guns by some accounts, then attacked the prison staff-sergeants, at which the prisoners rioted, turned on their "screws", as they are more commonly known, and severely mauled them. Even the camp commandant is said to have been dragged from his office and beaten up.

'Now, the most dreaded feature about this iniquitous prison is its Walking Wall, an institution which makes the hardiest of ex-prisoners blench merely to be reminded of it. In brief the Walking Wall is a high wall of sandbags which tours the perimeter of the prison parade ground, because the prisoners are made to pick up sandbags at one end and race over the top to deposit them at the other, thus having the effect of making the wall "walk". It is an exercise in futility, designed by a sadist and perpetuated by a whole legion of equally sadistic men.'

Offer whistled when he read that. 'Iniquitous prison' . . . 'exercise in futility' '. . . designed by a sadist', these were interesting and significant observations.

He glanced at the by-line: 'From our Cairo Correspondent Hugh Atherton.' Atherton? Offer frowned. He knew the name. During his spell as Entertainments Officer for troops in Jerusalem—the happiest time of his life—he had come into contact with most journalists arriving in the city. He was sure the name Atherton rang a bell . . . Suddenly it came back. Atherton, an oldish boy, knocking on fifty. A thin man with a sardonic humour. He remembered liking the fellow.

Offer read on, held by this report which for once undoubtedly took the side of prisoners in the Glasshouse. The writer had even got hold of the O.C. Middle East Field Prisons' part in the riot. How the brigadier must have tried to hush up that one, chuckled Offer. But the next sentence was news to him.

'Now it is rumoured that all prisoners, whether taking part in the riot or not, have been given a minimum extra twenty days' detention.'

'The bastards!' growled Offer, and by God the screws would be merciless with the subdued rioters. But there was more about Field Prisons to surprise John Offer.

'I know what I am talking about,' he read, and Offer whistled at the next bit. 'During World War I I served a sentence in a notorious Glasshouse, that most terrible of Field Prisons at Al Sheereh on the road out from Alexandria. They all say it, but I had done no wrong . . .'

A boy of nineteen, an evil sergeant of the guard. Night, and the sergeant doing things to him and he struggling and suddenly an accident. A jerk of the head, the sharp rim of Atherton's helmet catching the sergeant across the nose. Blood and a broken bone and it all had to come out, and the sergeant swearing that Atherton had assaulted him, and it was his word against the boy's.

'I came out of Al Sheereh a bad soldier, turned against military authority and the army in which I had to serve.' Atherton would not be the most popular war correspondent in the Middle East after this revelation.

'I do not pretend that all who enter Glasshouses are victims of injustice, or are clear of villainy. What I do say is that no nation aspiring to being civilised should allow such places of punishment to continue. There are other means of exacting discipline without breaking the hearts of boys and minor transgressors and turning them into anti-social beings.

'I say quite flatly that the real criminals in a Glasshouse are those men who are prepared to ride through the war on the sufferings of others—I am talking about the screws and their superiors, as high up as you like to go.

All have been corrupted by the system. Many of them I met were the last people to be chosen to have power over their fellow creatures, warped and sadistic men, men more fitted for observation in a mental asylum than caring for prisoners.'

John Offer put down the paper and licked his lips. By God, that was strong stuff, a wonder any paper dared publish it, especially in wartime. And people would dismiss it, he thought, refusing to believe that anything like that could really happen.

But it did happen. And this man, all these long years later, could not forget it any more than he, Offer, could.

'I'd like to meet you again sometime, Atherton, old boy,' Offer murmured to himself. It took something for a man to write like that and publicly proclaim that he had done time in jail, even in an army prison.

Two nights later a perturbed and even alarmed Weybright brought another surprise for Offer. It was a signal from Cairo. The same signal was repeated every night at the same time for the next seven days. It was openly addressed to him. It ran: 'Captain John Offer. You are asked to come to G.H.Q. Cairo urgently. You are required for a very special mission. You are guaranteed immunity from arrest and will be allowed to return to your commando. Top priority air passage awaits you at Benghazi Airport.' It was signed Captain Roger Tansley.

*

There is truth in the saying about birds of a feather. It applies to generals as well as wild life, and in Cairo there was much meeting of Top Brass, not always for conference but at times informally. Of course they still continued to talk shop, even in the most informal of times because military minds of their stature generally live only for military careers.

At one such gathering—just pink gins and Tom Collins or whiskies-and-soda—the major-general found himself talking about Sharafim and John Offer's roaming commando.

'It's unbelievable,' some general said, almost snorting into his gin. 'Fellow makes himself a captain, creates a riot in a Glasshouse, then goes joy-riding where he likes over the desert.'

'Joy-riding?' The major-general most curiously these days became a little defensive of Offer, almost as if he were his protégé. 'Hardly that, not round Kufra and Siwa, and he's one of the few men in this world who has crossed the Great Sand Sea, you know. I doubt if many Bedouin have ever tried it.'

With his fellow generals the major-general rarely put on his earthy act; that was to impress the lower orders.

'He seems to have occupied his time rather usefully, too, harassing an enemy garrison at Siwa, rescuing some of our P.O.W.s, defeating a pursuing German force in the Sand Sea, and most recently destroying nine aircraft on the ground, as if he were the S.A.S.'

The other general, a full-blown lieutenant-general, was very abrupt at that. 'Don't care what the fellow's done.' Clipped moustache and very clipped speech. 'Should be tracked down without loss of time and sent for life to jail again.'

'The question is finding him.' The major-general was a little nettled. Lieutenant-generals always tried to nettle officers rising to their own level. 'Last heard of he was in Benghazi, but who knows where he is now? Maybe a thousand miles away, or even here in Burkha Street.' That was the brothel quarter.

Captain Tansley had come up with the information that Offer had been spotted in Benghazi. 'Then why the devil wasn't he arrested?' exploded his major-general.

'Because the M.P.—a lieutenant—was kidded by a phoney name and some phoney papers about a Field Salvage unit. The lieutenant kept thinking about that Field Salvage Company and later checked with his H.Q. He was told there wasn't such a unit. Back the lieutenant went to pick up his man, but the bird had flown.'

''How do you know he was Offer? Could be some other guilty bird.'

Tansley smiled, a slightly superior smile. 'The name the fellow gave the M.P. was Robin Raeburn.'

'Well?'

'That was Offer's stage name. Pretty convincing, eh?'

It was.

The full-blown general had to put a touch of impatience in his voice. 'Oh, come now, don't say the whole army's incapable of finding one man.'

The major-general got his own back. 'Matter of fact, I'm not trying very hard to find him now. Instead, I've just invited him to drop in on me for a little talk.'

'There's a time for joking, Toby,' began the senior general ominously, but his junior was full of confidence now.

'Look here, what good does it do us to stick this fellow away in chokey for life?' He didn't wait for an answer. 'Won't help the war effort. But the chap—him and his ruffians—have ability. They keep demonstrating it. So why don't we turn it to advantage?'

The Top Brass spoke very carefully, so that afterwards he could say he had never heard such damn' nonsense. 'I don't know whether you appreciate what you are saying, Toby. You are suggesting that a bunch of criminals might be employed in some way better than orthodox soldiers?' He let his voice rise at the end, to finish on a note one decibel short of scoffing.

'Not better,' the major-general admitted. 'But instead of . . . Look here——' He had a habit of requiring his audience to look here. 'There's one very important job for someone to do. Everyone thinks we're going to run old Rommel right out of Africa, but we know we've shot our bolt already. Our lines of communication are now dangerously long, while his have been compressed—now he has the advantage. We know he is pouring tanks and guns and men in via Italy, and we know it is only a question of time before he chases us out of Benghazi once more.'

It was getting monotonous, in and out of Benghazi every few months, shoving their surplus salt down the wells to make the water unpalatable for the newcomers.

'Now, how far will he chase us if he hasn't got the oil and petrol?' He fixed his senior with a very bold stare. Give him his due, the old boy didn't take umbrage, even slightly, this time. His military mind had begun an instant appreciation of the situation, based on a sudden intuition that his major-general was on to something.

'Go on,' he ordered. 'Let's have it.'

'Rommel's building up big fuel dumps at Agheila, bringing it down by road from Tripoli in Italian petrol tankers. I want a commando to get in at that fuel and blow it up,' the major-general said simply.

The senior officer said, 'It's a notable ambition. What's your plan, Toby?'

'To use Offer and his Glasshouse Gang.'

A pause to let that one sink in. Then—'Why Offer?'

'Because he's expendable.'

'Ah!' Light began to dawn on the lieutenant-general.

'Look here, this Offer is an incredible chap. I've really begun to get an admiration for him. His nerve is colossal, his ingenuity remarkable. And they seem to be very effective desert raiders. All right, why waste time chasing the buggers——' A slight check to his speech. He knew the big general disapproved of swearing, as if in some way it reduced a man's ability to kill his enemies. 'Why slap them in clink, a burden to everybody including the taxpayer back home? Why not make 'em earn their feed like all good soldiers?'

'So you want him to have a crack at Rommel's oil dumps? It's a tall order.'

'Offer might do it. That fellow really has a clever mind.'

'The place is guarded more strongly than the Crown Jewels.' An enormous understatement, they both knew. 'If he gets in, I'll bet he doesn't get out alive.'

'That,' said the major-general, 'is why I have picked on Offer for the job. I agree with you. Why sacrifice some S.A.S. patrol on such a suicide mission? If Offer does get in and do the job and is knocked off trying to get away, he'll have done his bit for the war effort and won't be a menace to any more Glasshouses.'

The big chap said, almost cordially, 'It's very good, Toby. Very good thinking. But how are you going to get him to take on the mission?'

The major-general spoke with such ruthlessness that he descended to earthiness for once. 'I'm going to put the fear of Jesus Christ into the little bastard! By the time I've finished with him, he'll *want* to have a smack at the job.'

'I hope you're right, Toby. Hope you're right. You say you've invited him to meet you?'

'Every day this week I've sent a signal for his attention. I've promised him he won't be arrested if he takes a trip to Cairo, and I'll keep my word.'

'He won't come,' said the big general gloomily. 'You say the man's no fool? Then why should he trust you?'

*

John Offer was a very restless man. It seemed uncanny to keep getting that message addressed to him by some man he'd never heard of. Which was why, though his instincts suspected a snare, his mind kept thinking about the signal. He had a feeling of things closing around him, and he was now in a condition to grasp at straws.

They had his name, maybe the names of some of his men, too; and the way the M.P. lieutenant had come scrutinising everyone at the Hotel Berenice showed they also had a close description of him. There were times when Offer's spine went ice-cold. Ultimately, he felt, the inexorable army would track them down, and then . . .

When the seventh signal came, John Offer's nerve snapped, just as the clever major-general had prophesied to his aide. 'Keep sending it, Roger, my boy. In time a fish gets curious and just has to have a nibble.'

Captain Offer spoke about it to his R.S.M. because he had to—O'Keefe would be in charge during his absence. Weybright was also in on the conversation, because he knew all about the situation, anyway.

Offer said, 'I don't suppose I'll be away more than three days at the most.'

O'Keefe, bred to cynicism by army experience said, flatly, 'They'll have your guts for garters. It's a trap.'

'You may be right. But I don't intend to shove my head into it.' He had worked out his own fail-safe devices. 'We go tomorrow. You'll drive me to the airport. Don't let any men out of camp while I'm away.' He didn't trust the blighters.

That night he shaved off his moustache. Next morning before they took to the truck Offer sent for Arab Ward, their medical orderly. 'I want a nice piece of Elastoplast to go across my nose,' he said, and Ward obliged within a few minutes.

So, in the simplest of manner, the former actor disguised himself thoroughly. If anyone was on the look out for a flat-nosed bristly moustached army captain at Benghazi Airport, they wouldn't look twice at the clean-shaven officer whose nose configuration was hidden by humble Elastoplast.

O'Keefe was quite admiring of the simplicity of the disguise. 'No one would recognise you now, sir.' And then he spoiled it by adding, artlessly, 'I think you look better this way.'

Offer had mentally debated other aspects of disguise. What he really needed was a safe identity. Inspiration came to him, and he called to his batman, Pomegranate Face, that inveterate collector of many things including knuckledusters. Among Pom's collection were exactly the insignia for his needs. Confidently Captain Offer assumed them—no need even to change rank. Then O'Keefe, still highly dubious, drove him to the much-bombed Benghazi Airport, where they said goodbye, and Offer was touched to see how reluctantly O'Keefe took his departure.

In spite of his confidence in his inspired disguise, Captain Offer felt a decided tightening of the stomach as he pushed through the crowd into the shattered concrete building to which all passengers had to report. Not that he was going to report as Captain Offer and pick up the top priority seat they had promised him. He was going to Cairo under his own steam, in this new identity, and he would visit this mysterious Captain Roger Tansley only when he had taken out an insurance policy. Long ago he had learned not to take any chances with the military.

He kept his eyes skinned and saw several M.P.s strolling majestically about the crowded hall. He hadn't a doubt they'd been tipped off to watch out for him. To arrest him? Probably not if he was intent on catching that plane. But certainly to follow him, in case he was taking advantage of the free flight to get out of a suddenly unhealthy Benghazi to Cairo where he might lose himself again. Oh, yes, they'd try to pick him up here and keep tabs on him.

Well, they weren't getting on to him this early morning, he thought grimly, then relaxed and strolled up to the inevitable trestle table behind which sat a couple of R.A.F. types—pilot-officers—handling all enquiries and shovelling papers out by the bucketful. A very busy place, Benghazi Airport, now that it had changed hands once more.

When it was his turn, Offer the Actor said, very briskly, 'I'm Tansley.' Tansley would have been shocked if he'd heard that. 'Medical Corps.' The perfect disguise he had worked out in the night. Doctors were above humanity; no one ever suspected a quack. As an army doctor he'd have instant respect and attention, because instinctively ordinary mortals kowtowed to medical learning. So it was now.

Offer put on the right brisk tone of voice, that manner which says from the start it is certain he'll get what he asks for.

'I've no authority, old chap, but I've got to get to Cairo Main Hospital today. There's a new technique for handling greenstick fractures being demonstrated, and you know what a hell of a lot we've got going gangrenous up here.'

And you know . . . Flatter a man by telling him he's in the know and mateyness is instantly established. The poor young R.A.F. sod hadn't a chance against Offer's practised wiles. He didn't even try to put across the usual, 'I'm sorry, sir, there just aren't any spare seats. There's a queue a mile long for anyone with less than Priority II . . .'

A doctor. Urgent medical matters. Gangrene. He winked. 'I'll fix you, doc. Oughtn't to do it, y'know, but——'

'Good show,' said Offer, but even then in the manner of a man getting only what he had known he would get. 'Must be back day after tomorrow, though. Can you fix it? A lot of surgery waiting on me.'

So that was fixed. The P.O. was glad to oblige a doc. He looked sympathetically at the plastered nose. 'Looks as if you've been in the wars, too, doc.'

Offer spoke confidentially. 'No.' Shaking his head quickly. 'Fell down a bloody hole, that's all.'

It made the pilot-officer laugh. Nothing like humour of an anti-climatic nature, thought Offer. When the great—and doctors were minor great—tumbled, the world was cheered. The P.O. was going off duty. 'You've an hour to wait. How about a snifter in the mess?'

'Bit early,' said a triumphant Offer, but allowed himself to be persuaded. Much safer in the mess than out here, though he felt very confident in himself now.

Leaving the echoing, battered hall, they had to pass a couple of Military Police stationed at the door. They gave barely a glance at them, Offer and the R.A.F. type chatting amiably. But Offer deliberately, though casually, as if not premeditated, caught one Red Cap's eye and nodded absent-mindedly. As a major-general in G.H.Q. Cairo had remarked, Offer was a cheeky bugger.

So Army Doctor Roger Tansley flew to Cairo, and the same young pilot-officer reported that no one answering the name of Captain John Offer had picked up a Cairo passage that day, reserved for him by highest authority in the Middle East.

It was a tedious journey, sitting on hollowed-out metal seats that ran the length of both sides of their DC3. Passengers sat facing each other across a great pile of kit and God-knows-what which occupied the middle of the plane. They were cheered with a carton of sandwiches each, and thermos flasks of tea and black coffee circulated, but four hours solidly sitting sideways was an ordeal worse than the Great Sand Sea, decided the new Captain Tansley long before the descent into Heliopolis Airport, Cairo.

In Cairo, Offer's first act was to visit an old friend in the native quarter, out of bounds to all troops, of course, but Offer never noticed such warning signs. He needed new documentation. Never again could he risk being Robin Raeburn, Field Salvage (Forward Area) Coy, and with the hounds on to him it wasn't much good being Captain Much-wanted Offer, either.

Now he rather liked the Medical Corps. Something very safe and reassuring about being a doctor. He thought he would continue as Captain Roger Tansley, R.A.M.C., and his obliging forger friend promised him authentic documentation within twenty-four hours. He also invented two more identities to be on the safe side.

Still Offer did not venture near Cairo's G.H.Q. After a most pleasant evening on the town, dining at Shepheard's, of course, surrounded by Top Brass, he called the following morning on Hugh Atherton.

John Offer guessed his man would be attached to the Public Relations Unit, a civilian and paid by his newspaper but stuck into the green-and-gold tabbed uniform of an accredited War Correspondent because the army didn't like civvies up Front. The correspondents had their club and Offer knew where to find it. Whether he would find Hugh Atherton there was another matter. Atherton, quite likely, was nosing out stories in the Benghazi area. Still, there was just a chance he was lingering in Cairo.

He was. Luck was with Offer that day. Atherton wasn't at the Front because a bout of malaria, picked up a year before in India, had laid him low. A day later, Atherton said, and he'd have been off to the new fighting zone.

Offer spotted him, very relaxed in a cool basketwork chair on the balcony overlooking Sharia Solomon Pasha. He knew him on sight, thought the chap looked desperately thin. Offer simply sat down opposite him, smiled, and gently peeled off the Elastoplast.

Atherton came to slowly from his thoughts, fixed his eyes on Offer and frowned. Memory came back. 'Ah! Now, who is it? Ray Something? Raymond?'

'Raeburn,' assisted Offer. Atherton had met him at a time when he was using his stage name because even then military authority wanted to lay their hands on John Offer, the absconding quartermaster sergeant. 'Robin Raeburn.'

'Mmmm,' said Atherton, his eyes on the insignia on the tunic. He was puzzled. 'Didn't know you had a medical history, Robin.'

'I haven't.' Offer's policy with Atherton was to keep nothing back. 'This is disguise, old chap. All the bloody M.P.s in Africa are looking for me. By the way, my real name's Offer—John Offer.'

Very slowly Atherton withdrew his thin legs from their footrest and sat more erect. He did it as if he were muscle-weary, but his manner, all the same, was now alert. He was a newspaperman scenting a story.

'And why are they after you?' Atherton was remembering some scandal about Raeburn. Something about a court martial, and wasn't he even then masquerading under a phoney name?

The actor in him had to make Offer present the situation dramatically. 'Remember that griff about some commandos taking over Sharafim Glasshouse? You wrote about it some time back.'

Atherton nodded. He was painfully alert now, instinctively knowing he was on to something big.

'Well, Hugh, my friend, I was the bloke that thought that one up and led the raid.'

The *Observer* man sat in silence for quite a time after that, his eyes never leaving Offer's smiling face. And then he spoke, and of course his reaction was unorthodox. 'You have my congratulations, then. All I would ask is for you to do the same some day for Al Sheereh.'

John Offer relaxed then. He knew he had Atherton on his side. He said, very easily, 'Let me start from the beginning, shall I?' And he did. He told the whole story, and in his way Offer was an honest man. He never tried to varnish himself or his companions, simply telling the truth as he saw it. In the end he did attempt to summarise the situation in his own terms, however.

'I got out of gear with the military machine and can't get into mesh again. I'm not making excuses. Sure I flogged Q stores, but you know it didn't seem like stealing. I wouldn't take anything of yours, for instance. It was rather grand, too, being able to feed my rep friends. It's a little difficult to resist playing the grand man, Hugh.'

'But,' Atherton reminded him gently, 'you committed a crime. Don't you have to pay for crimes?'

Offer wanted to say, 'But do you have to pay so hard? Do these "crimes" really merit such barbarous treatment, and in the end does it make for a better army?' But what was the good of talking like that, even to Atherton who was wholly in sympathy with him. He sighed and said, 'Of course,' and with that dismissed the subject, and went briskly into his real reason for wanting to meet Atherton.

'Hugh, I'm here to get your assistance.'

'I had a feeling there was some compelling reason.' Hugh Atherton could be a very dry man.

'G.H.Q. want me, Glasshouse John, for some special mission.' He saw how startled Atherton looked at the revelation. 'It came by wireless signal, and they've asked me to go to them and have promised me immunity from arrest if I do. But I have a nasty, suspicious mind, Hugh; I've learnt never to trust army promises. Is this a trap, an easy way to entice me back into the Glasshouse? I'd say they're capable of it.'

'Not so sure,' said Atherton, looking at the pencilled signal Weybright had written. 'It's got some ring of sincerity.'

'That's what I thought. All the same, I come to you to take out an insurance policy. I want you to know I am responding to this invitation and am going to G.H.Q. If the next thing you hear is that I'm on a court martial for a long list of offences, or in the Glasshouse already, I want you to kick up a stink about it.'

'Would that do you any good?' Atherton showed his doubts. 'Wouldn't it be too late, if they'd got you inside?'

'It's all I can think of,' Offer admitted. But if they knew the Press were cognisant with the situation they might walk a little more circumspectly.

'I think you'll be all right.' Atherton looked again at that signal. 'It's a truly remarkable situation, Robin——'

'——John.'

'John. This mission, now that does sound like a story to me.'

They got their heads together after that. Atherton wanted a story for his paper and he got it. What he also wanted was exclusive information on future developments and activities. 'You're a newspaperman's dream,' he told Offer. 'Whatever you do now is bound to turn into something sensational. You've got to keep me primed.'

'I'll do that . . . Maybe we'll write a book together?' Offer, crafty man, could see money in the situation.

'You'll have to be out of the Glasshouse before that can be published,' Atherton told him, and it made Offer wince. They parted, arranging a meeting in four hours' time. If Offer didn't turn up, Atherton would cancel his flight to Benghazi next day and start some awkward enquiring.

*

Offer did hesitate outside G.H.Q., and for a few moments looked on a world as a man would who expects he might soon lose his freedom. He was still wearing the rank of captain, but now his Medical Corps badges were in his pocket. No sense in letting G.H.Q. know more than they need, he thought. Finally, almost jauntily, he ascended the few broad steps and went inside the old building. It was a bit like Benghazi Airport, busy with people hurrying in and out, faded, tatty and with an appearance of neglect.

John Offer, ex-jail-bird, army deserter, bogus in the rank he displayed, a man now wanted for an impressive list of crimes against the military, was given the most extraordinary V.I.P. treatment at G.H.Q. when they knew he was there. In days his name had become notorious, his deeds probably magnified, and the circumstances of his presence within G.H.Q. was so astonishing as to merit the highest curiosity from all.

Officers up to the rank of colonel found reason to come hurrying from their bare-looking rooms, excusatory bits of papers in their hands, their alibis as they hovered where Offer waited in the entrance hall. Offer knew why they were there and kept a straight face but was a bit tickled by it all. But if the glamour of the moment hadn't been upon him, the moment it left him they'd have no time for him and would trample him down . . .

The young handsome Captain Roger Tansley came down and introduced himself to the man who had recently been Captain Roger Tansley. That pleasant smoothie's eyes twinkled as he surveyed his man.

'I must say it's a surprise,' he said. 'You didn't pick up your V.I.P. ticket at Benghazi.'

Offer said, very courteously, 'I didn't. Too many people were waiting to see me do it.' And at that Tansley stiffened slightly, like a man caught out in some act of impropriety, and showed guilt.

But he smiled again, almost as easy as John Offer. 'How did you get here, then?'—pumping Offer and Offer saw through it. Give them nothing to go on, he was telling himself.

'Camel,' he said. 'Frightfully slow, y'know.'

Tansley gave up and led him in to meet the major-general. Offer saw a big, bulking man behind a desk, elderly, as most generals are, bushybrowed, and yet, curiously, not intimidating. The major-general waved him to a seat, and his manner was courteous, which was a surprise to Captain Tansley who had expected something different. Even so, being a general he had to soften up his man by cataloguing the crimes laid against him.

'I must thank you for responding to my invitation, Offer, but let us get things clear from the start. You are a man on the run, a deserter. You have committed many crimes in the military calendar, and someday you'll have to pay for them. Your worst, of course, was mounting an attack on Sharafim Prison.'

Offer's heart sank at the words. Oh, Christ, did they know about that, too? How much else did they know about him?

'I must tell you that our legal boys are looking into this matter, for you were bearing arms, you know, and in time of war what you did is probably treasonable conduct. You know the penalty for treason?' The question shot out, and for a second the courtesy had vanished and the eyes were hard.

Offer panicked, then held it down. Resolutely he faced the bigger, older man. 'You're not telling me that you've invited me here to face a charge of treason, that I'm going to be arrested?'

The big, grey-haired head shook. 'No. When I promise immunity I don't play with words.'

John Offer relaxed, and hoped his sigh wasn't audible. 'Then what do you want of me?'

'Offer, we're in a sticky hole. By we I mean our armies in the field here in North Africa. Now, what I am about to say to you is of the highest confidentiality, and I want your word that you will not divulge any of it to anyone else.'

Offer was suddenly at ease. 'Of course.'

The major-general looked beyond Offer and barked, 'Roger!'

Offer turned and was startled to find that all the time Captain Tansley had been quietly seated immediately behind him. But of course a general wouldn't confer alone with a criminal of known violent habits.

'Get me the gubbins.'

'Yes, sir.'

The gubbins was a thick collection of files, ragged with an assortment of protruding papers. But while Tansley was opening them on the big desk, the general had something else to show his unusual guest. He rose, picked up a stick and crossed the room to where a huge map of Libya adorned the wall. The stick tapped at a place marked El Agheila, at the deepest part of a great bay named Gulf of Benghazi, though until the British came it had had the old name of Gulf of Sidra.

'Know what that is, Offer?' Offer was cautious and shook his head. 'It's the enemy H.Q. It's where Rommel is. And it's where you're going, *private*——' A very nasty reminder of humble rank. '—to do something for King and Country and make minor amends for all the trouble you've been causing us.'

Offer remained untroubled. He had a feeling he was beginning to get the measure of this big chap. There was that hint of humour that could be played upon . . . 'What do you want me to do with Rommel?'

'Destroy his oil supplies.' The major-general came out with it, as simply as that. He resumed his seat and shuffled around with some big aerial photographs. 'Oil is king in this desert war. Destroy his oil and it's like destroying his tanks. Without oil a modern army is helpless and cannot fight.'

'I thought Rommel was on the run?' The papers were making loud noises about hurling him out of Africa within three months.

The general gestured impatiently. 'Don't you believe it. All our Intelligence reports speak of a massive buildup of Axis strength. Any day now he's going to burst out and we'll have to retire if only to shorten our lines of communication.'

He went back to the map. 'This is why oil's so vital. Rommel's getting supplies for his army via Italy and Sicily through the port of Tripoli. I know it is still four hundred and fifty miles from Tripoli to El Agheila, but it is a good road and compare that with our problem. Our main supply base is along the Nile, and that's almost a thousand miles away. Every desert mile which you have to transport men, guns, tanks and everything an army requires adds to your oil requirements. On top of that, of course, we have to bring everything round the Cape, and that's another twelve thousand miles, mostly in oil-burning ships, too. Compare that with a couple of hundred across from Sicily.'

He swung his head round to face Offer. 'Do I make clear the vital importance of oil in this war, or do you add mental affliction to pronounced criminal proclivity?'

Offer said, easily, 'If I did not know it before, you have convinced me now.' He would not say sir. If he was out of the army, he need show no outward respect for its major-generals.

'Well, Roger, we seem to have made progress.' The general tossed the stick on to the table, then resumed his seat and fanned out the photographs. 'Rommel ships all his oil through Tripoli, then brings it by road-tanker to an oil dump outside Agheila. Come and look at these.'

Aerial photographs always need interpreting for the uninitiated. The general obliged. 'Here he has a whole complex of oil storage tanks, part sunken in the ground and concrete-protected. He inherited them from the Italians who created them when Mussolini got ideas on a North African empire.'

Offer could see the neat capsule-like shapes, grouped in fives and dispersed irregularly. Over twenty of the big storage tanks, he thought.

'Even that's not enough. Rommel has an army of over half a million men now, counting his Italian allies. He needs a lot of oil to keep 'em moving.' The general's finger stubbed at shapes on a photograph. 'These look like other oil dumps, too. Improvised ones, of course, petrol and oil in forty-gallon drums, and probably in tens of thousands of jerricans. There's oil everywhere here. If we can destroy this oil he won't be able to move, and that'll give us time to consolidate our positions outside Benghazi preparatory to another push up the coast.'

Offer was thoughtful. 'I'd have thought bombers would be best for this job,' but the general shook his head.

'Agheila is formidably defended, and our main bomber base is far away at El Adem.' That was about five hundred miles from El Agheila. 'The Luftwaffe has been massively strengthened in the past month, and gets plenty of warning when our bombers take off. Rommel's fighters come up like hornets the moment there's an alert. They've time to get altitude and play havoc with our bombers. No, I'm assured there are real difficulties opposing the idea of successful bombing. Of course the R.A.F. will try.'

'And you want someone—me—to blow 'em up on the ground?' Offer let the general see he thought the idea amusing.

'I do, and you're going to do it because you've no alternative.' The general was blunt.

'You have other commandos, nice clean-living types. Why pick on us?'

The major-general debated that question for a moment. 'You have revealed a pattern of originality which commends itself to me. To get at this oil demands an inspiration which I'm not sure we have even in our brave S.A.S. It's just a hunch, Offer; just some little niggling thought at the back of my mind that if you're forced to do it you'll come up with something simple and brilliant that'll do the trick. I don't know why I have that feeling—probably a waste of time, but . . . Well, there it is, and we're in a mood to try everything.'

'Meaning, you've talked to the S.A.S. and they've said it can't be done,' Offer thought. Aloud: 'And if we did pull off this miracle, what's in it for us? A King's Pardon for beating up the screws and going A.W.O.L.?'

The general's mouth hardened. 'I'm promising you nothing. You'll have to make some atonement for being bad soldiers. But . . .'

'You'll lop forty years off our sentence and all we'll do is fifty in the Glasshouse.' Offer thought he understood.

'I don't even offer you forty years' remission. I'm just telling you, things might be made easier for you and your men if you co-operate a bit more with the war effort.'

'And if we don't?'

'We shall remember that you've had your chance and turned us down. We'll go after you without mercy. If you think you can get away with desertion indefinitely you're wrong in your head.' His tone became ruthless, unrelenting. 'I do not exaggerate, Offer, when I say we are probably well able to prove you guilty of treason. Treason is a country's most serious crime. Nowhere in the world would you be safe from retribution. You would die, Offer, you and your men, because we would hunt you down, and I would have no compunction in ordering your death.'

Offer looked at those bushy eyebrows and thought, 'No, you wouldn't.' Death had little meaning to generals, except their own.

Offer said, his voice sounding more comfortable than he felt, 'It's quite a job you're proposing. It means coming in out of the desert, penetrating their defences—and I've an idea they'll be quite a hurdle—doing our stuff without enemy co-operation, and then,'—Offer paused, looking hard at that heavy face before him. Softly—'somehow getting out of Agheila.'

The general nodded slowly, his eyes unmoving on Offer's. And Offer knew that the respectfully silent Roger Tansley was watching him no less intently.

Very slowly Offer said, 'No one's going to get out of there alive after blowing up the oil installations.'

'That's one reason why we prefer to use you and your men and not send the S.A.S. on such an operation.'

'I see.' John Offer sat back to consider the situation. 'You've put it bluntly. You're proposing a suicide mission. Wouldn't I be a mug to undertake it? Wouldn't it be better for me . . . us . . . to keep on the run and enjoy life even if it's only for a few more months?'

'Could be.'

'Then why waste your time? You must know my answer?'

The general sat back, big hand toying with his stick on the desk. 'Do I? Do you?'

He was a clever man, that general; now he demonstrated it though neither of his audience saw what he was attempting to do. Instead of pursuing that line of conversation he pushed a drawing over for Offer to see.

'Look at this. It's a map of the Agheila area based upon the most recent aerial photos. You can see that the oil installations are central to the whole defence system—that's how vital oil is to Rommel. They're here——' That finger stubbing again. '—and I don't doubt there's a special guard mounted day and night over them. Ringing the whole of Agheila are several lines of defences, apart from 88 mm anti-aircraft batteries. Here's a line of forts, and we can see a trench system linking them. What we can't see is barbed wire, but you can bet it's there thirty foot deep.

'A bit farther out——' His finger traced a line. '—there's another defence system. Dragon's teeth.' A concrete antitank trap. 'And here we can see where artillery are dug in, ringing the landward side of the town, and just as strong to the west as anywhere else. You can say, with certainty, that for five and maybe ten miles around the oil dump you couldn't move without being detected.'

'Yet you think someone can slip through and pop a bomb in his oil?' The general saw that Offer was very thoughtful and knew he had so far succeeded. He had got his man intrigued by a problem, and when a man is intrigued he begins to work on solutions. It had to come from within, the general knew, for a man cannot be made to find answers to apparently insoluble problems.

'You know, Offer, all military history is a tale of the impossible and of men finding ways to overcome it. Theoretically, advancing infantry cannot survive against massed machine-gun fire, yet it is done—in various ways they find means of countering it. Theoretically a creeping artillery barrage should wipe out all human life in its path, yet quite simply, by digging slit trenches, for instance, enough stay alive to make it a most expensive way of killing one's enemies.'

'You're saying that though it looks impossible, you think someone can find a way of getting through?'

'Undoubtedly. I'll bet, if only we knew it, there are a dozen ways of doing it. The thing is to find a dozen men of such original imagination that they can work them out. I only know one—you. And of course I'm not even sure of you.'

'And I'm expendable,' said Offer with equal bluntness. Yet the problem did intrigue him. He studied the ground map, and his fingers traced the roads in and out and he thought of the barriers across them and the guardhouses and road blocks. He said, 'You forgot to mention the mine-fields.' They weren't marked on this map, but they'd be there.

'I thought you take them for granted.' Captain Tansley smiled dutifully at his general's dry humour.

'A cat couldn't get in there.' Offer pushed the plan away.

'But a cat hasn't the resource and diabolical imagination you've shown.' Or your curious courage, the general could have added.

The talk went on for a good two hours. They kept coming back to the maps and the photographs, and when Offer said, 'Suicide!' the general riposted with, 'I'll get you shot if you don't start thinking.'

It ended still on that level, and yet Offer must have been nibbling at the hook, for he asked if he could take the ground plan with him. The general shook his head. 'You can study it in forward H.Q. at Benghazi if you're interested.' But it wasn't going out of G.H.Q.'s possession. He took a sheet of headed notepaper. 'You'll need an authority to see it——' His eyes lifted quickly from the paper on which he was scrawling with a scratchy pen. '—and a further guarantee of immunity from arrest.' He was going to play fair, Offer realised.

He looked at the G.H.Q.-headed notepaper. 'Captain John Offer is on special work for me. He must have all assistance and freedom from H.M. military supervision.' It was signed by the major-general.

'That's as far as I can go in saying you're not to be arrested. I'll call off the M.P.s the moment you say you'll have a crack at the job.'

After that the general took Offer into a large room where the Top Brass gathered for its morning drinks, and paraded him rather as if he were a war trophy. Here again they all knew about John Offer, and wanted to see him, this rogue of a fellow who had created military history. 'Did up Sharafim, you know,' introduced the major-general making an unnecessary explanation.

The C-in-C said, 'That's nothing to be proud of,' but the major-general appeared to be prepared to stick up for his protégé.

'Oh, I don't know. Personally the place gives me the shudders. It doesn't seem quite twentieth century . . .'

Offer looked sharply at the general. He was a man of unsuspected depths.

'And Brigadier Thorbury?' Irony, very heavy. Brigadier Thorbury who had been caught up in the Sharafim riot and had been roughly handled.

'Thorbury?' The major-general's voice was very cold. 'Can't say I feel sorry for the fellow. Never did take to him.' Junior officers might, but more astute men had always seen through the man, and others in that room murmured agreement.

It was not a warm reception, and John Offer did not enjoy the polite hostility to his presence. When they got out of the room Offer said, 'After that, getting inside Agheila won't feel all that bad.'

'I knew you'd take on the job.'

'Are you kidding?' But Offer was thinking around the problem when once again he stepped out into the Cairo sunshine. He stood there for a moment, blinking against the sudden intensity of light, and he realised that he had been under great tension in the past hours, for all his seeming aplomb. At the back of his mind all the time there had been the gnawing doubt of treachery, that he would never be allowed out of G.H.Q. as a free man. Yet here he was, and in relief his mind exulted.

He began to walk towards the native quarter, and his mind dwelt upon his recent hosts. They'd played fair, but what they had proposed was ridiculous. They couldn't expect him to tackle that one, certain suicide—it was too long a shot. And they must know he wouldn't co-operate.

So, he thought, right now they'll have someone following me, so that if I don't say yeah they'll know where to find me when I turn 'em down. Did they think him a sucker? he jeered to himself.

So as he walked the busy sharias of central Cairo he acquired a great interest in the fashionable shop windows. He kept stopping as if to look in, but all the time he was angling himself so that he could reflect the scenes around him. If the fellow was a professional who knew his stuff he'd follow from across the street. If he was an amateur he'd keep behind, on the same pavement.

After a few stops and careful scrutiny he began to notice the same fellow idling in the rear. An amateur, same pavement. And to himself, again he scoffed. The chap was in civilian attire, but very clean, very British. Short curly blond hair, scrubbed pink-and-white cheeks even in this sunshine, and so erect he gave away his military training.

Offer studied him. Young, keen and intelligent. A subaltern, of course. But not very smart for all the appearance of intelligence. The sort of career officer who would somehow rise no higher than lieutenant-colonel, Offer decided, but he was being a bit mean at the time, down on army officers. Yet the major-general had impressed him.

When he was sure he was being followed, Offer simply walked on into the out-of-bounds native quarter. That was the easiest way to get rid of anyone following him. Of course the chap had to come in after him—duty, one might say, knew no bounds—and Offer led him well into the place before doing the dirty on him.

Quite suddenly Offer right-about-turned and went marching back down the narrow, crowded street. He saw his tracker, and knew the fellow was momentarily nonplussed by the manoeuvre. As Offer came up the chap pretended to be looking straight ahead, and was walking on.

But John Offer planted himself in front of the young chap. Instead of addressing him, however, Offer began to shout and wave his arms, his words a mixture of the little Arabic he knew mixed with some English. The whole amounted only to gibberish. It was sufficient.

'Mizkin!' Offer shouted, gesticulating like mad—the beggar's cry for 'Pity me!' 'Ye-la! Imshi! Igori! Ruh!'—various ways of telling a man to get the hell out of his way quickly. 'Silly young sod, thinking I didn't know! Feluss mafish!' Horrible Arabic, real soldier's stuff—'My money is finished'—but what did it matter?

The Egyptian is a man of insatiable curiosity. In any event, in any part of the world, to see a uniformed British officer turning on a startled English civilian and shouting that he had no money and was to be pitied would undoubtedly attract some attention. So it was now. Suddenly every male Egyptian within hundreds of yards came running to the scene of the commotion. In no time the pair were close-pressed by skull-capped and tarboshed Egyptians, faces avid with excitement, big eyes bright and brown at the prospect of trouble between the Master Race.

Offer saw the unhappiness on that clean young face but had no pity. He leaned forward, 'Now, get yourself out of this mess, lieutenant, and tell the general I'm disappointed in him.'

He turned and barged his way through the crowd and because somehow he exuded a cheerful good humour no one took umbrage. Yet when the very erect young Englishman tried to follow, for some reason the crowd grew nasty and jostled him a lot and shouted quite frighteningly at him. He got away in the end but they picked his pockets clean of everything in them.

When the discomfited lieutenant reported how Offer had turned the tables on him, the major-general seemed to chuckle, heartlessly amused. 'This chap might do the trick for us yet,' he told his aide. 'Clever little devil, this Offer chap. Pity he's got to go to jail, if not worse.'

*

The documents were ready for him. Excellent work. 'I feel a new man,' Offer told himself, three new identities in separate pockets, and confident now he sought out the newspaperman.

They sat together. 'What's this mission?' Atherton asked.

Offer said, 'On my way here I've been doing some thinking. Isn't it curious? I'm on the run, wanted by the army, but because the general asked me not to talk about it, I can't tell you.'

Atherton said it was to his credit and made no attempt to pump him.

'You're going to have a crack at it?'

Offer shook his head. 'Not if it's real suicide. Think I'm that daft, Hugh?'

'But if you think you have a chance—that inspiration the general talked about? Will you have a go?'

'If I can see a way of getting out alive, maybe.' Still not committing himself. He rose. 'I'm going back to Benghazi tomorrow.'

He must buy himself more Elastoplast; for certain they'd be watching out for him at Heliopolis and at the Benghazi end. He'd buy a stick, too, a heavy one with a rubber tip like hospitals issue. A wad of folded paper inside one shoe and he wouldn't need to act a limp, it would be there naturally. No M.P. in the wide world would bother with an army doctor, looking as if he had just come out of hospital himself.

'Where'll I contact you in Benghazi?'

Offer gave him the name of the small hotel. 'The lady owner is one of my admirers,' he said with modesty. 'Incidentally the only person in Benghazi who knows me by the name of Offer.' That made him thoughtful. Next time he would have to talk to her winningly and get her to sign him by another name. She would do it, Offer thought complacently; she had loved that night and had begged for more sweet moments. 'French,' he added.

'In Libya?'—surprised.

'She married an Italian. When we marched into the town he panicked and cleared off to Tripoli, leaving her to manage. Which she does, first-class.'

'You be careful he doesn't return and find you comforting her in bed,' Atherton warned. They parted, each very determined to keep the other's friendship.

John Offer passed his second evening in Cairo most pleasantly. True, he was not faithful to his new lady love in Benghazi. A nursing sister from Cairo hospital with a thing about doctors, especially doctors wounded in action, picked up with him at the first inviting smile from the quack.

'Got it under fire,' he told her modestly. 'Had to go out to give morphia to some of our lads pinned down. Stopped a bit of something in my foot when I was dragging the third one back.'

Her eyes were wet with adoration at his heroism. What else could she do but support his slow footsteps—'Right up to the side of my bed,' Offer chuckled when he told Atherton about it later. And then it was too late for her. Not that she wanted it otherwise.

'But, Angela, my dear, just one thing. If we spend my last hours in Cairo together, there must be absolutely no talking shop.'

She promised. The girl would have promised anything. So Offer's medical knowledge was not put to the test that night.

*

O'Keefe met the limping M.O. at Benghazi airport and was raucous about the stick. It had been an uneventful journey, plenty of M.P.s at both ends looking for a chap with a flattened nose, but Offer was so far sure of himself now that he hardly bothered to glance at them.

Driving back the R.S.M. said they'd had a bit of bother in camp while he was away. 'Oh, what was that?' Offer was removing the wad from his shoe. Yet he thought he could guess.

'Some of the chaps wanting a night out in Benghazi, already browned off with hanging around camp. They got stroppy about it, too.'

'Who were they?' No prizes for guessing right.

'Sibrett, Skipper, Dodge, Cruiser and Busker,' intoned O'Keefe. But not Bannister, this time. He could do well without those bastards, Offer thought, though he had a soft spot for Cruiser and Busker. They'd shared the same cell in Sharafim, and though they were out-and-out villains, there was this bond between him and them—a fragile, tenuous thing, but undeniably there. Pity it didn't stretch two ways these days, but the former fairground bullies ran too much with Sibrett's pack, easily led if excitement was promised.

'Did they go?'

'No.' That was interesting. Suddenly all the other men had turned on the loud-voiced and truculent Sibrett and told him to pipe down and he wasn't going into Benghazi while their captain was away. 'They said they weren't going to have that shower bringing more trouble on them. They'll never forget McTone and the way he pulled the plug on us at Siwa.'

That was heartening. Offer felt good. He had the loyalty of most of his men, it seemed.

'But you'd have managed them, R.S.M.'

O'Keefe, honest man, was doubtful. 'They're hard men, sir. When they get it into their heads, they're not to be stopped by a brass badge on a man's arm.' O'Keefe tapped his R.S.M. wrist badge. '*You* can quieten them, but I'm not so sure they'd take much heed of me.'

When they drove into the camp, evening close upon them, it was like coming home. There was the usual activity around that time, the cooks going at their work, men wandering across with mess tins and mugs, some fellows playing around with a new pet which had wandered into the camp. It was a baby pig and it was being made a fuss of and seemed quite to like the attention. Offer saw they had drawn rude designs on its pink back, and had improvised a sergeant-major's wrist strap for a collar. 'The bastards,' said O'Keefe, but amiably.

The lads smiled at Offer, too, glad to see him back, and it brought home to him that he had responsibilities towards them and mustn't let them down. After the evening meal, grouped around a camp fire, for it grew mighty cold in evenings so high in the Green Mountains, John Offer brought them up to date with events.

'I've been off and you don't know where I've been,' he told them. 'Well, I've just had a trip to Cairo at His Majesty's expense.' Astonishment. 'What's more I went there on the invitation of a major-general, and I was his guest at the War House.'

They didn't believe him. Sitting there in those mountains Offer found it difficult to believe himself. G.H.Q. . . . a proposed suicide mission . . . in his pocket a note promising temporary immunity. And Angela, of course. Angela of the adoring eyes and instinct to nurse the wounded. Now, why couldn't Angela nurse him here in these beautiful mountains!

'True,' he told them, shutting up the hubbub. He was going to tell them everything, but not that bit about the assault on Sharafim being treasonable conduct with the death-penalty potential for every man concerned. No need to bother their heads about that.

'G.H.Q. wanted to meet me because they had a proposition for me. In brief, they've got a high regard for us as commandos.' What would G.H.Q. say if they knew that a lot of the Glasshouse Gang's claims to desert successes were a bit of a leg-pull? 'They've asked me to undertake a mission which obviously they don't even believe the S.A.S. could pull off.'

'What's in it for us?' First thoughts of men inherently suspicious of army proposals.

'In the long term, I'm not sure.' Offer was frank about it. 'You can bet if we pulled it off it would count in our favour, but how much that would reckon against desertion and raiding Sharafim, I don't know.'

'Must be something.' That was Palfreyman, the former solicitor's clerk. His voice was quick and eager. There were some men like Palfreyman who worried about their position and a clouded future which seemed they'd always be on the run from the Military Police. Tulger, the Devonian, was another a bit like him, a good chap who never ought to have been thrust into the Glasshouse in the first place.

'Must be something,' agreed Offer, but most of those sods couldn't look further into the future than tomorrow.

'What's the short term?' There they were, hands out already for whatever they could get from the deal.

'Short term? Temporary immunity from arrest if we say we'll take on the job.' No one had asked yet what the job was. 'Which means we can move into camp close to Benghazi and can go on the bash every night and the M.P.s won't dare lay a hand on us.'

That had them gasping. Offer saw how their faces lit up. For some this was almost the millennium. Great and glorious booze-ups, openly done, and with two derisory fingers cocked up the snoots of any Red Cap who tried to run them in.

'We're on!' shouted battered-faced Charley Crookshank in delight.

'We're not!' said Offer firmly. Not committing themselves to the mission, anyway. He shut them up with an impatient wave of his hand. 'It's no picnic what they propose——'

'What is it?' Someone got round to the question at last. It was Weybright, of course.

'I'm not telling you.' Just as firmly. Tell these sods about the mission, then let them loose on a bender? Why, half Benghazi would know about the proposed raid before the first drunken night was over. 'Not just yet. You'll know only if I decide it's worth undertaking. Then I'll tell you all about it, and if you don't like the smell of it you can drop out. Fair enough?'

It was. So then he gave them the good news.

'That doesn't mean to say we can't have a bite at the cake.' He'd worked this one out on the Dakota flying west. 'I'm going to look into the proposition. That means accepting an invitation to study maps and information here at Forward H.Q. To do that I'll have to go there daily'—shoving his head into the lion's jaws—'and that can only be conditional upon our having temporary immunity from arrest. So until I make up my mind, Benghazi is yours!'

They cheered wildly, and some danced around, randy young sods, unable to contain their excitement. John Offer made a last statement which brought forth one, final cheer.

'And don't worry, chaps. Even if eventually I turn it down, I'll stretch this research as long as possible. We ought to get a few weeks at least in Benghazi.'

*

The camp in the Jebel, then, proved of short duration. It was beautiful, almost heavenly, and they had thoroughly appreciated their two weeks' lay-up in its brisk climate. But all the same, every man leapt at the chance to get closer to crowded, smelly Benghazi. Women were there. Young soldiers will swop every scene of Nature's beauty for a few minutes with a willing girl.

They moved the following morning, and the noisy, cheering truckloads of men that descended the Jebel were the happiest bunch of warriors in all Africa that day. Driving into the town, every time they saw a Red Cap they set up that chant from their childhood, 'Can't touch me!'

There was a big camping area south of Benghazi, with everything—food and water and Naafi beer—laid on, so they took over some tents and that was their new home. John Offer immediately went off to find Intelligence at Benghazi H.Q. He had to introduce himself to a Colonel Easterham, whose forename was the old-fashioned Joseph and who did not like the familiarity of Joe.

Easterham knew all about him. He was a big and intelligent man and his greeting of Offer held no reservations in spite of his knowledge of his audience.

Offer said, 'I've to report to you my decision regarding a certain mission. I have decided, very cautiously, I might tell you, to look closer into the matter. This does not mean that I am committing myself to it, just going into it to see if it's worth a damn.'

'I quite appreciate your attitude.' Easterham smiled and it was a warm smile. Offer knew he and the big chap would get on well together. 'In fact, I'd call you a bloody fool if you didn't tread cautiously.'

'You think it's a rough deal?'

Easterham was frank. 'I can't see anyone pulling it off.'

Well, the Glasshouse Gang would at least get a holiday out of it. 'Let's see all the latest information about Agheila,' Offer invited. There wasn't much beyond aerial photographs and the inevitable L.R.D.G. reports from their celebrated and invaluable Road Watch, now somewhere between Agheila and Tripoli. He and the colonel got together over them, talking over points and getting nowhere. Late that afternoon they parted.

Offer was despondent. 'There doesn't seem a hope in hell. But someday I might go scouting down to Agheila to see if anything suggests itself. If I do I shall ask to be supplied with Jeeps.'

He had been impressed with the S.A.S.'s new vehicles, much better than ordinary trucks for desert rigours. The colonel made no promises but said something might be done about it.

Few of the Glasshouse Gang spent that night under canvas. O'Keefe cleared off very quickly to see his nimble lady, and Offer, this day a captain in the artillery according to his badges, went to exchange pleasantries with a certain French hotel-owner. He took in a few brandies en route because what was the hurry, and they made him feel expansive and full of confidence in life, and that was the right mood in which to visit a lady, separated from her husband by two mighty armies.

She greeted him with unmistakable joy, and was quick to bring coffee to his room, and he was quick to take advantage of it, though the hour was early, and again the coffee regrettably was allowed to go cold.

Later he dined with the lady, and she was an excellent cook, and he told her very quietly that on the previous occasion he had been working for Intelligence under a false name and his real name was Roger Tansley. Having found such a cosy billet, Offer wanted to keep the name of Offer clear away from it. There was no knowing when he might want to have some pleasant place at night if or when he went on the run again. The French lady might or not have believed his story—French ladies are not as easily taken in as major-generals or Intelligence colonels—but so long as her charming British officer delighted her in bed she wasn't bothered what he called himself.

Every day Offer reported himself to Intelligence, and every day he dutifully reported himself to the Military Police, too, to bail out erring followers who had got themselves into trouble the night before. For once R.S.M. O'Keefe, with his ferocious antagonism towards M.P.s, was not one of them. He had a sleek and contented look about him; his lady besides being nimble was also a fair cook.

In the M.P.s' barracks, Captain John Offer became an object of sardonic humour with the Red Caps. 'Not another of your shower!' they'd moan as he came in and laid claim to some hopeful body, often sorely bruised but remarkably cheerful under the circumstances. 'What's all this about immunity from arrest? Who are you—Christ's fuckin' disciples?'

Offer would look shocked and reprove them and simply say the magic words, 'We're going on a very special mission and you can't have him.'

'Well, go,' urged the M.P.s, 'and the sooner the better!'

But Offer wasn't in a hurry. The longer he stretched out on this affair, the more enjoyable it became. Not that he saw any light emerging from all his talks with Easterham and other Intelligence officers. Every day they went over and over the same ground, arguing about possibilities, starting afresh from a new angle, and always coming to the same conclusion. It was impossible.

Finally Colonel Easterham said what Offer had said much earlier. 'It can't be planned from aerial photographs. You'll have to make a reccie on the spot.' His manner suggested the result would be the same.

John Offer, that man born for comfort, did not want to uproot himself from the pleasures of Benghazi. However, he couldn't stall indefinitely, and anyway, a now tired O'Keefe was beginning to talk about a desert trip as something recuperative. Other men were also beginning to yawn about the same round of activities, all too often ending in sapping hangovers. They too would welcome action.

So, because there was nothing else he could do about it, unless they sheered off as deserters again, Offer indented for seven Jeeps and hoped they wouldn't come to him in a hurry. Within four days, however, miracle of miracles, they were there to be collected.

Now Captain Offer called his men together again. 'Your bed-bashing days are over,' he told them. 'Temporarily, at least. We've got to go on a trip into the desert. I'm still not telling you what it's about, only that even now I'm not committed, and we shall only be looking at the lie of the land.' That was all the men need know. 'We shall be right behind the enemy lines, however, so it's a case of volunteers only.'

He looked hopefully at his three black sheep, Sibrett, Dodge and the mean-faced Skipper, but they made no demur at accompanying the mission. Later, Offer deliberately tackled Sibrett and said, quite bluntly, 'You don't need to come if you don't want.' He was almost telling him he'd be glad if he opted out of the party.

Sibrett, eyes dirty with malice, said, 'Why shouldn't we come? Think we're scared?'

Captain Offer walked away disappointed. That Sibrett had cunning. He'd probably worked it all out. What would happen to him if he cast himself adrift from Offer's party? For the time being Offer's men at least had immunity from arrest. If he left them the M.P.s would pick him up and have him in the Glasshouse before you could say court martial. Offer had proved he could keep them out of the hands of military law, and probably instinctively Sibrett knew he hadn't the resource to do it himself. What applied to Sibrett applied equally to his unpleasant cronies.

But Offer didn't try to ease out Cruiser and Busker. In a tight corner, villains though they were, their brute strength could be invaluable. He needed them.

*

They moved out from Benghazi one early morning, seven smart new Jeeps spanking along at exhilarating pace. Why, if these delightful American toys got sand-stuck they could simply lift them out! They were admirably designed, almost purpose-built for desert work.

Offer's French lady had been desolate at his departure. No, she would take no money from him. (Marvellous to be loved, thought Offer, the happy rascal.) When would he return? She could not leave without her Rogeair! She wept copiously, and filled the hotel with drama on his last visit. And never was any brave soldier so comforted as on that last night in bed. Other subdued men appeared to have had more or less similar partings.

O'Keefe had planned the route and led the way. What had once been an amateur bunch of inepts in the desert was now a compact and efficient commando, as good as the best at surviving even under the most inhospitable circumstances. What was more, they had made light of conditions which had once almost killed them, taking everything in their stride as if barely noticing the hardships.

For over a day they travelled due south, deep into the desert. Then O'Keefe navigated them westward so that on the third day he told them they were level with Rommel's H.Q. at El Agheila. He and Captain Offer had a conference then, a brand new desert map between them. In the end they decided to continue further, so as to approach Agheila from the Tripoli side. An enemy presence was less likely to be suspected from that direction, was their argument, so once more the engines were started and the Jeeps bowled along.

Next morning they established their base in the desert. This was one of many wadis with which the arid land was riven. What was so good about this one was that it had a massive overhang of rock along its course, so big that all seven Jeeps could crowd under it if necessary. O'Keefe, ever conscious of air attack, said he couldn't think of a better place. Five of the Jeeps were run under it and the camouflage nets draped over them. The other two Jeeps would be moving on.

For his crews Offer found himself selecting the original members of the Glasshouse Gang. Why he did it, he was not sure. There were sounder men than his batman-driver, Pomegranate Face, for instance, yet when the time came he just said, 'You'll drive,' to Pom, and that was that.

His new sergeant, Eddie Walker, his most loyal and devoted follower, could not be left behind, of course. He drove the second Jeep. The massive bulking Cruiser and Busker took over with Walker in his Jeep, and Offer told Charley Crookshank to hop into his. They needed one extra man for each vehicle—four was the right number of crew. They were required to man the Bren guns, and Offer picked on Lashley the Australian for his Jeep and Jimmy Wilborn for Walker's.

O'Keefe had insisted on the Brens. When he learnt they were to get the Jeeps they'd asked for, he became very vigorous about the machine-gun to mount in each. 'Vickers? Lewis? World War I stuff! If they offer them, sir, tell 'em to stick 'em. We've got Jeeps and we must have the best in Mgs. Brens, sir, take nothing less than Brens.'

Primed with this injunction, Captain Offer refused to let them swing old weapons on them and finally came away triumphant with Brens. Very lovingly R.S.M. O'Keefe saw to the mounting of each himself, and when he had finished one would have thought he had made his Jeeps invulnerable forever to any hostile intention.

The two Jeeps travelled through the night, Offer aiming to strike the coast road about ten miles out from Agheila towards Tripoli. It wasn't hard going, most of the time, just the usual unexpected setbacks, the big holes encountered which shouldn't have been there on that flat coastal plain, and the equally unexpected outcrops of ugly rocks.

But long before dawn they came in sight of the road. When they were a good ten miles away they began to see lights slowly crawling across the horizon, and knew them to be the headlamps of vehicles. The lights were masked, but trucks had to have lights at night and no amount of masking could completely screen out their hooded beams.

Soon after they saw the distant lights, Offer gave the order to halt. Intelligence had reported large areas of salt marsh to the west of El

Agheila, and he didn't want to get stuck in a bog. So they set a watch, then settled in their blankets, grateful for them against the night's stinging cold, and slept so peacefully no one would have imagined they were over two hundred miles behind the enemy front line.

The dawn sentry brought Offer out of sleep at the first hint of daylight. Breakfast was all ready for him, and he took it at leisure, watching the sun come up and the world take familiar shape once more. They appeared to be in a safe position, no one and no building anywhere in sight. They were on a wide-spreading plain, with just a few low hills north-east of them, and nothing in between right up to a tiny patch of white on the horizon which would be El Agheila.

Offer decided to head for those tiny hills—mounds, more like, they were so small—and see what advantage they gave him. They had the merit of being a couple of miles nearer the town, anyway. It took very little time to reach them, but they were disappointing, just an area of rolling land, and unworthy of the name of hill. Climbing cautiously, Offer and Walker came up to the skyline. Nothing over the other side. They relaxed and got out their glasses.

The binoculars were almost useless. True, they brought the buildings of Agheila astonishingly close, but Offer needed much greater altitude if he were to study the territory surrounding the town.

The trouble was that modern defence positions were discreet and unobtrusive. If they're not they are useless. Everything would be dug in and camouflaged, he thought, his glasses slowly ranging over the drab grey scrubland around Agheila. They revealed only hints of defences. After a while he could make out some blockhouses or forts, but even then not very easily.

But wire was there. There was so much barbed wire looping its way around the town that Offer thought even a ferret would get scratched unless it was particularly emaciated. That was almost the only thing visible, the several deep fences of wire, but they gave a measure of the defences unseen.

Offer dismissed as impracticable any idea of crawling through the wire, finding the oil dumps in the huge area contained within, and blowing them up with a couple of hand grenades, Italian or German guards obligingly watching on. Well, if creeping through the wire was out of the question, how else could they get in? Parachutes? At night? But how do you get *out* of a stirred up hornets' nest if you parachute in? Offer looked coldly on any plan which did not provide for his safe escape afterwards. Anyway, he'd never done any parachuting and was pretty sure he'd hate it if he tried.

All that day was wasted, roaming the area south and west of Agheila. What surprised Offer after a time was that some distant pair of binoculars didn't pick them up and get interested in them, but no one came bustling out of the town to see them off. If anyone did, they'd just have to run ahead of the pursuit, Offer thought, and was confident that his desert guile would now keep them safe.

They camped for the night far out on the plain again, and over a tasty meal of American canned stew followed by delicious canned figs—they'd done well out of stores at Benghazi—Offer brooded over the situation. He found himself exasperated by the day's ineffectualness, quite put out because he had made no progress.

At that moment Offer was full of inconsistency, yet never saw it himself. He was a man strongly imbued with a sense of looking first after himself. He had been turned against the army and all it represented by adverse experience, though always he would admit he had brought it on himself. He felt he owed nothing now to the uniform he wore, and anyway it was a fraud, and he would have looked cynical if he'd been told he would ever risk his life in contributing to his country's war effort.

Yet here he sat propped against a Jeep wheel, the night's darkness profound around them, brow furrowed in something like dejection because he saw no way of obliging Cairo by destroying Rommel's oil dumps.

The truth was that Offer was a man with a quick, ingenious mind, who just had to solve problems when they were presented to him. He had entered on this mission light-heartedly, using it as a means to enjoy himself in Benghazi, but in time the problem had begun to intrigue him and had got him interested. Now, sitting so near yet so far from Agheila, Offer felt put out because he couldn't get close enough to see its weaknesses. He felt thwarted. They'd wasted a day and gained nothing from it. Worse, he couldn't see what else they could do unless he flew over in a fighter to study the ground at first hand. Not that that would be any damned good, he thought disgustedly. They would still have to come in on land.

By the time the rapidly cooling night drove them to their blankets, Offer's logical mind had found a partial solution to his problem. They couldn't learn anything from that distance. Therefore they had to get closer to their target. He decided to go up and have a look at that road.

Hauptmann Kurt Braunschweig was on stand-by twenty-four hours of every day, and was not very pleased the way things were going. He was an impatient man, and while this new duty had promised a lot, in fact precisely nothing so far had happened to bring his force into action. The British were surprisingly quiet.

Waiting, though, had produced the usual change. He was not a man who could carry hatred for long, and though he still remembered with horror that time in the quicksands, his desire for vengeance became muted and he began to forget about Glasshouse John. Of course it would return if he ever clapped eyes upon the fellow. Right now he champed impatiently at the need to hang around Agheila when he could be with his regiment at the Front.

To subdue his feelings of frustration, the big Hauptmann abruptly decided on a hard exercise in the desert. It would tone them up and get them in prime condition when they went off after any desert marauders. He would be in constant touch with the Afrika Korps H.Q. in Agheila by radio, and never more than a few hours' drive away if he were needed.

*

Offer's two Jeeps came trundling brazenly to within a mile of the road, and there parked cautiously where a clump of fierce-barbed camel thorn put a screen between them and the traffic. Walker came over. He liked Offer's company. Together they trained their glasses on the busy road before them.

The road was Mussolini's. The Italian dictator had caused it to be built, one thousand miles of it, stretching from Tunis to the Egyptian border, in furtherance of his African empire-building. It was an excellent road, stones every kilometre, marked with the familiar bundle of rods with the axehead in the middle, the fasces, symbol of a corrupt and brutal Fascist regime. Mussolini, the Pontine Frog, had planned to extend the road through to the Nile, and even had a white horse specially trained to carry his short, stumpy, be-medalled body in triumph into Cairo. Unhappily, this small army of British obstinately refused to get out of Africa, and in fact by now had captured over a half a million of Italians, so that Hitler, contemptuous of his junior partner, had had to send Rommel and the Afrika Korps to help him out.

The surface of the road, never properly finished here near Agheila, was beginning to crack and sink under the weight of military traffic along it.

Offer was awed by the constant flow of vehicles mostly in one direction, towards the new fighting front.

Long tank transporters crawled endlessly towards the town, keeping in the side lane as befitted a speed of eight miles an hour. Motorised guns—the celebrated, versatile 88mm, he noticed—swept by the tanks with heavy majesty. Armoured cars came through in swift forays, like flights of birds; half-tracks rattled by, as did machine-gun carriers, flame-throwers, patrol vehicles, and others they could not identify. But outnumbering them was the soft transport. Almost bumper to bumper they sped down the coastal highway, truck after truck full of supplies and oil, of ammunition and men.

Offer thought, 'Tripoli must be a busy port.' His eye caught a convoy of petrol tankers, still bearing their Italian brand name, ponderously rolling along the busy highway. 'That's the nearest we'll ever get to Rommel's oil,' he thought.

Far down the long straight road towards the town, culverted where it crossed marshland, Offer could see a road block. Even with glasses it was still too far away, though, to tell what was really happening. They could see traffic stretching back for a mile or more, though, as if the inspection at the road block was being very rigorously undertaken.

Finally Offer shoved his glasses back into their case. 'We're wasting our time, Eddie. We're not learning anything from this distance.'

They would have to go still closer. Offer looked at the road and thought, 'Why not?' It was the last place the enemy would think of, looking for them there, and what had he learned? If it was outrageous enough you got away with it.

'We're going to move on to that road.' They'd park by the side of it, so close to the road block they might see into the town, though Christ knew what good it would do them. What Colonel Easterham had said nearly three weeks ago held true at this moment. The bloody job was impossible.

'We'll have the bonnet up, as if we've broken down.' That would explain their stationary presence by the roadside. Two British Jeeps two hundred miles from their own army? No one would look twice at them. Offer had seen more than one Jeep in the past hour scudding west towards Tripoli, captured stock pressed into use by Axis officers delighted with their trophies. For that matter a depressing number of Leylands, Scammells, A.E.C.s, Chevrolets and Fords were on that road doing their bit for Fascism. Offer even saw a solitary Shell petrol tanker, familiar in its red and gold, travelling west at speed, empty and headed for Tripoli.

So the two Jeeps went bumping over a plain that was not quite as level as it looked, heading for a point on the highway not half a mile from the road block. At exactly that moment in El Agheila, Hauptmann Braunschweig gave the order to his patrol to move out.

Offer, first tactfully removing the pips of officer rank from his epaulettes, drove openly to within thirty yards of the Tripoli road and parked there. They were so close they could see the faces of the round-limbed, vest-clad Italian drivers, who drove most of the trucks, and the dust-goggled observers erect in their armoured cars as they swept close by. It was impressive and at first awesome to be so close to the enemy, to feel their weight and might and see how many they were, but in no time remarkably they took little notice of them.

Big Busker and his oppo, Cruiser, lifted a bonnet and did nothing with a spanner or two wielded at intervals to suggest mechanics at work. Offer saw no reason why they shouldn't make their stay as comfortable as possible and told Walker to have a brew-up. It would look quite natural, anyway. Pom got out the firecan and then, assisted by Lashley, decided to make a pukka meal and got busy with a can opener. Even a few American food cans found later wouldn't give them away, for Rommel's first successes in Libya had yielded any amount of British and American foodstuffs. For that matter the British taxpayer was subsidising the Axis war effort with so many KD shirts and shorts, captured in Tobruk, that half the German army appeared to be wearing them.

In a time of uniformed men it was difficult sometimes to know which army was which.

John Offer himself added further to the naturalness of the situation by picking up a shovel and marching determinedly into a clump of camel thorn forty yards away. But screened by the bush, John Offer dropped the shovel and took out his glasses. These he focused on the road block. After a brief glance he swung his glasses, slowly surveying the scene beyond.

There was nothing for another mile inside the barbed wire perimeter fence except dusty, scrub-covered plain, though Offer wouldn't mind betting on the trenches that were hidden there, the anti-tank gun emplacements, the machine-gun nests, and the camouflaged observation posts where men with glasses kept watch and might even now be interested in him, behind this bush.

Beyond that mile of seeming nothing was a straggle of poor huts, the usual Arab hovels that preluded most towns, and then came more substantial buildings, looking very square and white and Italian in that sunshine. They were built on a slope, so that the buildings rose tier by tier, though irregularly, but a fat lot of good that did for him, he thought. The oil dumps wouldn't be in the town, anyway.

His glasses came back to the intervening stretch of road between the road block and the first of the buildings. There was some sort of turning there, for he saw traffic diverging, some plunging on into Agheila, others—all the fighting vehicles at least—pulling away at right angles from it. Of course, the military camps would fringe the town.

Something caught his eye where the roads diverged. At first it was an oil tanker, bearing right. Then he saw there was a tall signpost behind it, bristling with the usual army corps, regimental and other signs. Out of interest he brought the signs clearly into focus, and almost immediately he saw the word, OLIO. Oil, he was sure of that. Offer had learned Italian in his youth when he aspired to becoming an opera singer. Ambition had faded with a breaking of a youthful voice, much admired in the church choir. His Italian was in poor shape now, but olio was hardly a word to forget.

Under OLIO was another big word. It looked like DEPOSITO, and Offer thought, 'I'll bet that means depot.' Oil Depot. There would be further signs, he guessed, posting the way right through the camps into the oil depot.

'All I've got to do is follow the signs.' It sounded like the Underground at Piccadilly. Yes, but first he had to get through this road block, and there might be others along the road to the military camping grounds.

He concentrated his attention on the road block. It was manned by Germans. His glasses brought them so close he could see their lips moving as they looked up at drivers in their high cabs. They were being very, very thorough, papers being carefully examined before return, all vehicles having to stop, even important-looking Staff cars. But not oil tankers. They were waved through without halting.

Hauptmann Braunschweig and his patrol of *Kubelwagens*, those versatile offspring of the Volkswagen, came through the focus of Offer's glasses just as he decided to return to his Jeeps. The German Desert Task Force was halted at the road block, vigilance as sharp upon vehicles leaving as upon entering the town. It would be some time before the Hauptmann came level with the Glasshouse Jeeps.

Offer tramped back through the soft hot soil to the roadside. He felt weary, the sun after the very cold night seeming to bear him down, his muscles tired. He recognised the symptoms. He was out of heart, oppressed by a sense of failure and futility. They were thoroughly wasting their time here, and he craved to be back in Benghazi.

He thought yearningly of those shaded balconies, tables set out in the coolness, the smiling Arab waiters with their tall glasses of iced and sodaed drinks, the cheerfully busy, highly aromatic cafes in the entrancing narrow shopping alleys. And he thought of his charming French lady and her willingness to go to bed with him and the joys of night manoeuvres under the soft cool sheets.

'We're wasting our bloody time,' he thought out of temper. 'If they want to get at that oil they'll have to use bombers.' Too expensive, too uncertain, Colonel Easterham had said, but the thing sticking out a mile was that there was no way of getting at the oil storage tanks otherwise.

He took his seat in his Jeep and accepted with gratitude a mug of strong army tea. Sugar being short in Benghazi at that time, Pom had shoved half a pot of raspberry jam into the brew. It made drinking an adventure, retaining the pips and ejecting the tea leaves.

Cruiser shoved his big flat face round the open bonnet and said, plaintively, 'How much longer, sir?'

John Offer removed the mug from his lips. Amazing how much better a fellow felt after a drop of the old char. 'Not much longer. Half an hour.' Or more, if he saw anything that looked at all useful to him. He settled back to watch the traffic rumble by, heading for the road block, the queue outside it seeming as long as ever.

Hauptmann Braunschweig was coming through it at that moment.

Offer's mind went over and over the same old thoughts. There was no getting in through the wire anywhere around the town, and anyone who could bluff his way past that road block was a good 'un. A German guard on it . . . they only had Weybright speaking German, and Offer wondered if it would pass for native. And if it didn't? Anyway, what were those papers they showed? No, the road was no good as a means of getting inside Agheila.

The Hauptmann and his patrol were coming along the road towards the two Jeeps, moving at a faster pace now.

Offer began to think, 'If the R.A.F. say they can't get 'em from the air, and I say we can't get 'em from the land, that leaves only one thing.'

The sea. Perhaps, after all, that was the only way into Agheila. If it was, they could count him out. John Offer was no sailor. So here he was, set with an impossible problem, but the moment he admitted it to Cairo he became a hunted man again. This time a known hunted man, with the hunt narrowed for him and his men, and their chances of freedom apparently severely limited.

He glanced towards the road. He had not seen armoured cars moving in this direction, out towards Tripoli, before.

Hauptmann Kurt Braunschweig passed him at that moment. His eyes were on the Jeeps. Even American Jeeps were not proof against mechanical failure, he was thinking. He liked the Jeep—he had driven one for a brief while—but he could not understand the British choosing them for desert journeys. He, being a well-trained German, put his faith in armour, even light armour such as the *Kubelwagens* had, and concentrated machine-gun fire.

His attention moved from the Jeeps after a brief glance, and lifted to the face of the man at the wheel. Braunschweig was only forty yards away. The face was turning away, abruptly, as if startled by some unexpected voice beside him. A man was standing there wearing a broad-brimmed New Zealander's hat. He, Braunschweig, had one too, picked up at Sidi Resegh, but he wouldn't wear it like a lot of Germans, though they said it was sensible and cool to the head. Braunschweig was keeping his as a souvenir, to hang in his study back home when the Wehrmacht had achieved final victory.

Braunschweig caught a glimpse of that face in the driving seat of the Jeep.

*

Someone said, 'What are you doing here?'

It was one yard from Offer, spoken in an English that wasn't quite Home Counties. The shock of that strange voice had John Offer jerking round in an instant. His heart was in his mouth, and his mouth as dry suddenly as the Libyan desert behind him. Cruiser heard the voice and came round the raised bonnet, fists balling to strike immediately, and Walker, standing beside the Jeep, whirled, grabbing for his tommy.

John Offer looked into a lean brown face under a broad-brimmed New Zealander's hat. The eyes were grey and regarded him humorously. 'Easy,' drawled the voice. 'I'm L.R.D.G. Anything to drink, mates?'

It took seconds to get over the shock. A Fiat truck had quietly freewheeled up behind them. Just as quietly the New Zealander had walked across to where Offer sat, attention concentrated on that busy road block. Pom brought tea. The New Zealander's companion, who wore the peaked cap of the Afrika Korps, wandered over and joined them. They were part of an L.R.D.G. New Zealand patrol keeping watch on the road twenty miles towards Tripoli.

John Offer had two astonished questions to ask. 'What are *you* doing here?' was the first one. Driving boldly in broad daylight within a mile or so of Rommel's H.Q.

A shrug. 'We thought the ride would do us good.' Later the New Zealander said they rarely took such risks, but they wanted to see closer to the town in case there was anything—new anti-tank defence positions, for instance—which ought to be reported back to Cairo. Not that they could see anything from the Tripoli road, they'd also found out.

'How did you spot we were British?' The Jeeps? After all, by their uniform, though so many Axis troops wore it now?

The New Zealander shrugged. 'Don't know. It just stuck out a mile.' Something in the way they sat or moved around or made gestures. Something indefinable but instantly recognisable to one of their own kind.

The Hauptmann drove on because all he saw was a face turning away. But for the New Zealander's timely interruption the Hauptmann and John Offer would have found themselves staring into each other's faces forty yards of ground only between them, and Kurt Braunschweig would have known Offer in an instant.

Five miles up the road the German *Kubelwagens* drove off the highway and took to the desert. Though he did not intend to stray far from the Afrika Korps H.Q., all the same Hauptmann Braunschweig intended to undertake a most rigorous desert exercise. They would drive west parallel to the coast road, he had told his two Feldwebels, a distance of a hundred kilometres or so, then return paralleling their tracks though deeper into the desert. They would make hard journeys, some by day and some by night. They had to simulate the real thing.

*

The New Zealander hadn't much to tell that was helpful. The Road Watch was screamingly boring, he assured them, but how valuable it was, particularly at this time with all Rommel's supplies coming up. The nightly radio report by the Road Watch to Cairo must have been a Godsend to the planners of Middle East Command.

He couldn't see a cat in hell's chance of anyone getting into Agheila, he told Offer, when asked. So Offer asked what was there along the road towards Tripoli? Nothing helpful to his mission, by the sound of it. There was a Staging Post—that was the Road Watch's name for it—about thirty miles back. A place where men and machines refuelled and sometimes camped overnight. It didn't sound very attractive and Offer couldn't see how it might be of use to his plans. His plans? He hadn't any, he thought, and was surprised by his own dejection, as if now he really wanted to get inside that perimeter fence.

'What do you want inside Agheila?' The New Zealander asked, and in the same breath said, 'But I won't ask you.' And then said one word, 'Oil.'

'I'm glad you didn't ask,' said Offer. 'It might have embarrassed me.' Smart chaps, these L.R.D.G.

They parted in time, the New Zealander warning Offer not to linger too long as an Italian road patrol sometimes came by and they might become inquisitive. So Offer cleared off, too, wandering around the dunes again, getting closer to the perimeter fence, this time in rough country, and finding nothing to help him.

The following day again they pottered around and again every hour was a waste of time and Offer knew he might just as well be back with O'Keefe and his men. Yet something kept him fretting around those defences, the mouse trying to get at the cheese but, not daring to poke his nose too far forward.

The next day he determined to be their last, an announcement which was greeted by ironic cheers over supper that night. This time again he took a risk and parked alongside the road, and again he studied the road blocks and the town beyond and the scrub territory in between. And again it all looked hopeless. Without papers they could never outwit that road block, and even if they had them, was Weybright's German good enough to get them by those vigilant guards?

'Oh, the hell with it,' he said at last, though he had lingered on and now it was late afternoon. 'It's stupid, hanging around. Come on, let's make camp and trek back to the boys first thing tomorrow.'

And then they'd go to Benghazi and have a great and marvellous orgy of a time, and there Offer would report failure to Easterham. End of immunity from arrest. Start of desert wandering again. Not the brightest of prospect.

So they took off and made camp for the night.

*

Hauptman Braunschweig had put his men through a gruelling time. They had slogged for something like three hundred heart-breaking kilometres, deliberately seeking hard country, something to try men and vehicles alike, and both had come out well. Some part of the exercise had been in the hottest time of daylight; at other times they had moved in the dark, chilly night, and they were not sure which they hated most.

Finally, travelling east, the column of *Kubelwagens* came across Offer's distinctive Jeep tracks. They crossed without noticing them, for this happened to be one of their night marches.

*

For Offer's men it was a cheerful supper. Back to O'Keefe in the morning. Back in Benghazi two days later. Then booze and bints again, they told each other; and they had forgotten how booze and bints had become boring and they, God help them, had even looked for a break by way of desert travel. Now it was the desert that bored, and Benghazi sin that attracted.

Only John Offer was without cheer. He wasn't yet oppressed by the future, after reaching Benghazi, but just depressed because he did not like to admit failure. It would annoy him, the annoyance lingering for days, he knew, because he was always like that, and even now his thoughts kept returning to Agheila and its impregnable defences and the road block with its queue of patient waiting traffic.

He rolled into his blanket, and in his sleep great never-ending columns of Axis military traffic swished by in his dreams, guns and tanks, and trucks and tankers. Tankers. A Shell tanker was constantly scudding over the horizon of his night thoughts. Empty and going like the clappers.

And when he woke next morning he knew how to get into the town.

O'Keefe was glad to see them return. He'd been having trouble. Waiting while their commander absented himself had been no picnic. They were in a dry wadi in an area riven by dry wadis, no blade of grass anywhere, not even a bunch of tough camel thorn surviving in this desiccation. For the men left behind, life was most uncomfortable; even travelling the desert was better than this.

There was so little they could do. One man sat on a look-out point for one hour only, and with so many men their watch came round only once a day. The rest of the time they hung around the wadi, never straying because there was nothing anyway to stray for, and most of the time they kept within the shadow of the overhang and lay on their backs and tried to drug their minds so that time would pass without their noticing it. None of them succeeded.

Even lying in that shade was hot and miserable. What air circulated in those wadis was over-heated. There was always dust, too, even on days when seemingly there was no wind. Lying on the ground gave them no chance of escaping it, and it rose and filled their nostrils, and Weybright always thought it created a smell as if he'd suffered a nose bleed. Nothing to do, and no comfort in doing nothing.

Most of them would have taken it with that curious philosophy of the long-suffering British serving-man, but always there's a griper in every bunch and such a man has an unsettling influence.

As early as the day after Offer's party had moved off, Sibrett was moaning unpleasantly to his R.S.M. He was the perennial fault-finder. 'How much longer, s'arnt-major?' was his first sour gripe. And then, each day, he got increasingly awkward.

For one thing, he raised doubts among his comrades, a thing no good soldier should do. He began to have arguments with his oppos, and the theme was, why were they waiting there? Who was to say Offer's party hadn't already been shot up? If so, they were wasting their time in this blasted hole and ought to be moving. Worse, if Offer had been picked up, the Boche or Eyetie would start back-tracking along Offer's tyre marks, and they'd look bloody fools, suddenly seeing Germans and Italians driving into this wadi. He gave an impression that anyway he didn't think much to Offer's capacity for keeping out of trouble.

'Bloody tow-rag,' was his vague denunciation, and some men were irritated by him, Sibrett, going on and on with his pessimism. Some who would normally have survived the boredom were rattled by him and made too upset to settle down. In time, therefore, as the days went by and Offer hadn't returned, these men began to join Sibrett in his gripings.

Finally the R.S.M. snapped at them, 'Come on, out with it! What're you driving at?' They moaned, he told them roughly, but made no positive proposal of alternative action. 'Are you working up to saying it's time we went, and bugger the captain?'

Of course they were, but a man doesn't come outright with that. He sows the idea in higher authority's mind and hopes it will act, not them. Higher authority in the shape of a very loyal R.S.M., said, briefly, 'We don't move from here without him, so you can stuff your griping. What's five days, anyway?'

'It's a long time for a reccie,' said Sibrett, made further truculent at being tackled head on. 'Something's happened to him, he's stupid enough for anything.'

The sergeant-major said, 'Shut up. And he'll be back tomorrow, I'm willing to bet.' Offer had water and rations for only a week. If he was capable he wouldn't be long in returning.

John Offer, in fact, was with them less than two hours after sunrise. At the first possible moment he had an earnest conversation with his R.S.M. The object of their mission was the destruction of Rommel's oil reserves, he began, and his problem had been working out a plan which wasn't plain suicide.

'You know, sergeant-major, any idea that isn't absurdly simple is useless when it comes to these sort of operations. You've got to dream up some plan so ridiculous in its simplicity that you kick yourself for not having thought of it before. Personally if the plan were at all intricate I wouldn't have anything to do with it. I intend to come out of this do with a whole skin.'

And the way to get inside Agheila without arousing suspicion had been staring him in the face ever since he'd dropped that shovel behind the camel thorn and focused his binoculars on the German road block. It had taken a night's dreaming, though, to see it.

'You can forget any heroics about crawling through the wire to get at the oil. Where there aren't defence posts and guns, you can bet there are mines. If we count out a naval landing or a parachute drop, it leaves only the road if we are to get inside Agheila. Right?'

'Right,' nodded O'Keefe, who had such faith now in the smaller man's resource that he listened without any doubt that Offer had cracked the problem.

'If we are to get past that road block'—Offer told him how tough and vigilant the guards were—'it's got to be by cunning; yet it will have to be openly done, for we'll need one vehicle at least and how do we get in past that block?'

And here had come the inspiration. Somewhere at the back of Offer's mind a memory had lingered. A long queue of military vehicles held up for examination by the road-block guard, and a loaded petrol tanker being waved through without halting.

'Tankers are the only vehicles to get past that road block without showing papers. I'll bet it's the same coming out.'

Tankers were always in a hurry. Offer remembered the way the empty Shell tanker had gone screaming up the Tripoli road, urged on by an insatiable army to shuttle fuel between shipping tanker in port and the Agheila oil dump.

The R.S.M.'s eyes were shining. 'By God, you've got something there, sir.' His mind leapt to possibilities immediately. 'All you need is a road tanker and we're in!' To him with his Long Range Desert Group education, knocking off a tanker was a piece of cake.

And once inside the perimeter fence there'd be signs to direct them by most economical route to their target, the oil dump. Getting out? 'If we can hang on to an empty tanker we ought to be able to nip out past the road block without trouble.'

When Offer told his men the mission was on, they gave full approval to the plan, frustration and boredom again making them reckless, so that hardly anyone there thought of the danger to those penetrating the defences.

That, in fact, was a problem and created quite a bit of rancour. All the men clamoured loudly to be with Offer when he cracked the Agheila defences, but he wanted three others only beside himself to go in. He had worked out that he'd need two tankers, one loaded with petrol, the other empty, though this latter would have to simulate loaded going in. He'd need four men, again including himself: one driver and his mate to each tanker. But he'd need other personnel to ferry them in and out by Jeep, and that meant two more men to each of two Jeeps. Eight altogether, the same number as he had had on his recent reccie. One of them would have to be Tiffy Jones with his box of tools.

Captain Offer would not take the same crews this time. Weybright with his German would be with him, driving the loaded tanker. 'Sergeant-major, I'd like you to go with the empty tanker.'

O'Keefe showed his delight. If he'd been left off this trip he would have been a bitter and humiliated man. The O'Keefe's of this world, thought Offer, were the crazy men, always seeking excitement however deadly it might be. But he wanted O'Keefe for that second tanker, because he had to have someone quick in reaction and completely dependable. He decided that Tiffy Jones might just as well ride as mate with O'Keefe.

Two Jeeps would carry them to the Staging Post, where they would knock off the tankers. 'Busker, Cruiser, Lashley, Pom, you come up with the Jeeps.' Two good drivers and two good machine-gunners, and Busker and Cruiser had other qualifications for the night's sortie.

When they knew they were to be left out there was mutinous talk from some of the other men, and a lot of—'Why can't we have a break, sir? You took them blokes with you last time.' Except Weybright and Tiffy.

'Because I think they're the best men for this job,' Offer told them bluntly. 'Now, do stop this bloody arguing. You know you can't all go. This needs the barest minimum of men, four to go in and four to stand by to bring us out when we've done the job. We're going to do it tonight, and with a bit of luck we might be on our way tomorrow before daylight.'

A most perturbed Sergeant Walker came to Captain Offer after the briefing. He said, tragically, 'I'm not going with you this time?'

'Can't find a place for you, Eddie. Sorry.'

'You're leaving me in charge here? With these bastards?' The N.C.O. most lacking in ideas on maintaining discipline was rendered aghast by the prospect. To be truthful, John Offer didn't think it a good idea, either, but he had to take O'Keefe with him, so Walker would have to remain behind.

'It's only for a few hours.'

'They'll play me up!'

'Then get stuck into them,' said Offer, exasperated. 'What are sergeants' stripes for?'

'I never wanted them in the first place. You talked me into having 'em.' And Walker's expression said he bitterly regretted his weakness that day in the Siwa palm grove.

Offer just let him moan on, and then they all got to preparing for the attack that night. Offer's two Jeeps were most carefully serviced and refuelled, and the mounted Bren guns closely checked and cleaned. After that there was nothing to do except lie up in that barely tolerable heat and wait for the sun to go down.

*

Captain Offer's two Jeeps bumped away down the wadi with one hour left of daylight. 'With luck,' he told Walker and the envious men who'd been left behind, 'you'll hear us come in some time before midnight.' That left several hours before dawn, and if everyone in the wadi was packed and ready to move out they might put those hours of darkness to good advantage.

When night rolled quickly on to the desert, Offer's Jeeps were within sight of the road. Another half-hour and they reached it. Now, supremely confident in themselves, certain that no one was going to challenge them, they turned west and went scudding along the Tripoli road for an hour to where the New Zealander had said was the Staging Post.

It was like a miniature town. There were some small squarish permanent buildings stuck back from one of the mightiest car parks Offer had ever seen, with a whole forest of tents stretching in lines around them. Between the road and the buildings was parked every kind of vehicle a modern army might use. Offer saw tracked and wheeled vehicles by the hundred, if not thousand. Columns of trucks were constantly pulling in and finding space to halt, while other vehicles were just as constantly pulling out and heading east towards Agheila. Over everything hung the stench of oil burning off over-heated engines, but with it also the permeating odour of food being cooked.

This night Offer reduced risks by parking well into the darkness a good two hundred yards from the more frequented area. He was again wearing a shirt without marks of rank, and thus inconspicuously attired he and Weybright went to reconnoitre the big car park.

They were looking for suitable tankers, and within a few minutes they realised it was going to be easy. A whole lot of them were parked more or less together, as if tanker drivers sought each other's company during such halts. They were dispersed, of course, in case of air attack, and that was to Offer's advantage. There was also little difficulty in telling which tankers were loaded and which were empty. You knocked on the side.

Offer and Weybright stood in the darkness and for half an hour watched what happened. In all cases when tankers drove in, whether loaded or empty, drivers and mates, always Italians so far as Offer could see, and most of them wearing their long thick topcoats against the night's cold, climbed down and set off towards the buildings. Generally they carried mess tins or mugs and plates, and clearly this was for most of them a halt for a meal.

When the Italians returned, often quite boisterously as if they had had their bottle of vino with their meal, they sometimes drove off straightaway, at other times the tankers were driven for refuelling to rows of petrol and diesel pumps under screened lights to one side of the parking area.

When Offer thought they had got the procedure well understood, they returned to where the rest of the party sat huddled in their Jeeps, quite difficult to find because of the darkness. They had a few minutes together, Offer telling what they had found and once more going over the plan, then again they set off. This time all four who would take in the tankers—Weybright, Tiffy Jones and O'Keefe, as well as Offer—went silently into the parking area, together with the big men, Cruiser and Busker.

Offer had given long consideration to the next part of the plan. His first inclination had been to commandeer two suitable tankers and simply drive off in them, but second thoughts had decided against this idea. If they followed that plan, the drivers would raise the alarm when they found their vehicles were gone. If that happened, Offer might find the road blocked to all tankers as well as other vehicles.

Regretfully Italian drivers and mates had to be disposed of to keep them quiet. Hence his thugs, Busker and Cruiser.

So six Britons came to the tanker park and in the darkness made their selection of vehicles. It was easy. No driver ever removed his key from the ignition switch. It wasn't necessary. They made their choice. One was loaded with petrol, the other was empty. Posting all others on watch, Tiffy Jones opened his tool bag and took out a metal drill. He began to bore holes in line across the underside of the large-bore flexible metal hose through which the petrol would be pumped.

Twice the operation was interrupted by returning Italian drivers and their mates, but fortunately none of them came close to claim the tankers Offer had selected. Finally Tiffy Jones came to his captain and whispered that the job was done; he'd drilled enough holes for their purpose. So now the Glasshouse commandos stood together, hardly to be seen in the dark, and waited.

Fifteen minutes later the first pair of Italians came up to the loaded tanker. They were talking as if in argument, and were very noisy about it. When they were sure these were driver and mate of their selected vehicle, Offer gave the signal and his men closed in.

The driver was getting up into his seat when he felt a gun jabbed hard into his mouth and he was hauled to the ground. A terrified Italian found himself surrounded by dimly seen men, all of whom were carrying weapons.

The driver's mate reached his seat and was turning to close the door when John Offer shoved a gun barrel under his chin and said, softly, 'Un silenzio di tomba, signore, per favore.' So softly spoken, but with that gun barrel pointing, a convincing command.

Busker's big hand reached beyond Offer and lifted the trembling mate out of his seat.

'Okay, they're yours,' Offer told them and Busker and Cruiser went off into deeper darkness with the unfortunate driver and mate.

While they were away the other driver and mate returned. Offer and his men collared them both together where they stood peeing against the rear offside wheel of their tanker. It was the last time they would ever relieve themselves. When Busker and Cruiser, the hard men, came padding back through the darkness, Offer handed over their new prisoners.

'We'll see you at the rendezvous,' Offer told the fairground bullies. That would be about the place where Offer had been surprised by the New Zealand L.R.D.G. man. Here, later, they would abandon their empty tanker, and take the Jeeps, which would be waiting inconspicuously by the roadside for them. That is, if they came out alive.

Captain Offer saw Cruiser and Busker march off with their second lot of prisoners. Both carried knives in their hands, as well as tommies. It was not a job he would have liked to do, but it did not seem to have affected his big followers.

Offer hauled himself into the cab, heavy, lumbering Weybright clambering in at the far side. He switched on the hooded headlights. A little distance away they saw other lights go on and knew Tiffy Jones and the R.S.M. were ready to move out, too.

Then Offer saw three other tankers creeping across the parking area towards the road and told Weybright to hold it a second and let them get out first. When they had rocked up a little slope and gained the road, Weybright went grinding slowly after them. O'Keefe would bring up the rear.

On the road, Weybright accelerated, catching up on the other three tankers, doubtless Tiffy Jones closing up behind, too. Offer felt there would be safety in numbers, and anyway it solved problems inside the perimeter fence. There'd be no anxiety over perhaps missing direction signs and getting lost far from the oil dump. All they would have to do was follow the rear light of the tanker before them.

Weybright looked in his mirror and said, 'It's okay, the R.S.M.'s behind.'

Offer looked at the red light of the tanker ahead and said, 'Do you have a feeling this is unreal, that it isn't really happening?' Weybright was the only man in his commando to whom he would speak like this.

Weybright laughed. 'Of course it's not really happening. This is a dream we're sharing. We are not in enemy territory, heading for the inner sanctum, there to risk our lives in a hazardous and clearly suicidal action. Begging your pardon for doubting your ability as a planner, sir.'

He laughed, and Offer laughed, too. Weybright was getting used to the controls now and wasn't so hard on the gears. He said, 'I'm one of the world's biggest cowards. If this were true I'd be dying a thousand deaths in anticipation of the real one.'

Offer said, 'You're not the world's biggest funk. That's me. And I don't know how I came to be here, but here we are and we're going in.'

Planned back in the desert, away from this busy Tripoli road, everything had seemed beautifully simple. Nothing could go wrong with his plan, he had assured himself, but now, committed to it, the road block only hundreds of yards ahead, Offer's bumping heart told him his confidence was only surface thin.

The tankers ahead began to slow. They had run level with parked army vehicles, the long queue whose head would be at the barrier. Weybright came down rather noisily through his gears, decelerating, too. Now they began to crawl.

Suddenly, Captain Offer became very, very alert, in his mind those warning bells of danger ringing. Previously tankers had swept through the barrier; why then this night were they being held up? Still, they were crawling, unlike the trucks and armoured vehicles to their right which seemed not only stationary but had the appearance of having been halted for some time.

There were men standing away from their vehicles, just off the road, dimly seen in the starlit darkness, hunched figures moving restlessly and stamping their feet. Looking out Offer could see into drivers' cabs, and apathetic faces looked back at him. Sometimes the faces yawned, and some of the drivers had their heads on their arms resting on their steering wheels as if snatching sleep.

Their column now halted, too. Offer said in a swift whisper, 'There's trouble.' He could feel the tension radiating from his companion.

Then a vehicle came up from behind, and then another and another and another. Four of them, almost silently gliding down the centre of the road. Offer looking across Weybright, saw helmeted figures on motorcycles— combination motorbikes, he realised, the sidecar on the 'wrong' side and looking odd to his English eyes. He didn't know what it was about the

Wehrmacht combination motor-cyclists, but they always looked menacing and brought a chill of fear to him.

The motor-cyclists went slowly on, some road patrol, Offer guessed, perhaps the one the New Zealander had mentioned, only this was German not Italian. The tension began to ease out of Offer. Then it returned, worse, much worse, suddenly almost too tight to bear.

The last of the patrol had revved up noisily and swung in a swift circle in the centre of the road. It was returning. Instinctively Offer knew it was going to halt beside them. It did. Offer saw a face under a coal-scuttle helmet looking in beyond Weybright, face just above the door level. He must have been standing on his footrests. The German spoke, his voice harsh and angry and highly unpleasant.

*

The look-out at the wadi in the last hour after Offer's departure had done a bad job. Instead of watching in all directions he had allowed his attention to be held by the departing Jeeps and had followed them, glimpsed occasionally, as they crested slopes and became smaller with distance. To reduce the boredom of his watch the sentry tried to see how long he could keep the Jeeps in sight, and even after they had disappeared from view he still kept staring northwards for several minutes until finally deciding they had gone.

He turned his gaze in other directions now. The sun was on the rim of the horizon, throwing long black shadows. The heat was going from the day, but it was still painfully hot, perched up there on the crag.

His eyes brooded over the wasteland. Then he saw movement. A column of armoured vehicles creeping up from the south.

'Jesus Christ!' he said in a panic, and began to scramble frantically down to the overhang, but he felt it was too late.

*

Braunschweig gave them a hard day because this would be their last. Another night's camp in the desert and then they would return to whatever joys Agheila had to offer. The Hauptmann was a good soldier and took whatever came in his stride, but he could not say he roamed the desert out of choice.

That last day Braunschweig sought out the hard places, so that every hour was one of toil, digging out, hauling and shoving, and the heavy *Kubelwagens* weren't as easy to move as the unarmoured desert raiders' vehicles, the Hauptmann thought. Perhaps the British were right to choose vehicles primarily for their value in covering bad ground at their fastest. Perhaps armour wasn't the answer. He hoped they would soon put the question to a test.

They were an exhausted patrol, then, very late in the afternoon, muscle-weary and aching for rest, yet Braunschweig kept them at it right up to the last. And just before the end, Braunschweig's patrol saw tyre marks crossing their path.

All tiredness left them. Down leapt the Hauptmann and his Feldwebel. Without any orders, his *Kubelwagens* faced all directions, machine-guns trained and readied in case an enemy was near.

Braunschweig's eye measured the width of the track and his heart exulted. No vehicle in the Axis armies had such a narrow measure. And the clear imprint of the tyres wasn't German or Italian. They were also recently made, he knew, because ten days ago there had been a big sandstorm. The Hauptmann's eyes lifted, following the tyre marks. They were heading directly north. He made a calculation. If they continued, that way they would hit the Tripoli road somewhat west of Agheila. He thought this confirmed his opinion that these were enemy invaders of their territory and not someone using captured Jeeps. Anyone returning to Agheila—where else could they head for in this desert?—would surely go directly for the town, not waste time aiming for the road west of it. Of course they might have come from Agheila and be heading into the desert . . . There was only one thing to do, anyway. Follow the tracks and try to close with the makers of them.

Braunschweig was so cheered by their discovery that he ran back to his wagon, and felt no tiredness as he did so. He rapped out an order to his sergeant-driver, and the *Kubelwagen* turned to follow the Jeep tracks.

Five minutes later there weren't any tracks to follow. The wily R.S.M. O'Keefe had sought out hard ground before finding their wadi hide-out, so that no tracks led towards it.

Braunschweig's elation subsided as his cars quested around trying to pick up the trail again. Once they did so, just a short track across a small area of soft grey earth, but here, where the stony ground began to give way to a labyrinth of water-eroded rock-walled wadis, the trail really ended.

Baffled, Braunschweig gazed around him, his eyes probing into the long shadows. Now the heavy tiredness of the day returned. In a few moments there would be nothing to see. Braunschweig made a decision. Less than half a mile from where an alarmed Sergeant Walker and patrol stood to their guns under the camouflaged overhang, he ordered camp to be made for the night.

He also radioed a warning to Rommel's H.Q. 'Enemy patrol believed to be operating in Agheila area.'

*

His heart in his mouth, Offer stared across Weybright into that hard, seamed German face. What was he saying? How had he rumbled them?

Weybright began to talk, and he had the same aggressive manner as the German. Then he swung open the door and got out, leaving a shocked and apprehensive Captain Offer to sit with his hand on his revolver.

But Weybright only went to the bonnet of the tanker and did something to one of the lights, and then he came clambering back and the motor-cyclist revved up, whirled around and followed his companions, receding up the centre of the road.

Offer said, 'Great grief, what was all that about?' He still could not relax.

'It's a road patrol, a special one put out this night. All he did was to come and tell me the hood was askew on one of the headlamps. Against regulations, and get something done about it or you'll be in trouble!'

'That was all?' The tanker ahead was beginning to crawl forward again.

'That was not all,' said Weybright grimly, shoving in a gear and lurching clumsily forward. 'I asked him what was up, this queueing for tankers and their special patrol. You know what he said, sir?'

Offer said, 'I can take any bad news. Go on.' Even the simplest, most fool-proof of plans could come unstuck.

He saw Weybright's big face as a round greyness in the dark of their cab, light glinting from somewhere on the steel-rimmed specs. From that face came words that shocked John Offer. 'They know we're here, sir.'

'They know *we're* here?' Sheer incredulity in Offer's voice.

'That's why the special patrol's out. He said there's a British party of about half a dozen Jeeps somewhere in the vicinity, and there's a general alert to find them. He asked me if we'd seen any Jeep patrol coming in. I said no.'

Offer found words again. 'How the devil do they know we're here?' He could only think that someone had spotted them that day at the side of the Tripoli road. But it couldn't be—they were looking for half a dozen Jeeps, and that day there had only been two together.

They were grinding slowly along. Weybright said, softly, 'What do we do now, sir? Scarper?'

Out of the question. The Jeeps wouldn't be in position to pick them up for another hour. Besides, how could they abandon two tankers in the fast lane; even worse, what would happen if they started to turn round, out of the queue? That patrol would be up and wanting to know what was on, and next time they might pick on O'Keefe's truck and him not speaking Italian or German.

Offer's agile thoughts were trying to cope with the disturbing situation. 'What's the hold-up at the gate? A search for everyone?'

A shake of Weybright's head. The tankers were picking up speed before them. 'Someone bumped someone a little while back. One of the trucks took fire. So the road's narrowed, holding everyone up. Now it looks as though it's been cleared.'

As simple as that. Why the devil, though, had some German or Italian decided to have a prang that night of all nights!

Offer said, suddenly determined, 'We're going in, Art. We're going to follow the plan. Right?' Because what else could they do? John Offer, all the same, wished he was many, many miles from Agheila at that moment.

'Right,' said Weybright without enthusiasm.

They were closing on the barrier, a red and white banded tubular bar raised aloft before a wooden guard-house. The entrance was flooded with light. In fact there were quite a lot of lights ahead, but they would all go out if they had an air raid warning, Offer knew. By the light they saw a brisk-looking guard at the checkpoint, the German equivalent of British military police. Fortunately they were concentrating on vehicles other than tankers, which now swept through the gate at quite a fair pace.

They were inside the defences of Agheila. The enemy might know of their patrol in the vicinity, though how the devil they knew, Offer couldn't imagine, but they did not know that four Britons had cracked open the stronghold with the simplest of ruses.

The turn-off. The tankers ahead swung right. Weybright followed. A glance in the mirror told him that O'Keefe was hard on their tail. There was a confusion of signs, but without much difficulty they kept seeing OLIO DEPOSITO, though following the tankers meant that now they did not need this assistance.

For close on two miles they drove along an excellent new concrete road, and all the time a brightness in the night came nearer. Quite suddenly they came under the lights, and ahead of them they saw the oil installations.

They were there.

Tension, acute and painful, gripped them again. Their mouths were dry with fear. Within minutes would come the testing time. If things went wrong they might only have moments of life within them.

The road had opened on to a great concrete apron. Along one end was a massive pipeline, doubtless leading off to all the huge oil storage tanks. Offer saw tankers ahead, one after the other pulling into a half circle then reversing on to the pipeline. He saw the mates hop down from the cabs and haul upon their hoses and make a connection with the pipeline. That would be his rôle. He explained things to Weybright, having to concentrate on his driving. In fact the routine of the procedure, and the example of those three tankers ahead dictated what should be done.

Weybright brought the roaring tanker into a short curve. A halt. Reverse engaged, Weybright hanging out of his cab door pulling back against the pipeline.

Offer took one swift look round before descending. There were buildings in the background, but they were far away and might be unconnected with the oil dump. Closer at hand, though, was one wooden shed into which drivers or their mates appeared to report. It was all very brightly lit, and Offer saw figures about—too many men in uniform, in fact. Some were sentries on patrol, rifles slung over their shoulders. Others were workers at the depot, men carrying bits of paper, and always hurrying and looking important.

John Offer gave one last reassuring pat at the bulges in his pockets and descended. 'We've got about two minutes,' Offer jerked back at Weybright. 'You'd better get down in a moment.' There'd be no petrol tanker to drive when they'd done their job. Weybright nodded. He seemed past speech, Offer thought, his face very white. But Weybright would be all there when he was needed. Offer had great confidence in the man who was half-German.

Offer dragged on the connecting hose. He knew how it was done from his old days in the Territorial Army. He saw where to make the connection and it was a quick bayonet type, plugged in and half twisted and there it was. He gave the signal to Weybright who started the pump. Then Offer got well out of the way.

Tiffy Jones was driving the empty tanker, and Offer saw his face as he leaned out to reverse against the pipeline. To his astonishment Tiffy was grinning. How on earth could anyone grin at a time like this? he thought.

Then the face came closer and it wasn't a real grin; this was a caricature, quite without humour.

The empty tanker halted. O'Keefe would be down at the far side going through the motions of connecting up. Offer said softly, 'When I give the word, Tiffy, start to move. Any minute now . . .'

He could smell petrol very strongly. The hose would be leaking badly where Tiffy Jones had drilled those holes, and the concrete platform was still hot from the day's sunshine so that the petrol vaporised almost as soon as it touched it. By God, the stench of it! It was strong . . .

Offer saw a hatless German soldier hurrying by with a pad of paper in his hand. The man seemed to hesitate, and then his head turned towards the leaking hose and his attitude was that of a man sniffing the air.

Weybright got down at that moment and joined Offer. His captain had removed one of the bulges from his pocket. The German began to come, almost running, towards them and then he started shouting.

'He says we haven't made a proper connection and the petrol's spilling,' Weybright translated swiftly. 'Says to stop pumping immediately or we'll have a fire.'

'We'll have a fire,' agreed Offer. 'Get cracking!' His head jerked towards the cab of the empty tanker. 'Tell O'Keefe. I'll count ten.' Then they had only another ten seconds in which to make safe distance.

Weybright clambered into the empty tanker beside Tiffy. It was going to be crowded in the cab with four of them in it. Offer heard him call to O'Keefe. The German clerk was alarmed and agitated, running now, coming up to the tanker. Offer looked beyond him and saw that the shouting had attracted attention. Someone had come out of the small hut and was standing there watching the scene. Blast it, his plan didn't call for any witness to his next act.

John Offer pulled the pin of the Mills bomb in his hand and rolled it under the tanker. The second one was dragged from his pocket, primed and rolled after the first. They were specially-timed ones that Tiffy Jones had supplied for this operation, with a delayed fuse that would detonate after ten seconds and not the usual four.

The empty tanker was moving, leaving its hose behind. The running German saw it, and seemed to understand that something was seriously amiss, for he halted and half turned and began to shout back towards the hut. A guard came running forward from the shadows. Perhaps everyone was on their nerves this night, warned to watch out for British saboteurs known to be in the area.

John Offer caught the moving tanker and was hauled into the crowded interior by Weybright. He was counting, '... three ... four ... five ...'

Someone was bellowing and Offer got the word '*Halt*!' but Tiffy was giving the tanker the gun and making a big noise about it. Two other tankers coming in swerved out of the way and Tiffy got an earful of voluble Italian.

'... six ... seven ...'

Offer was sweating with fright, telling himself, why hadn't he asked for twenty seconds? Ten seconds in a slowly accelerating vehicle got them nowhere. When the bang came they'd go up with it.

'... eight ... nine ...'

And then it went up. Two explosions merged into one. Then followed a roaring sound—that would be the petrol vapour exploding. And then an explosion of such violence that everyone in that cab felt concussed by it. The tanker behind was a roaring pyre of flame. Electric lights were unnecessary now, the petrol fire as bright almost as the day's sun.

Following the blast from the explosions came a mighty wave of hot air from the inferno where their tanker had been. Debris began to fall from that last great explosion, bits of tanker cascading upon them and over the concrete road ahead.

But their own tanker was still going. That was the dominating thought in Offer's mind. Tiffy Jones' foot hadn't even eased on the accelerator during the past two seconds. They were coming off the apron and pulling on to the road. Offer turned to look back. A broad river of fire was rolling across the concrete apron in pursuit of them. It was travelling at incredible speed. If it enveloped the empty tanker that would blow up, too, because an empty tanker was filled with petrol vapour.

'Faster, faster!' urged Offer, almost screaming, but the tanker couldn't be made to get into better speed.

Then they were on the road and the flames were being left behind, and Offer was thinking that they had done some damage at least to Rommel's oil supply. But would that wave of petrol get into the tanks and blow them up, too? That was the object of their sabotage, the storage tanks, not just to set fire to one tanker in the oil depot. John Offer prayed that if the tanks did go up they'd have a couple of minutes' grace ...

The biggest bang yet went up one minute later. They must have been half a mile from the storage tanks, but the shock wave rocked the empty tanker so much they felt it lift off its suspension and roll uncontrollably for seconds. Then Tiffy got it back on the road, and they were running away again from the heat and light and the roaring of a mighty oil fire. Sirens began to oscillate wildly in all directions. The noise was savage, frightening.

The junction. Only a few hundred yards to the gate. Still tension, but exhilaration creeping into their veins. They'd done it, got at Rommel's oil. Five more minutes and they'd be in their Jeeps and romping off across the desert.

Ahead was the road block. No one would be surprised to see an empty tanker belting away from the scene of the fire as fast as it could go. Someone might call out, asking them what was happening in the oil depot. Offer found breath and said to Weybright, 'Be ready if they stop us at the barrier.'

The red-and-white banded barrier *was* down across the road when they got there. Offer, momentarily aghast at the sight, thought, 'Someone's phoned through about us.' Either that or it was standard drill to stop all traffic leaving if there was a hint of sabotage.

Tiffy saw the barrier and yelped, 'What do we do, sir?' He was in panic.

Offer said, 'Charge the bloody thing!' What else was there they could do?'

The guard was in a crowd across the barrier. With them were drivers and other soldiers from the long queue of vehicles that still stretched up the road, watching the distant inferno. Offer had a nasty vision of them running the gauntlet when they crashed the barrier and alerted that long queue of parked vehicles to an enemy presence.

The lights were still on over the road block. Quite clearly they saw the faces of the men ahead, and saw how swiftly their expressions changed. One moment they were staring at the tremendous fire behind, then the approaching tanker got in the way of their view. Offer saw uncomprehending faces, and then as the tanker roared up without dropping speed, alarm came and then fright and a mad scramble began to get out of the way of the charging vehicle.

They hit the barrier, stoutly housed in concrete posts. The tanker seemed to stop, then the posts snapped off at ground level and the tanker went riding on, the red-and-white banded tubular post being carried a few yards before suddenly flinging to one side, scything into the little crowd trying to stumble away.

The line of halted vehicles ahead. Two lines. Some tankers stationary in the fast lane before them. No one sleeping in the queue now, not with that racket and the vivid orange glow of the fire.

Another mighty explosion behind and even at that distance, seconds later they could feel the blast of air which hit them hard. Behind the wheel Tiffy Jones cheered, but he was the only one. They were still in danger. Offer was sure they were being shot at by the guard from the rear. The bulk of the tanker behind would protect them, but what if the bullets got a tyre, or those startled men standing out beside their vehicles caught on and opened up as they drew level.

But the Axis soldiers all grouped on the far side of their vehicles did not catch on until too late. Their attention was held by the leaping flames in the oil depot, by the noise of sirens and explosions, so that one empty tanker fleeing from the area seemed not out of place to them. It was only when it had passed that they realised the gate guard was firing after it, and when they had run to their weapons they were mostly too late.

Not entirely. The empty tanker roared past the end of the queue. Half a mile and they should find their Jeeps. Not easy, Offer was thinking, not in this darkness. Thank God it was dark, though. Vehicles even now would be pursuing them, and light would have been helpful to their enemies.

There was a sudden alarming noise, a wild flapping, and the tanker began to lurch across the road. Tiffy got it under control. He shouted, 'Sod it, a tyre's gone!' Some bullet had found its mark.

There was no stopping to change a wheel. The tanker kept going. When Offer thought they were at the rendezvous he called out, 'Pull over!'

The Jeeps would be on the south side of the road. Tiffy hauled on the wheel and shot across the road in front of a startled German driver of a big truck. The desert, rough ground and all darkness, and a lot of violent bumping at that speed. Everyone anxiously staring out to catch a glimpse of the Jeeps, and not succeeding. Panic began to rise. Christ, suppose they weren't there!

The tanker hit something very solid. It almost came to a complete halt, hurling them forward in bruising contact with the unyielding metal interior of the cab, then it rode up on one front wheel and came to a stop in imminent danger of toppling over.

'Out!' yelled Offer, and they all fell out and on to the ground. The empty tanker had ended its usefulness for them.

On the ground they looked frantically around. That mighty glow to the east, the sirens oscillating and inspiring frantic pandemonium, vehicles, lights showing, racing up the road from the direction of the guard-house. And darkness all around them and no sign of the Jeeps.

Offer began to run, because they couldn't just stand there so close to the Tripoli road. 'Sod, sod, sod it!' he was saying inside him. They'd pulled it off, gone in and out and done for Rommel's oil, and now the bloody Jeeps weren't there . . .

Engines started throatily, near and disconcertingly loud. Headlights came on, hooded but seeming tremendously bright under that starlight. And a voice—harshly Australian but cheerful and so welcome—'This way, mates!'

The Jeeps had been there all the time, so close. They turned thankfully and stumbled over the rough dark ground and found them. On the road the pursuing vehicles saw their lights and opened fire with machine-guns. Lashley switched off the headlamps immediately. They all piled in. The Jeeps shot away, out to make distance from those machine-gunners and the hell with the rough ground.

It wasn't all that dangerous. They had reccied this area on previous visits and mostly it was just rough ground but without many bad holes and awkward rocks. So they blinded along and trusted to luck. Second gear work, and ten to fifteen miles an hour, but Offer was willing to bet no pursuing vehicle would charge through the blackness after them at that speed. Every minute put them closer to safety. Thank God there was no moon so early.

Captain Offer had reckoned they would be two or three hours finding their way back to the wadi. Before that he reckoned they would be safe from pursuit and could use their headlamps. Well, he thought, listening back, they seemed to be dropping their pursuers already. There was no more firing now, and the lights of those vehicles steadily receded.

At one stage Cruiser, bright thick-head, said, 'Let's have a bash at 'em with the Bren, sir!'

And betray their position in the desert? 'Don't be a bloody chump, Cruiser,' Offer advised, and they bumped on, every revolution of their wheels taking them farther and farther away from danger.

When they had been travelling for close on half an hour, more sedately now for there was no sense in pushing their luck with reckless speed, Offer said they could use their headlights. That bucked up their rate of travel, and they all felt good and very contented with their night's work. But only a few minutes after they started using their lights, they heard the sound of an aircraft, not too high, approaching.

'Switch off,' said Offer resignedly, and out went their headlights. The plane seemed to fly directly overhead. All at once their desert world was turned from blackness into a brightness as the sunshine of the day. The aircraft had dropped a parachute flare.

Both vehicles instantly halted. They felt naked, sitting there in that brilliant white light, exposed for all to see. Their only safety was to remain still; if they moved, they would attract attention.

Offer got out his glasses and looked back. He saw vehicles moving where the road would be. Armoured cars. He saw them stretching out, extending their line and knew they were moving into the desert to search it. Rommel wasn't going to let the daring saboteurs escape following this night's work.

Offer lowered his glasses and told them what he had seen. The second Jeep had crawled slowly up alongside, so that they all sat together and could talk. He said, 'When the flare ends, use your lights and make as much ground as possible.' Their tail lights were disconnected and so wouldn't betray them to pursuers.

In time the flare died away. They shot off, driving at reckless speed again, and making good progress. Then they heard the plane return and doused their lights. Another parachute flare was dropped, and again they had to halt.

The tactics were continued all through the night. Sometimes a succession of flares were dropped, and for long periods the commando could only sit anxiously and pray there'd be a spell of darkness to follow. It was cat-and-mouse game. When the flares illuminated the desert the mouse had to stop and crouch and wait for darkness, while all the time the cats—those armoured cars—steadily advanced across the plain towards them . . . yet not seeing them, they knew, or the tracer would be flying.

And when there were times of darkness, the mouse shot away, using headlamps to make all the speed until that damned aircraft made its return run; and now it was the turn of the cats to halt and wait for light so that their advance could be resumed.

It slowed the pace of the commando tremendously. In time it became obvious that it would be well past midnight before they were back at the wadi; then as the hours passed it began to look as if they would still be on their way at daybreak, and the thought worried them.

Offer, apart from the worry, was dismayed now, because having so magnificently achieved their objective it seemed particularly hard luck that they should be pinned down when they ought to be fleeing gaily out of enemy territory.

It was big, sharp Weybright who again brought hope back to them. He said, a long time later, thoughtfully, 'I've got an idea we're getting away from them. Those flares are dropping behind us.'

When they thought of it, it did seem as if the aircraft continued to drop its flares over the same ground, nearer to the road, a big enough area, true, but they were managing to crawl out beyond the pool of brightest light.

'They must think we're still back there.'

Offer bucked up at the thought. So long as they didn't attract attention, perhaps in time they might drive completely out of the radius of the flares. He shivered. There had been times in the night when those armoured cars had seemed to be getting uncomfortably close.

He looked at his watch. Four-thirty. Oh, Lord, they'd just about make it to the wadi. Then the best thing would be for them to hole up for the day under the overhang. If they took to the desert in daylight they would not escape the attentions of the aircraft searching for them. A pity, though, they weren't able to put good distance between them and Agheila, for their chances of escaping aerial detection improved tremendously with every mile away from the coast.

He looked again at the flares. We'll have to take a risk, he decided, and said, briskly, 'Okay, use your lights. Douse 'em if you hear an aircraft.'

They drove faster now, and ignored the floating parachute flares and it seemed Art Weybright was right. They must have been at the extent of good visibility and soon Offer knew they were dropping their pursuers. Twice, even so, they made long halts because of overflying aircraft, and that made them fret with anxiety, for dawn was already paling the eastern horizon.

Finally they came to the escarpment, the area of eroded ridges and wadis. The noise of their straining engines seemed magnified as they climbed, but they were confident their enemies behind would not hear them.

Offer eventually gave the order to halt, and they switched off their engines. They had come to the top of the escarpment and Offer wanted to climb on foot to the nearest height and try to spot their overhang hide-out. The faithful O'Keefe went climbing up through the cold darkness beside him. He said, cheerfully, 'I think we've given the buggers the slip, sir.'

*

Less than a mile away a German sentry had heard the sounds of the approaching Jeeps and had promptly wakened his commander. Captain Braunschweig immediately ordered every man to be roused, then they sat quietly and waited for dawn. By the sound of it the vehicles appeared to be coming almost head on towards the German patrol.

The Hauptmann had no doubts that the vehicles were enemy, for apart from his own patrol he could see no reason why any other Axis force should be in this vicinity.

Before midnight, Braunschweig had been hauled out of slumber by his Feldwebel reporting a big orange glow towards the north. All Braunschweig's men stirred at that and rose to see the phenomenon. It was a fire, they decided, and a mighty big fire. At times the glow brightened, and a long time later they heard a sound which suggested an explosion.

'That's Agheila,' the Hauptmann knew. Such a fire could only mean a big oil conflagration, and Braunschweig's thoughts immediately leapt to sabotage. After all, there were these recent tracks of an enemy patrol in the vicinity and it wasn't hard to link them with that great if distant inferno.

Later the sky took on a different brightness, this time hard white, and they knew that parachute flares were being used. This again could only mean a search for an enemy in the desert, confirming his first thought of sabotage.

And now the German patrol could hear approaching motor engines, and the Hauptmann rejoiced for it seemed that the saboteurs were returning along their former tracks from near Agheila. His men were standing to their guns in silence, watching him from below where he had taken up position on some high ground, waiting for the light to get better.

Then the distant roaring of engines faded and went into silence. Braunschweig's heart leapt. Did this mean they had gone to ground? If so it would not take his Task Force long to dig them out.

*

No one had slept in the wadi that night. Knowing that an enemy was so close across the escarpment put an end to all thoughts of kip.

After the dark they came and sat out in the open and had a talk. It got them nowhere. It was a time for leadership and Walker, Offer's unwilling N.C.O. wasn't the man for such an emergency, excellent though he was in so many other respects. In the end they decided on the obvious. There was nothing they could do about the situation, therefore they would do nothing. When Offer came he would make all the decisions for them.

Walker told them, unnecessarily, they must make no noise, for sound travelled far in those silent lands. In fact they were quite sure on one occasion they heard metal striking hard rock, and guessed it was from that enemy force, no doubt encamped uncomfortably close to them. Walker very sensibly put out a strong cordon of sentries to guard against possible night attack.

No one was allowed to smoke, either, for from past experience they knew how far the odour of tobacco smoke could carry. That created a lot of bother among the hardened smokers, who argued against the ruling, but Walker had the support of a majority of his men.

The inevitable Sibrett and his close allies tried to bully the easy-going Walker, but Walker lost his patience and in a manner not approved by the generals in Whitehall, warned them of the penalty if they disobeyed his orders.

'Smoke,' he warned, 'and I'll kick the fucking tab down your fuckin' throat and your fuckin' teeth after it. Right?'

It was crude, repetitious in delivery, but effective. Walker, the old palais bouncer, was a big man and hard with it. They did not smoke though they suffered all the withdrawal pangs of the nicotine addict while the night hours dragged by.

Offer had said they should be looking out for him around midnight. A flashing torch could guide him in. 'You'll hear my engines long before I get up the escarpment,' he had said.

When midnight came and went, and then two o'clock, three o'clock, four and later, the tension within that silent wadi grew to almost insupportable dimensions, until something like panic prevailed. In time everyone was sure Captain Offer's party had met with trouble. They too had caught the distant orange glow that made them think their comrades had got at Rommel's oil. Then they saw the white glare of the parachute flares and knew there was a manhunt out there.

'They're being pinned down in the desert,' some men argued, 'that's why they're late. They won't get here, you'll see. Jerry is holding them at

Agheila and when it's light they'll have every man out hunting for them, and all the Luftwaffe, too. They won't get away. If they have made it, why aren't they here now?'

It was an awkward question. By three o'clock, and thoroughly demoralised by the long waiting, a faction had grown which wanted to scarper while the going was good with some darkness to hide them.

'They'll hear our engines.' *They* were that force half a mile away. 'They'll follow us.' That was Sergeant Walker, torn between anxiety to look after his own interests and loyalty to John Offer.

Skipper, venomous as a cornered viper, snapped, 'So what? If *we* don't move before daylight they'll get *us*.'

'If we just lie up quietly here we'll stand a better chance of keeping out of trouble.' Sergeant Walker, uncertain but putting up all the arguments in favour of staying because they couldn't let their comrades down by not being there when Offer's party reached the wadi.

A lot of men joined in at that, and at times they began to forget the nearby enemy and their voices rose in argument until Walker ordered them to shut up.

'If we just lie up here we might find ourselves fuckin' surrounded,' Sibrett mouthed, and that had them all stirring nervously and looking along the darkness of the wadi, as if fearing to see an enemy already upon them. With considerable perspicacity Sibrett said he'd fuckin' bet the fuckin' Huns had followed their fuckin' tracks right across a similar desert.

'They're sitting back there in camp because it grew too dark to see our trail.' Which wasn't quite true but near enough.

In the end Walker told them flatly they weren't going to make a run for it. 'Suppose they turn up just after we leave? And which of us knows how to navigate through the desert?'

That seemed a clincher, though Sibrett finally came up with—'I'll take my chances. I can use the sun, and we all know the North Star if we move at night.'

Inevitably, without trying, they'd learned a few tricks about desert navigation from their R.S.M. It wasn't as if they were deep in the desert, anyway. The sun and the night's stars could keep them on a south-by-east, then a north-by-east course and eventually they were bound to hit the Mediterranean coast behind their own front line. Still Walker refused to change his mind.

So Sibrett gathered his friends around him and quietly told them, fuck Walker, he knew what he was going to do.

'I'm going to grab a fuckin' Jeep and get to fuck out of here,' he told Dodge and the ugly, mean-faced Skipper. Sibrett was intent on looking after himself, not Captain Bleedin' Offer. 'Who's with me?'

Skipper and Dodge, reckless for anything, said fuck Offer, they was going to scarper, and they played with their guns in a manner which said they would use them if anyone tried to stop them. When they spoke to Joe Bannister, as wild a spirit as they, he too said count him fuckin' in. They didn't want more, though they knew there were quite a few others who would jump at the chance to join them.

'Don't let on,' Sibrett warned, and the four quietly made their preparations and waited their chance.

But things didn't go well for them. The five Jeeps were parked bumper to bumper under that rocky overhang. If they were to make a sudden exit down the wadi they would have to take the first Jeep of the close little column. Frustratingly, Sergeant Walker decided to hold court in that particular Jeep. He sat behind the wheel, camouflage net thrown back, the other men perched on the bonnet, or standing against the vehicle, all talking, all speculating with increasing pessimism about their chances of survival.

'Whatever hour he comes, if he comes at all, Jerry will hear him.' By now the men in the wadi had decided that their neighbours must be Germans. They were right but had no reason to be. Private Palfreyman was doing the talking. 'So where does that leave us?'

If Offer did ever arrive at the wadi he would alert the enemy. If he never turned up and they themselves had to move, their engines would immediately draw enemy attention upon them, and they shivered when they remembered those armoured *Kubelwagens*.

Finally, to everyone's relief the sky began to pale. At that Sergeant Walker made a move. Stiff with cold, he alighted from the Jeep.

'Let's have a dekko from up top,' he said. 'Keep your heads down.' Mustn't be seen on the skyline. Walker began to climb, very softly, making no noise. Other men followed him, but not Sibrett and his close companions.

'Come on,' whispered Sibrett hoarsely. 'Now's our fuckin' chance!'

They started to board the Jeep, throwing in their few personal belongings, and at that moment they began to hear the approach of Offer's

Jeeps. Now came new anxiety on top of old. Offer's party had betrayed the presence of an enemy in the area. Would his engines bring the Germans out looking for them, and in the process stumble on this wadi? In a few minutes it would be broad daylight.

Then Offer switched off his engines, before Walker and his men had even climbed to the look-out position, and after that Germans and British had to sit there and wait.

Within a few minutes there was no waiting for any of them.

*

Sibrett took the wheel, but for those few minutes did not start the engine. If they were to run from the enemy in daylight, they might as well start when the light was good enough for them to take off down the wadi at speed.

Sibrett said, 'With a bit of luck Walker will come chasing us.' Walker would think that their starting Jeep had betrayed the hide-out to the enemy. Anyway, he wouldn't want to stay on and risk it, Sibrett said, and had the thought that Walker and the others, their nerves rotten after the long night's suspense, would make a panic move.

That would be right up their alley, he told his companions grimly. The bloody Boche would pursue anything that moved. But they, Sibrett and cronies, would have a start on all of them, and if Walker's lot tore after them they'd be between Sibrett's Jeep and the Huns. It would be Walker who would have to fight them off and indulge in a rearguard action, all of which would help Sibrett's party to get away.

Sibrett gave no thought to the position of Offer's party. If he did it amounted to no more than, 'Sod bleedin' Offer!' Offer could look after himself. Sibrett would do likewise.

When he judged the light to be just good enough Sibrett started the engine. The roar was a shock to everyone, the sound cascading round the walls of the harsh little ravine.

Sibrett shouted, 'Hang on!' and came pulling out into the wadi. Then he began to make tracks over the escarpment, heading east.

*

Captain Offer, perched up on a tall rock, heard the distant Jeep and was mystified. 'What the hell is happening?' Had Walker's lot grown tired of waiting and picked this moment for pulling out? In daylight? They'd be spotted in no time when Rommel put his aircraft up. He must catch up with Walker and bring him back to the security—if anywhere was going to prove secure in the next twelve hours of daylight—of the wadi and its overhang . . .

Then they all realised they were listening to the sound of one engine only and that puzzled them even more.

The light was fast improving. Already they could see a quarter of a mile across the eroded land; a few minutes more and they would see half a mile away, then a mile, then right to the horizon.

And now they heard the sound of other engines, more distant. It came rolling across the ragged escarpment, and the trained ears of the men with Offer told them these were no Jeeps.

Offer thought, 'Christ, that must be the Hun!' Or Italians. Whoever they were, they were close, only a mile or so from Offer's party, huddled there just below the skyline, and in direct line with Offer's proposed way of escape into the southern desert.

Two groups of men less than a mile apart, clustered on two look-out points, were now witness to a scene which almost had the elements of having been staged.

Offer and O'Keefe had topped the escarpment, perhaps half a mile east of the wadi where the other Jeeps were. Before them was a long dry basin which was probably a lake in time of rain, a basin which ran east and west for several miles, hard rock and boulder-strewn. Everywhere wadis emptied into this shallow basin, so that when it was filled with water it would have the appearance of sharp fiords around its edge.

Suddenly, on to this natural stage they saw a Jeep emerge. Both Offer and O'Keefe had their glasses up immediately. The light was getting better . . . they saw . . . Sibrett, Bannister, Skipper and Dodge. The Jeep was roaring away in second gear, picking its way round the great boulders.

Then other movement caught their eyes and their glasses swung to a point directly opposite. They had a glimpse of the tops of armoured cars moving along a shallow wadi and saw immediately that where that wadi entered the basin was in the line of flight of the Jeep.

It was a race—would the Jeep get past the wadi mouth before the first of the armoured cars barred the way? The watchers, would know very quickly, within three or four minutes, though that could be a long time for men witnessing the fate of other men. Now, attracted by the noise, Busker, Cruiser and the others were clambering for a look, too.

Offer's glasses turned to that column almost hidden amid the rocky ground across from them. Something was happening there. The column had stopped, as if it had encountered a place of difficult traverse, or perhaps one of the vehicles was playing up and barring the way for the others.

Then Offer saw movement much lower down towards the basin, and realised that one armoured car had got through and was ahead on its own. The race now was between one Jeep threading its way along the boulder-strewn basin and one armoured car descending the wadi.

O'Keefe said, concerned, 'That car's going to get there at the same time as the Jeep.' He began to rise, very hurried in his movements.

'Where are you going?' Offer demanded, suspicion in his voice.

'To get a Bren. We might hold the armoured car in the wadi and give our boys chance to get past.'

Our boys. Sibrett & Co? Sibrett who had left him to the enemy near Siwa?

'Hold it, sergeant-major.'

'Hold it?' O'Keefe spun round, startled.

Offer, still looking through his glasses said, 'Yes, we're not going to give ourselves away, not for the sake of Sibrett's shower. What are they doing on their own, anyway?'

His glasses had swung to the point where Sibrett's Jeep had emerged into the basin, and he recognised the place. That was the wadi where they had left Walker and the others. His glasses moved fractionally, taking in a higher place. Yes, that was their look-out point, and he could see figures crouching on top.

Offer snapped, 'Sibrett's done a bunk and left the others to look after themselves. Okay, let them take their chances with that armoured car, and they might do us a good turn in the process.'

Already Offer was thinking, 'Sibrett, the sod, might lead that armoured column a dance and give us a chance to slide out without them knowing we're here.' And coldly he thought, 'Sibrett, you bastard, you're expendable!' Sibrett could do something good in his life by dying to save his comrades. So, no warning him of danger, and no help to hold back his enemies. Offer explained his views tersely, and O'Keefe simply sat down and said, 'You're right. Let's hope Sibrett leads 'em right out of the country.'

So they watched, eight men now together, and saw the Jeep a mere six hundred yards away dodging along the basin floor, with a glimpse occasionally of one armoured car trundling down the wadi opposite, the two vehicles fast closing in on each other. Now the other armoured cars were moving, too, the unknown obstacle overcome at last.

The Jeep seemed suddenly to find good ground and come on at a cracking pace. The armoured car now turned a bend in the wadi and they could see it completely as it came lurching on to the basin. And suddenly both vehicles were in view of each other.

Skipper on the Jeep machine-gun was quickest to react. They saw tracer, then caught the echoing sounds of machine-gun fire. The tracer went wild because of the jolting, and then the armoured car opened up and was equally wide of the mark.

The Jeep got by unscathed and put some rocky cover between them and the *Kubelwagen*, but a minute later the armoured car was right out on the basin and had a clear view of the fleeing Jeep. The commander of the car showed sense. He knew the nimble Jeep would beat him on this boulder-strewn surface, so the thing to do was to stop it before it got out of firing range.

He ordered his driver to halt. He himself manned the twin machine-guns. With a steady firing platform for his guns he could hardly miss, not at two hundred yards.

Offer and his men saw the manoeuvre and Lashley said, grimly, 'It's curtains for 'em,' and it was.

Tracer lashed across the basin. Too high. The German corrected his aim. The tracer came lower, lower, lower . . . on target. Skipper, futilely firing back, took a whole stream of lead including tracer through his body and it hurled him on to Sibrett at the wheel. The Jeep began to run wild for a moment, but the tracer crept after it. It began to chew through the metal work, and then it might have hit Sibrett for they saw the Jeep run straight on to a big rock and seem to demolish itself there. One man, thrown out, rose to his feet, both hands in the air.

Offer said, 'Wait!' as his R.S.M. rose as if to get down to start their Jeeps. He wanted all the armoured cars along the basin before they started their engines. He saw them come one by one out of the wadi and go chasing off after the first *Kubelwagen*, closing in now on the wrecked Jeep and the one survivor.

When the enemy was as far away as it was likely they would get, Offer stood erect, facing Sergeant Walker and his men on the look-out point, and began to wave. After a few seconds he saw someone wave back and knew they had made contact.

'If he's wise,' Offer said to O'Keefe, 'Walker will be all ready to move out when we go over the top. Come on, let's go!'

They clambered down to their Jeeps and started them. The Germans would hear the sound and be instantly alert, but Offer did not propose to rejoin his comrades via the basin. Instead they turned and ran back and took another wadi half a mile further west which would bring them on top of the escarpment right behind their own wadi.

Offer was not bothered about the German armoured cars. He had enough lead on this rugged ground to outdistance them with his lighter Jeeps. He'd rendezvous with Walker, and they would take off and get across this escarpment and down on to the desert. No good staying here, he knew. Whoever had survived that crash would talk, like McTone had done, and the Germans wouldn't be long in finding their hide-out.

What bothered Offer was the prospect of a long chase in daylight across a desert which would give them no cover from air attack. Rommel's aircraft would be up and searching for them any minute now, he was sure. No doubt the commander of those armoured cars would soon radio their position and home the Luftwaffe in on them. Probably they had only minutes in which to make their getaway. Offer wanted to be on more level ground before the Luftwaffe arrived, for if they were pinned down in these wadis, so difficult even for their Jeeps to negotiate, it wouldn't be long before the slower armoured cars came up to polish them off.

*

Walker was waiting, his Jeeps lined up, engines running, ready to fall in with them when they came by. Offer shouted as they drove up, 'Keep going, Eddie! We're up to our neck in trouble!'

Sergeant Walker grinned, a much relieved man because now he did not have the responsibility of making decisions. With sublime faith in his commanding officer, Walker pulled in behind Offer's two Jeeps and off they went up and across the top of the escarpment.

The sun was over the horizon suddenly, hot light warming them and they were grateful for it after the chill night they had passed through. Offer was in a buoyant mood. They seemed constantly to be getting away with murder. With a bit more luck they'd make it to Benghazi, and by Jove what a night of celebration they'd have when they did get there!

It was a rough escarpment face, a place no sane man would ever take a vehicle, but his men were inspired and there were times when they almost picked up their Jeeps and carried them over the toughest of obstacles.

Cruiser and Busker were really in their element. Between them they could hoist any Jeep over any difficulty, like a pair of human bulldozers, someone said. They seemed tireless, too, giving a hand with any trapped and stationary vehicle.

Three hours later they finally quit the bad lands and took to the desert beyond, but already the bombers had spotted them and were circling overhead like vultures. The spirit of jubilation fled within minutes.

Four bombers found them, three Bredas and a Ju88. Each in turn made a dive towards the Jeeps then pulled away without firing or dropping a bomb. It was a slightly puzzling manoeuvre, but Captain Offer didn't think of it as such at that moment. He was too concerned in deciding his next course of action.

When they first heard the bombers they came to a halt in a narrow rock-walled wadi that gave some protection, but Offer knew they could not remain there long. Those armoured cars would soon be in pursuit, and if the Glasshouse Gang didn't move it was only a question of time before the *Kubelwagens* were within range and turning their twin machine-guns upon them.

Offer had a quick conference with R.S.M. O'Keefe and Sergeant Walker. They finally arrived at the conclusion that, bombers or no bombers, they must try to make a run for it across the desert. The going would be good for a couple of hundred miles beyond the escarpment, they knew, flat, almost level ground, so they discussed tactics accordingly.

Offer finally gave the signal and the Jeeps started up again. Offer's Jeep led the way out of a wadi and on to the grey desert beyond. The moment they hit the plain every foot slammed down hard on their accelerators. The Jeeps leapt into top speed, exhilarating after the recent crawl, and tore along, line abreast, a hundred yards between them so as to offer dispersed targets when the bombs came and the strafing began. Six Jeeps, belting along at over fifty miles an hour, lifted great plumes of dust which hung for miles behind them.

And all waited for the bombers to come at them. Then each Jeep would weave and make violent changes of course in an attempt at evasive action. Offer wondered if even one Jeep would survive that day, yet continued to be hopeful because the L.R.D.G. had been through all this before and some of them had survived to tell the tale.

They drove hard, risking rocks and holes and encountering none, and every eye except the drivers' was intent upon the bombers now circling out over the flat wasteland, two thousand feet high, and just out of range of their Brens. At any moment they would level off and come in on a straight run at the Jeeps. The Bredas would have four machine-guns to strafe them, and the Ju88 would try to destroy them with cannon shells.

The bombers continued to circle. The Jeeps drove madly, like a herd of stampeding buffaloes over that great dusty plain. The bombers were still circling. After a quarter of an hour of this an astonished Offer began to accept that they had no intention of bombing them or they would have done it before. When this realisation dawned on him, perplexing though it was, Offer signalled to his Jeeps to slow down and take it easier. They settled at the safer speed of forty m.p.h. and devoured the miles between them and Benghazi in most satisfying fashion.

Offer, all the same, was a bewildered and unhappy man. Suspiciously watching those lazily circling aircraft, he had foreboding of evil times ahead. What devilment was the enemy up to? They must know that his patrol was responsible for starting the fires in the oil depot. Why, then, weren't they raking them with their guns and trying to blow the daylights out of them with bombs?

The bombers flew away half an hour after they had picked up the Jeep patrol. They flew off without a single hostile act against their enemy, and every man in those Jeeps, comfortably riding towards safety, thought it all too incredible to be reassuring. Had the war ended overnight? Someone even asked.

The bombers departed, then a tiny Fieseler Storch came buzzing up and settled down to a distant observation of the Glasshouse patrol. That was understandable. If the bombers weren't going to bomb, send them to base and save precious fuel. If the idea was to keep them under observation, then the Fieseler Storch was designed for such a purpose and was economical to operate, too.

Another two hours passed, hot hours now with the sun belting down and their throats craving for a drink and their bellies for a meal. Still that little plane accompanied them, and on that featureless grey desert there was no chance of giving it the slip. After those two hours the first Fieseler Storch homed off across the northern horizon and another Storch took up the watch.

Offer decided to call a halt. If they weren't in danger of attack from the air, there was no sense in running like mad and going hungry into the bargain. Whatever awful thing was being planned by the enemy, they might as well meet it well-fed.

His signal and slowing down were correctly interpreted and within a few minutes the six Jeeps had come together, No one left a Bren gun unmanned, however, and while others brewed-up and cooked a bully-beef hash, vigilant sentries watched the observation plane and the skies around it. If bombers came, the Jeeps would instantly disperse.

None came. They halted for twenty minutes over a hurried meal, during which time the petrol tanks were refilled, too. Offer had actually given the order to mount and move off when two further aircraft came droning towards them from the north. Their first reaction was that here came the bombers, but quite quickly they were identified as Ju52s, transport planes and possibly unarmed.

Still at a halt, and still highly suspicious, the Glasshouse Gang watched the big, slow aircraft fly east beyond them and in line of their escape. When they were some distance away, probably ten miles, the Ju52s spent some minutes circling as if making sure of a good landing place. Finally they came down and could hardly be seen even through glasses because of some swelling ground between. Ten minutes later the Junkers took off and headed north-west towards the airfields near Agheila. Simultaneously with their departure four bombers returned. This time they were Stukas, Hitler's dreaded dive-bombers. They began a vulture-like tight circling above the Jeeps.

Offer and O'Keefe held their usual conference. Captain Offer said he could only imagine that infantry had been landed from those Ju52s, perhaps in some hope of halting their flight. It didn't make sense, though, if the infantry were on foot, for his nippy little Jeeps would make a quick detour around them and leave them standing. What else, then, had those Ju52s brought?

Captain Offer said, 'Let's go—and disperse.' They began to wheel around and again took up positions a hundred yards apart, then at a steady forty continued their flight.

Offer was too canny a bird to continue on their old course, however, for that would have taken them on to where the Junkers had landed. He badly wanted to know why the aircraft had risked a landing in the desert, but he wasn't going out of his way to find out. His new course was south-east, taking them deeper into the desert . . .

Shocked, Captain Offer saw vehicles emerging ahead. They were travelling south in extended line formation like his own, and plainly they were intent on cutting off the British raiding force. They were armoured cars.

*

It was Bannister who was thrown out of the Jeep just a second or so before it disintegrated against a tall rock, Sibrett dead at the wheel. He had passed through a moment of awful terror, and was a wreck of a man as he scrambled to his feet, terrified of the advancing German armoured car, his hands high above his head, and his voice shouting, 'Don't shoot! Don't shoot! I give in!'

He had seen Skipper at the machine-gun go double as bullets shattered his body. He saw blood gushing and bits of human flesh come flying out of his fellow soldier, saw him fall on top of Sibrett who pushed him away frantically and in the same moment died as the stream of bullets found him, too. Bannister did not know what happened to Dodge, sitting passenger beside Sibrett. He could have been shot or he might have died when the Jeep smashed into the big rock seconds later. Bannister never knew because a bounce of the Jeep, seconds before crashing, sent him flying to the ground.

Hauptmann Braunschweig drove up to the quivering, terrified man and alighted. His other *Kubelwagens* were beginning to come into the basin now, making a tremendous din, but Braunschweig's concern was for his prisoner only. He had not time to waste and he wanted information.

He took out his automatic and pointed it at the demoralised man. 'Your name?' His Feldwebel was there to take it down. 'What is your unit and where are they?'

Bannister gulped and said, 'Bannister, sir. Fred Bannister. G.G.C.U.'

It was the Hauptmann's turn for shock. Then his pulse began to race fiercely. The G.G.C.U.! He knew those initials. These were the men above all others he wanted to meet. Well, he had one of them before him as prisoner, and now he was going to talk . . .

'Your leader is Captain Offer?'

Bannister said, 'Yes, sir,' not wondering how this German officer knew.

'Where are your comrades?'

Bannister pointed to the far end of the basin. 'Just there, sir.' He would talk, tell everything so long as he kept out of the bad books of this hard-faced German. Bannister was remembering what Offer had told them.

Don't let the Germans catch you or they'll give you real hell. The Glasshouse Gang was much wanted by the Afrika Korps.

Hauptmann Braunschweig wheeled, following the pointing finger. His armoured cars were almost up with him, making a tremendous echoing noise in this rock-walled basin. When they reached him they switched off, and when the engine noise died, Braunschweig was able to hear other engines driven hard, but they were a mile or more away beyond the basin.

'Too late,' he thought. 'They've taken fright and are on their way out.' His immediate impulse was to take off after them, and he even took a stride towards his wagon and then he halted.

He had a good brain, that Hauptmann, and he used it to purpose at that moment. He knew his heavier *Kubelwagens* could never hope to catch up with the fleeter Jeeps on that rough terrain, and would be even more outdistanced once his Task Force hit the flatland beyond the escarpment.

So Hauptmann Braunschweig called for his signaller and sent a message to his H.Q. in Agheila. He informed his superiors that he had stumbled upon the Glasshouse Gang, had killed three of them and taken a fourth prisoner. But the main party, including the notorious Captain Offer, had got away over the escarpment. He gave a precise map reference and then dictated a course of action for his superiors to follow if they wished.

He called for aerial observation of the fleeing commando, but asked that they should not attack the Jeeps. He wanted to capture Offer alive so that he could be tried for his crime against humanity in that terrible Sand Lake. Braunschweig was sure that his field-marshal would agree with this course. Then he ordered the Ju52s which had been placed at his disposal to fly into the airfield nearest to him now, which was west of Agheila. Hauptmann Braunschweig was unconcerned about the miles the Glasshouse Gang might make across the open desert. His Ju52 transport planes would make light of the distance and would put him and his armoured cars down in a position to intercept the fleeing raiders.

He made one more request, then he turned his *Kubelwagen* and led his vehicles north-west where, a few hours later, they arrived at the airfield to be told that his Ju52s would land at any minute now.

*

The bombers began to use their guns and bombs when Offer tried to outflank that distant armoured enemy. One by one they came peeling off to dive before the line of Jeeps, machine-guns kicking up a line of spurting dust in a manner most demoralising to the drivers. Instinctively they turned away, and that sent them heading towards the armoured cars racing across to intercept their flight.

Offer got them back on the old course, but again the Stukas came diving at them and this time two of them dropped one of their four 110 lb bombs, so close to the leading Jeep that it was almost overturned, and the blast and earth were hurled stingingly into their faces. That was even more demoralising, and once again they changed course, and now those armoured *Kubelwagens* were no great distance away, almost within firing range.

It took some time for the tactics to sink in, and then Offer realised what the strategy was. Still the bombers did not want to score direct hits; what they were doing was shepherding them on to the guns of the armoured cars. All the same, Offer had no doubts that if they did persevere on the new course he had taken, one which would turn the slower enemy's flank, the bombers would stop playing and would go in for them in earnest.

'They want us alive if possible.' The message had got home to Offer at last. Well, he wasn't going to be taken alive to face torture and death at the hands of the S.S. Neither did he intend to die from machine-gun strafing or a Ju88 bomb.

Offer pulled away from the armoured cars and began to drive back on his original tracks. He didn't like retreating, but if it helped to keep them alive he'd go right back to Agheila if necessary.

He was still puzzled by the situation, however. The hours were passing, and once darkness fell the Germans would never catch his patrol. So he had to use his ingenuity to keep out of trouble for the next several hours.

Offer did it by periodically feinting as if trying to turn his enemy's flank. Each time, the *Kubelwagens* changed course and strung out in line astern to intercept him, and though they were undoubtedly slower than the Jeeps, they weren't all that slow and Offer would have a job to turn their line and keep clear of their concentrated machine-gun fire.

It was the bombers, however, which refused to let them escape. Whenever the Jeeps made a show of racing for the flank they came screaming down, putting down a curtain of machine-gun bullets into which they could run and be destroyed if they were obstinately of that mind. And twice more, when Offer's feint looked dangerous, they dropped bombs in his path, and he knew four Stukas were more than a match for them. His gunners opened up whenever possible with their Brens, but did not appear to do any significant damage.

Finally, around four o'clock, Offer gave up all the manoeuvring and resignedly headed back north-west, his vehicles dispersed in line with him, and with an almost equal number of German armoured cars pacing them from the rear.

Offer said to his driver, Lashley now, 'I don't get it. What are they up to? They don't seem in a hurry. All they're doing is driving us back towards Agheila.' But darkness would descend long before they even reached the escarpment, let alone the coastal road into Agheila.

It was much later, when the sun was almost down on the horizon, that the problem was resolved. Still those Stukas maintained their vulture-like circling above them. Still those seven armoured cars came steadily on their heels, even more widely dispersed than Offer's Jeeps, almost a mile between the outside *Kubelwagens*. Remorselessly they seemed to be shoving the Glasshouse Gang before them.

Someone in the Jeep next to Offer's was calling, waving and stabbing frantically in a forward direction. Offer's eyes swung round. Instantly he saw what had excited attention. For some time now they had been able to see the rim of the escarpment, crossed so recently. Now, before it, a dust cloud had risen, telling of the passage of vehicles. It seemed to be extending across the horizon, as if they too were dispersing line abreast.

'Ease off,' Offer rapped to Lashley, and brought his glasses up. Quite clearly he made out another line of armoured cars and trucks. He counted—there must have been twenty of them. They seemed to be taking up a crescent formation, with the wings extended in advance of the centre vehicles.

Offer, aghast, could only say, 'Christ Almighty, we're done for now!'

In that moment he understood why the *Kubelwagens* had been content to shovel them forward across the desert, and why the Stukas had made no attempt to destroy them. All the time they had been waiting for massive reinforcements, and here they were, clear of the rugged escarpment at last. Within ten minutes at the rate everyone was going, the pincer grip would have got them, and they'd have been the target for a hundred machine-guns, and doubtless a few cannon and some mortars. Resistance would be suicidal, and sane men would give in and surrender, and that was what all this parade of might was for.

It was only at that moment that John Offer really appreciated how big a target he was in enemy eyes, and how terrible was their mood for retribution. Nothing would satisfy the Afrika Korps except to take him alive and try him and see him die with their own eyes.

Those quick, fleeting thoughts shook Offer, for it is unnerving to know one is the object of such hatred. But then his jaw came up. They hadn't got him yet. There had to be some way out of this trap. The sun was blinding in his eyes and he wished it had gone and there was darkness, for they'd never catch him and his desert foxes once light failed . . .

He knew what to do. He signalled for his Jeeps to close in on him, a manoeuvre which agitated the Stukas and brought them into tighter circles. No one dismounted, though they shut off their engines. Offer spoke to them standing on his seat.

'You chaps, you should know we're right up trouble creek. They want to take us alive, and if we don't do something within a few minutes it's either death or surrender for us. But they're not going to cop us. We're going to get out of this!' Well, maybe some of them; not all would survive. Perhaps no one would come through alive with those Stukas still with an hour's daylight left to destroy them.

He outlined the strategy, very hurriedly, because the two opposing lines of enemy vehicles were swiftly bearing down upon them. All agreed that what he proposed was the only course left to them. Engines were started, roaring into life, and the Jeeps began to manoeuvre.

Offer stopped retreating now. Lashley swung their Jeep south for a distance of quarter of a mile, and all the other Jeeps came in line astern, closing up on each other so that they drove no more than twenty yards between them. When he got himself in the right position, vis-à-vis the sun, and one Stuka had already peeled off into a power dive to head them back on course again, Offer gave an order.

Lashley swung the vehicle round so that they faced their original enemy. The Jeep howled through its gears, then settled in top, Lashley's foot trying to press the accelerator through the floorboards.

'Take the end one,' Offer ordered, bouncing in his seat. This time they were not going to try to round the enemy. This time they were going straight for him, were going to fight their way past them.

They charged the *Kubelwagen* at the extreme end of the line, the one deepest into the desert. Each Jeep behind Offer's drove through a billowing cloud of dust, hard on a driver's eyes, but it had some of the properties of a smoke screen, almost completely hiding the following vehicles.

The charged the last *Kubelwagen* because it meant that the more distant armoured cars were at long range with their guns, and in fact could not use them as their target closed on its victim for fear of hitting their own vehicles. If Offer had unwisely chosen to ram his way through the centre of the line, his Jeeps would have been the focus of a converging fire from both flanks.

But there was another reason behind that charge. Before the Stukas knew what was happening, the Jeeps were so close to the armoured cars that the Ju87s were unable to use either bombs or guns upon them. While they were racing to attack that unfortunate *Kubelwagen*, they were momentarily safe from air hostility.

Offer was taking a gamble. True, if they did break through they would have the Stukas after them with a vengeance, but there was only one hour of daylight left, and Offer had heard how more than once the redoubtable L.R.D.G., and no less redoubtable S.A.S. had run down the desert for a full day under air attack with a few survivors at the end of it.

. . . a few survivors. That, Offer knew, was the best *they* could hope for. But the enemy had that glaring sun to contend with.

Behind him his gunner opened up with their mounted Bren, a long burst at the *Kubelwagen* before them. His other Jeeps also started firing, but their targets were the second and third armoured cars, the ones so near they could do most damage.

Offer, hanging on and not able to do anything to help them, saw tracer flit from the twin Spandaus on the *Kubelwagen* and come zipping past them. The Spandaus must be aiming almost blind, though, with that flaming sun in the German's eyes. They were rocketing along, so close now Offer could see the head and shoulders of the German machine-gunner. For comfort, the *Kubelwagen* had been driving with the protective armoured screen and hood in an open position. All were being driven like this, all seven of the *Kubelwagens*; and in permitting it for once the efficient Hauptmann Braunschweig was in grave error. Heat or no heat, discomfort or no discomfort, those screens should have been up just in case the enemy turned upon them.

Before the *Kubelwagen* gunner's tracer could swing to take the Jeep head on, he died under the hail of bullets from Offer's machine-gun. Lashley swerved slightly to go outside the end *Kubelwagen*, now neutered by their Bren fire. The air was filled with tracer flashing from the other *wagens*, several of them trying to range on to the leading Jeep, Offer's. Around them bullets screamed in quick excited bursts. The air was hideous with the whizz and noise of spinning bullets. All at once the Jeeps had become the focus of a dozen machine-guns, and Mgs can hurl a startling number of missiles in the minute required to breach that line. What saved those who did get through, though, was undoubtedly the sun in the eyes of the most dangerous of the enemy, those two or three *Kubelwagens* nearest their comrade on the left flank. Those farthest away, unaffected by the sun, had the disadvantage of distance, though some of them opened up on the fleeing column while ever it was safe to maintain fire.

Offer's Jeep got through without a scratch. Not all were so lucky. The last Jeep collared all the flying lead, the driver was killed at the wheel, and out of control, the Jeep swerved and turned over and all that was left were dead and unconscious bodies to be picked up later by the Germans.

They were through, five racing Jeeps, though some men were also wounded in the later vehicles. They had out-witted and out-flanked the enemy, and that was an achievement. But now the real battle began.

Offer's men knew what to do. The moment they were round the *Kubelwagens*, the Jeeps swung wide of each other. Now it was every Jeep for itself. They had to survive attack from the air until they could attain the safety of night's darkness. The *Kubelwagens*, they guessed, would come hard after them, but they hadn't the pace unless the Jeeps punctured or had mechanical trouble.

The only enemy they really had to contend with were those Ju87s.

They came down, one after the other, as soon as the Jeeps were clear of the *Kubelwagens*. This time they dived in earnest. Now they must kill because they could not take the raiders alive.

They came in screaming power-dives, terrifying to hear, even more terrifying if one were the target. They unloaded their remaining bombs and strafed wickedly each with their four machine-guns.

It was a fierce, and to some an exhilarating hour. Everywhere across the plain five Jeeps sped, dust kicked up to hang in great, still clouds. Where they went, four Stukas came swooping to destroy them, the time for playing over. Now the radioed order was to get the Glasshouse Gang at all costs; they must not be allowed to escape, none of them.

Dodging, twisting and turning, employing every trick known to their drivers, the Jeeps used evasive action as the dive-bombers came hurtling down upon them. For those who witnessed the scene, a discomfited Braunschweig among them, it was a crazy sight. Jeeps racing along, Stukas peeling off and diving, guns blazing. Jeep machine-gunners doing their best to get a burst in, but it was pretty hopeless at that speed. Then at the last second a violent wrench on a steering wheel, a mighty skid and the Jeep would be off at right angles to its original course, as the bullets intended for it tore up the ground only yards away.

As time passed—precious minutes gained for the Jeeps—and the sun went down, the Stukas became more savage and daring. They threw their aircraft across the sky in desperate attempts to shorten the time between attacks, and when they dived they were increasingly reckless, as if getting exasperated at sight of the Jeeps evading them.

With cunning the Jeeps drove into each other's dust clouds, foxing the Stukas for precious seconds and emerging at unexpected angles. But not all could utilise each other's cover.

Occasionally a Jeep would come to a deliberate halt as a Stuka came flashing down for the kill—the briefest of halts, but a steady platform for a moment for their machine-gunner, as well as evading Stuka bullets. In that time they must have done damage to the planes, though for half an hour none was noticeable. Then one Stuka took a lot of Bren fire almost at desert level, as it was pulling up and away. It went on pulling up but probably the pilot was dead at the controls, for it maintained its arc of flight and finally power-dived on to the desert. There was a massive explosion, and a huge black-smoked oil fire rose skywards.

It cheered the Gang and gave them the courage to fight for their lives for yet another thirty minutes. Every minute gained was a victory, and every mile they travelled brought them nearer to the safety of their own lines.

The disaster to their comrade seemed now to induce some caution in the remaining Stuka pilots, for though they never ceased to attack, they took care to pull away before retaliatory fire could damage them. And then they started to work together in concert, no doubt talking to each other by radio.

Instead of each Stuka tackling its own evasive target, they concentrated on one Jeep and went for it, one after the other. The first was O'Keefe's. He saw the danger, took over the wheel himself, and tried to outsmart the enemy.

The first Stuka dived and bombed, but O'Keefe at the last moment had skidded completely round and was belting back towards the distant *Kubelwagens*. The second Stuka was too late to catch on to the manoeuvre and wasted ammunition in the dirt. The third, however, was able to change course and bore down upon O'Keefe's Jeep, yet again the wily man did an about-turn and again the Stuka missed. But they weren't going to miss all the time, O'Keefe knew, and though he held out for ten magnificent minutes they got him in the end. A stream of bullets caught the Jeep and it somersaulted over, and the others saw it from a distance and wondered whose turn it would be next.

It wasn't Offer; he was dead lucky this dying day. If they could have identified his Jeep from the air, the Stukas would, of course, have made him their prime target. As it was they picked on one driven by Private Salkirk—old Sally. With him were Jardine, Tulger and Gunner Rock. Sally wasn't lucky and they got his Jeep, which came to an abrupt halt. Three Jeeps running now, and about fifteen minutes of daylight still left. The Stukas were turning their attentions on a Jeep driven by Palfreyman.

Offer shouted, 'Back! Turn back!' He had seen someone moving by Sally's halted Jeep. Lashley threw the Jeep into a controlled skid, and went tearing across to where someone stood and waved. Arriving there, Lashley dropped anchor so suddenly it nearly threw everyone out of the car.

It was Sally. He was the only one to survive unhurt, the usual miracle of warfare. Jardine probably had his back broken and couldn't be moved. Tulger and Rock were both badly wounded, blood pouring from them, both unconscious.

Palfreyman, astute man that he was, was leading the Stukas a dance, and gaining vital minutes for them all. Offer took risks, stopping and putting bandages on his wounded men. They were too badly hurt to be moved and would have to be left to the tender mercies of the German. If the Afrika Korps lived up to their high reputation with the British army they would have mercy on the wounded.

By the time they had finished there was a *Kubelwagen* bearing down upon them. Sally scrambled into the front seat with Offer—the machine-gunners behind couldn't do with more crowding—and once more they took off.

Offer wanted to go over to O'Keefe's wrecked Jeep, but it was too near the advancing *Kubelwagens* for him to risk it. Reluctantly he ordered Lashley to head east again.

The Stukas got Palfreyman when only the sun's rim showed above the western horizon. Then they came after Offer, and for six or seven minutes they dodged and turned frantically, Lashley throwing the Jeep about as well as any motor-racing driver. Their ears were deafened by the battering waves of sound from the dive-bombers, and their hearts were in their mouths much of the time because of their closeness to death.

Yet all at once it seemed as if night fell upon them, for following a half-hearted attack, the Stukas zoomed away and kept going, heading northwest towards Agheila. The light was too bad to see down on the desert floor.

Offer said, 'We can halt now.' He felt suddenly exhausted. Lashley must have felt no different, for he put his arms on the steering wheel and leant his head upon them. In the back, his machine-gunners just slumped to the floor, the adrenalin that had sustained them all at once draining away and leaving them seemingly without strength.

Offer leaned over and switched on their headlights. He didn't think it would be much of a risk. If the *Kubelwagens* were still around they'd hear the distinctive Volkswagen engines approaching long before the Germans reached them. It grew very dark.

After a while they did hear an engine approaching, and they could tell the note anywhere. It was another Jeep. It too switched on its light and came slowly across to join the patrol commander.

Arab Ward, their medical orderly, was at the wheel. Crookshank, Pom and Jimmy Wilborn were with him. Ward too switched off and for a time no one spoke, resting, letting the tension ease out of their systems. It had been a long day and a trying one even for such hardy men, and now there seemed nothing to sustain them and they felt weary and depressed. In their thoughts were memories of their comrades who had died or had been injured back there. It spoilt the feeling of victory over the Luftwaffe.

Offer said, 'Now we'll go back.'

Abruptly he had vigour, and it jerked his men out of their slough and they too sat up.

'Back?' Arab Ward was a bit slow on the uptake.

'Maybe some of our chaps have survived and haven't been picked up by Jerry.'

So cautiously they toured back towards the scene of the battle. It was too dark to find any of the wrecked Jeeps, but when Offer thought they were somewhere close to them he risked putting on his headlights and driving several times in a tight circle before switching off and sitting silently in the darkness. If there were any survivors they would know where to head.

Ten minutes later he repeated the manoeuvre.

It was quite a bit nerve-wracking to have to sit there in dead silence, ears cocked for the faintest sound, always with the thought of enemy infantry stealing upon them in the night. They had no fear of *Kubelwagens* closing in, for they would hear their engines miles away.

Ten minutes later Offer made another circle, and within five minutes Wise and a tall thin artilleryman, Jack Redpath, came walking out of the desert. It was a joyful meeting, and everyone bucked up at that and hoped that more would come homing in on their headlamps.

But the night passed and that was all they saw of their comrades in the missing Jeeps. An hour before dawn Offer called off the search. They had a long way to go before they were safe, and he knew the Luftwaffe would be after them at daybreak. Much as he wanted to stay and search for his men, Offer knew his sensible course was to ferry the survivors out to safety.

They had a final meal and drink, still standing and listening, still with eyes hopefully searching the darkness. Then Offer said, 'Let's go,' and the two laden Jeeps went off at a steady speed towards Benghazi.

Just on daylight they halted and Offer emptied their vehicles of surplus food and water. Around the heap they built a cairn of stones and put a stick into it to which was fastened a not very clean vest. Still it was white and would attract attention, and if any survivors found it they would have food and drink to sustain them as far as the Allied lines.

An hour later they began to see aircraft. They bore the familiar roundels of the R.A.F. They had reached safety.

Two hours after dawn they ran into a South African gun site. Surviving some hostile challenges they were made welcome and given all the food and drink they needed. Then they slept.

Sometime in the afternoon Offer woke. He shook his signaller, Art Weybright, until his eyes opened, and then he said, 'I'm going back to look for the boys.' O'Keefe and Walker among others were missing. Both had grown on him, and he was curiously unhappy to think he might never see them again. Yet O'Keefe was a wily man and might still be alive and free.

'I'll come with you.'

They went out to their battered Jeep, and headed back into hostile territory. Once again the sun was setting far in the west. This time, though, the Luftwaffe was not in evidence—the hunt must have been called off.

And all at once they saw trudging figures. They accelerated joyfully. It *was* the wily O'Keefe with two men—Palfreyman and Tiffy Jones—he had picked up, a huge grin showing the gap from the missing front teeth.

They shook hands and pummelled each other and swapped stories. O'Keefe said they'd found the food cairn and 'God, sir, wasn't that water a blessing!' All day they had been hunted by the Luftwaffe, but simply by crouching close against odd thorn bushes they had managed to escape detection. Five men rode back in triumph to comrades who still slept the sleep of exhaustion. Seven Jeeps and twenty-eight men had set out. Two Jeeps and fourteen men returned.

Before getting their heads down again, Captain Offer made a signal to G.H.Q. Cairo. This time he was in no mood for exaggeration and his report went through unadorned with fancy.

Weybright took down the signal. 'Mission completed. Agheila oil set on fire. Fourteen men killed or missing. Five Jeeps lost. One Stuka shot down and damage done to enemy armoured cars.'

All the same it was an impressive report, and Cairo would know better than he from aerial photographs how much damage they had done to the enemy oil installation. Hours later the major-general sent a signal to Offer: 'Good show. Report immediately to G.H.Q. Cairo.'

Offer's response was classically Shavian: 'Not bloody likely.'

Printed in Great Britain
by Amazon